COMPANION
of EAGLES

I0672141

Regine Haensel

Companion of Eagles
Book Three of the Leather Book Tales
© Regine Haensel 2019

Interior design by Regine Haensel
Cover photo by Regine Haensel
Cover design and map by Meshon Cantrill
Printed by Amazon.com

Serimuse Books
Saskatoon, Saskatchewan, Canada
booksserimuse@gmail.com

Haensel, Regine, 1948-, author
Companion of eagles / Regine Haensel

(Book three of The leather book tales)
ISBN 978-0-9939032-2-9 (paperback)

I.Title. II.Series: Haensel, Regine, 1948- , Leather book tales;
bk. 3.

THE LEATHER BOOK TALES is a fantasy set in western North America. Four powers – fire, water, air and earth – reveal themselves in four young people, triggered and enhanced by a pair of silver bracelets. Their abilities grow as they overcome challenges and collaborate against forces that oppose and threaten them. Eventually the young people discover that they are part of an old and tangled tale, with risks not only for themselves, but for their world and its people.

The Leather Book Tales Series
Queen of Fire
Child of Dragons
Companion of Eagles
Daughter of Earth (forthcoming)

Other books by the same author (short stories)
The Other Place
A Rain of Dragonflies

Acknowledgements

A book is a product of many years and many hands. Through the years I've benefited greatly by being a part of the Saskatchewan writing community and the Saskatchewan Writers' Guild. Thanks also to my writing group, Visible Ink for useful comments at various points in the writing process.

Special thanks go to my two beta readers for this book, Kathy Fitzpatrick and Martha Mantikoski, who both read a draft near the end and provided helpful suggestions.

This book is dedicated to my grandson, Xavier William Cantrill, who, several years ago when I was telling him about one of the characters in Queen of Fire, Grandmother Wisdom, said that I should have a future character called Grandfather Frog.

COMPANION
of EAGLES

For Xavier

THE LAND

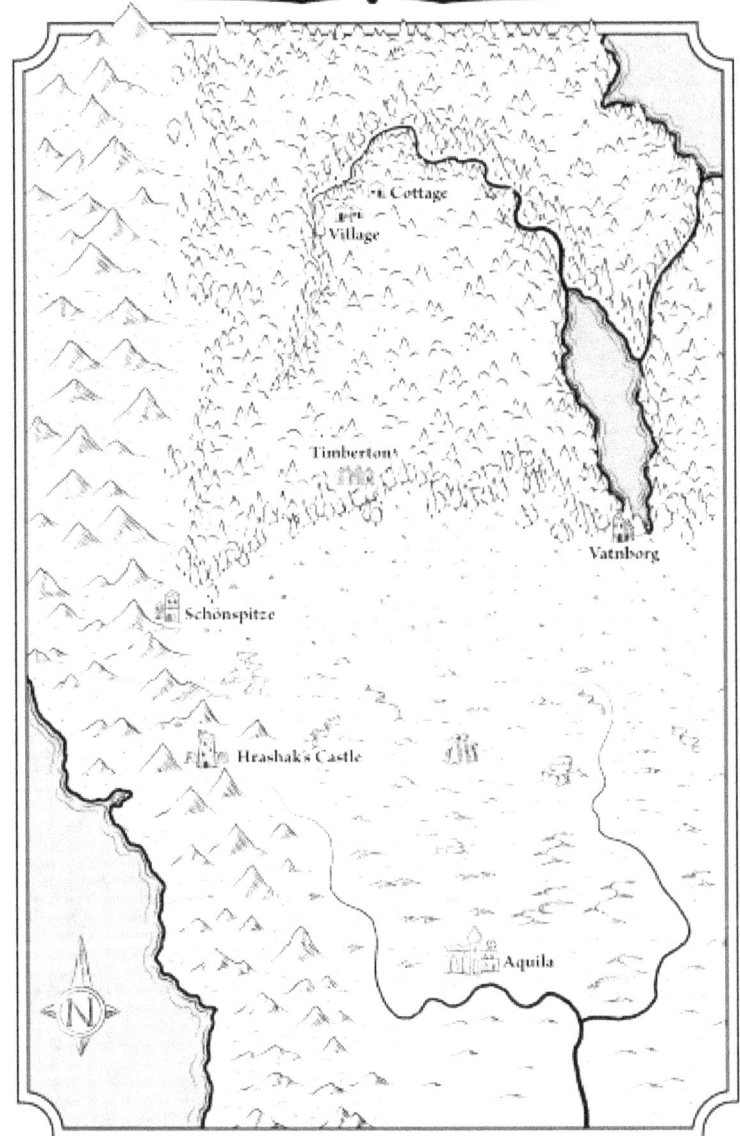

CONTENTS

Chapter I
Complications

The last thing I remember is drifting off to the distant drumming of the Lord's Militia signalling day's end in my room in Aquila, the house Papa and I share. But now my eyes are open wide seeing nothing but dark. No strip of moonlight through the gaps of my window shutters, no winking stars. When I press my eyelids down briefly there's not even the weird lines and sparks of light that usually show up. I turn my head this way and that. It's like a sandstorm at night hiding moon and stars, except there's no stinging grit against my skin, no song of sand and wind.

I stretch out my arms; groping hands touch nothing, no bed covers, no wooden bed frame. A chill breeze lifts the hair from my neck. I become aware of my cold and naked feet standing on a rough surface. Not a wood floor, maybe cobblestones? I could be standing out in the street in front of our house. Sleep walking? I've never done that before. It's unbelievably quiet – no leaves hissing in a breeze, no creaking branches. No squeaky wheels of a late-night cart, no footsteps. A speck of brightness off to one side draws my eyes. I squint as it slowly grows larger; hope by this light to see the outline of my window or the walls of a familiar house, but instead, dark shapes stand against an indistinct background. None of the shapes look like anything I recognize.

A whispering voice: "Samel."

I take a step forward. "Who's there?"

A sudden flare obliterates everything and my eyes swim. Quick as a darting fish, my fist knuckles the wet away. I'm just seeing clear again when icy liquid gushes over my feet, making me jump back and almost slip. But I spread my legs and get balanced. Flames blaze and steam rises as water meets fire. I flail at the mist, trying to clear it so I can see. Heat presses, wetness drips from my skin. I open and shut my eyes, take deep breaths. What is happening? Where am I?

When I open my eyes again, early morning light fills my bedroom. Familiar, ordinary. Just another dream, I guess. My fist pounds the mattress. What am I supposed to get from this? It doesn't make sense.

Bedding tangles around my waist and legs; my body's slick with sweat. I push at the scratchy blanket, but it's twisted into knots and won't budge. I stretch a leg; my toe rips a hole in the sheet.

"Talons and beaks!" My voice cracks the way it's been doing lately. Good thing I'm not wanting to be a singer. Voice going, skin itchy. Toenails too long – almost like an eagle's. I'm making a mess again.

In my head I can hear the other drum apprentices snickering. Yesterday one of them muttered to another, "Clumsy as a new born camel." Knew they were talking about me. Turned to glare at them. Don't know what I'd have said or done, but Tamtan, the drum master, walked in just then and we all bent to our work.

I frown at my knobby knees. They do make me think of camel legs. Except camel toes don't look like mine. I can hear Papa now: "If you'd pay more attention, you'd notice your toenails are too long. Cut them!"

The sheets are old, too thin. That'll be my excuse when I ask Papa for coin to buy new bedding. Still, he won't be happy about it. It's not like we're poor, though. Papa's stipend as a Lord's musician has always been enough to take good care of us. I'm sure Tamtan's other apprentices resent me partly because of that. None of their fathers are musicians of the calibre of Papa.

I shove all the bedding away. Too hot. The dry season is usually scorching in Aquila, but this is the worst I remember. Good thing Rowan isn't here – she'd find it harder to take than me, having lived most of her life in norther forests. Sister, where are you now? I should have defied Papal, snuck away and joined the caravan to travel with you.

Generally, I do what Papa wants, or I argue him round to my side. Man and boy, just him and me living together all my life, we don't always agree, but sort things out. I've been happy enough. That changed after Rowan came. And now she's gone again, who knows for how long? Life should be easier, but it isn't.

The dream. Was it about Rowan? Maybe she's in danger. I scramble out of bed, dragging the bedding to the floor and leaving it. Rummage in the wooden chest at the foot of my bed and pull out the silver bracelet of linked ivy leaves. Slip it onto my wrist. Mysterious, magical circlets that came from our parents, one each. I thump to the floor, struggle with my unruly legs, then settle. Close my eyes and think of my sister; picture her long hair, dark like Papa's, her grey eyes that I've been told are like our mother's. My concentration slips.

I'll never see Mother again, can't even remember her. Did I call her Mama? Did she ever sing to me? Maybe I got my musical abilities from her as well as Papa. I was too young when Papa and I left her and Rowan. And Mother's been dead for over a year now.

I scratch an itchy toe. Tailfeathers! Better cut my toe nails before they do more damage. Then get clothes on. The house is quiet though I can tell by the angle of the sun shining through my window that it's still early. Papa's either asleep or gone already to the river bank, to the old barracks of the Lord's Militia. They've been mostly empty for years, the grounds al-

lowed to grow wild, but Papa and his musician friends
along with other artists of Aquila are changing that.
They've joined designers, stone masons, carpenters
and labourers to turn the dilapidated buildings into an
arts school.

I sneak across the landing and peek into his room.
No Papa, bed made neatly, bedding stretched tight as
a drum head. It was under that bed I found my bracelet. It was Papa's really, but had abandoned him. He
wasn't happy about that.

I rattle down the stairs. No Papa anywhere. Why
didn't he wake me this morning as he's been doing
ever since Rowan left? Drag me along as usual with
him to the school when I don't have other duties. Not
that I'm sorry to be left at home. At the building site
I'd just be hanging around waiting for someone to
find tasks for me: carrying tools, cutting grass, cutting
brush. Scut work is no fun and not that good for a
musician's hands.

I search for a note. Today is supposed to be my
day for working with Papa – composing, playing the
flutes, cleaning and repairing them if necessary. If he
doesn't come back for that'll be the third lesson we've
missed since Rowan went. The arts school is important, but so am I!

The food cupboards hold bread, honey, butter,
a bit of cheese, figs. I'm not really hungry yet. Why
didn't he leave me a note? Even to say, practise the
flute or go get more food. I can hear his voice in my
head: "You're old enough to figure that out for your-

self." I'm not stupid and he's never said that I am. But we used to talk more, spend a lot of time together.

I wander into the living room. One of the big woven baskets the women from the Grasslands People brought sits there, full of sheet music. Some that Papa composed, some he copied with other musician's approval. I did most of the copying because I have a good hand, as Papa used to say. I leaf through a few sheets, put them back, finger the basket. It's well made. They could sell these for a good price in the market here.

The Grasslands People wanted help to find some missing children. That's what Rowan's gone to do, and I know they helped her when she was trying to find Papa and me, so I guess she felt she owed them. Still, it seems odd that they couldn't look for the children themselves. Would Rowan have gone if she'd been happier with us? My fault?

I'll try again to talk to my sister. Sit, breathe deeply, touch the bracelet, close my eyes and concentrate. Sometimes that will work, and I get some kind of picture, but today I wait until my knees start to cramp and my arms itch. No visions. Weird that I had that dream and now nothing. Still so much to learn about how and why the bracelets work and why they don't. Maybe Rowan doesn't want to talk to me. Was my dream influenced by the bracelet even though I wasn't touching it or was it just an ordinary strange dream? No answers just sitting here and my belly's rumbling.

I'm munching bread and cheese when there's a rat-tat at the door. Hope its Ali from across the street. I haven't seen her in a couple of days and she's always working on something interesting. I could help her, could use a distraction. Should practise the flute, though. A boy stands outside, a messenger from Papa: he does want me at the river bank.

***

I send the messenger ahead to let Papa know I'm coming, then saunter along cobblestone streets. The bracelet lies in my belt pouch as does the soprano flute that belongs to Papa. I'm also carrying a few dried figs, though there's usually food at the building site for anyone who wants it. I'm wearing a broad-brimmed hat to protect me from the blazing sun, as well as a light indigo tunic and baggy trousers.

"Samel!"

I turn to find Ali behind me. Her long, loose robes are patterned with palm leaves. She probably painted them on herself. A wide smile springs out on my face.

"Hey!"

"Going to the market?" she asks. "Mère sent me to look at wool for weaving. She's starting a new wall hanging."

"No, to the arts school."

"Could I come? I can get the wool later."

"If you don't mind being bored," I say.

"I like seeing how far they've come with the work; what new stones they've laid or painting they've done." Ali starts walking beside me. "Why are you going if it bores you?"

"Papa sent for me. I guess I keep hoping that if I hang around he might talk to me."

"Doesn't he talk to you at other times?"

"He works so much I hardly see him."

"Parents are like that sometimes," Ali says. "You should be used to it by now."

"It's different this time."

"How?"

"I don't know, just different." I pause to let a man riding a horse pass by, the hooves playing a march across the cobblestones. "Do your parents talk to you about the school and how they're helping there?"

Ali's parents, in fact her whole family, are artists. They draw, paint, weave, sculpt, and try just about anything that takes their fancy. I like visiting over there because you never know what you'll see.

"Of course! The talk at meals is all about the school. It's the best thing that's happened in this city! According to Mère and Père, in a long time. They talk so much about it I do get sick of it sometimes. We . . . Oh." She's caught my expression even though I'm staring straight ahead. "Your Papa doesn't talk about it?"

"I told you, he hardly talks to me at all these days! And we haven't played music together since before Rowan left. Haven't you been listening?"

"Don't grouch at me! Maybe he's worried about your sister."

"Of course he's worried about Rowan. I'm worried about her. I can't see her the way I could once, much less talk to her."

"The bracelet isn't working for you?"

Ali is the only one besides Papa that I've told about the magical circlets. "Doesn't seem to be."

We've reached the edge of the market with its clash of colours, cacophony of sounds, mingling of scents. Usually I like seeing what new fruits or cheeses have come in, what the musical instrument makers are showing, haggling with the stall keepers. Papa taught me to do the food shopping when I was quite young. I used to enjoy it all, loved coming here. Today I'm not in the mood.

I'm about to suggest to Ali that we turn to the right and avoid this crowded area when another girl stops in front of us. She's half a head taller than Ali or me, wavy blond hair hanging to her shoulders. Looks familiar, but just then I can't remember her name.

"Samel." She giggles. "I couldn't come to Tamtan's yesterday."

Then I remember. She's the drum master's new apprentice. The one who, on her first day, kept staring at me while I was trying to fix an out-of-tune drum. And on our break, she was giggling with one of the other apprentices. But I still can't recall her name.

"Oh, ah." I'm thinking about how to introduce her to Ali, but the blonde girl ignores my friend.

"Mother's waiting for me, have to go. Hope to see you tomorrow!" She flashes me a huge smile and walks quickly away.

"Who was that?"
I'm still gazing after the girl, but Ali's voice sounds odd, so I turn to her. "A new apprentice. Can't think of her name."

"She knows you for sure."
"She's seen me at Tamtan's."

"And you can't remember her name. Seems strange." Ali's staring after the girl, too, half turned away from me.

I nudge her shoulder with mine. "What's going on, Ali? Do you know her?"

She steps away. "How would I know one of Tamtan's apprentices? Anyway, your Papa's expecting us. We should get going."

And Ali rushes off to the left, past the market. I nearly have to run to catch up with her and she doesn't say another word. I'm trying to think what I could have done wrong. Is my best friend angry because I've forgotten a girl's name? Is there some other reason she's annoyed, something I've forgotten to do, something I should have said? I wish I could figure it out. Everything's too complicated these days.

Chapter II
Conversations

It's nearly mid-day when Ali and I have time to talk again. We sit tailor fashion on the riverbank near the old barracks. A slight breeze rustles the grasses and the leaves of the trees hinting at a tune I can almost catch. We haven't had to work too hard this morning. I raked grass and twigs and dumped loads in carts to be taken away. Helped clear an area that's going to be used as a garden.

Other than saying, "Finally, you're here!" Papa hasn't talked to me at all.

Ali bends forward stretching, her long fingers stained with green. They had her painting window frames. It's not until she touches me that I realize I've been bouncing my leg up and down. I pull away from her and lean against the trunk of the tree that's shading us.

"Why so jittery, Samel?"

Out of the corner of my left eye I see that she's flipped her brown hair over her shoulder and is twisting it. I don't answer right away, watch the dappled light under the alder tree play shadows across her face. She keeps looking at me.

"What do you mean?"

"Bouncing your leg, tapping your fingers. And on the way here you kept cracking your knuckles."

I want to deny it, but realize I've just flicked my thumb across a clump of grass. "Music in my head, wind in the tree," I excuse myself. Start clapping my hands gently, drum on my knees just to show her what I mean.

We've been best friends most of our lives, living across the street from each other, sharing our skills. My first memory of Ali is both of us scratching in dirt beside our houses. She paints, sketches, creates all kinds of art. I play flute, drums, harp, and compose a bit. We understand each other. And best friends know when you're not telling the whole truth.

"No," she shakes her head, sending hair flying out in dark crescendos. "This is different. It's more like twitches than music in your body."

I turn my back to her, pretend I'm watching the work not far from us. The renovations have been going on for weeks. In the beginning I was curious about everything, wanted to know how earth is cleared and dug, how mortar holds stones, how planks dovetail. Just because I'm a musician it doesn't mean that I'm not interested in other things, too. But Papa rarely answers my questions these days. Says he doesn't know or is too busy to talk. So, I've lost my enthusiasm. And right now I'd rather be anywhere else. I don't say that to Ali, though.

"Samel?"

"What!" I turn to my friend and she moves away from me. Maybe I spoke too loudly, and I guess my face isn't very friendly.

A grouchy face doesn't stop Ali for long. "You haven't been yourself for a while. Maybe since your sister left. Even when we walk, you're glancing here, there and everywhere. And you forget things." She pauses a moment, then continues in a rush of words. "Did that old sorcerer do something to you?"

I wrap my arms around my knees and try to sit as still as a rock. I don't want to remember the old man or the time in the castle. The way it ended.

But Ali won't let it go. "Could he um, have cast a spell on you and um, for some reason it's just coming out now?"

I sigh, and stop trying to hold back the memories. Papa, my sister Rowan and I were held prisoner in the mountains for several days about a year ago. We tried to reason with the old sorcerer who held us, but nothing worked. I think he was crazy. He wanted power and he thought my sister and I could help him get it. It was all about the silver bracelets we'd found. He wanted them. In the end Rowan used the magic of the bracelets to kill him and we escaped.

"Did you think I was different when we came back?" I can hear the challenge in my voice, but I don't care.

Ali ignores my tone and shrugs. "Maybe, maybe not. Lots was going on. Your sister upset and maybe sick. My sister's wedding. You'd been through an awful time, of course it affected you. But I wasn't with you at the castle and I never met the old man, so how can I know what he was like, what he might have done? I don't have any ideas about how spells work. I just see you're not like yourself."

Over near the main barracks people are yelling, running here and there. Some problem again, always problems, small or large – a wall crumbling, an axe needing sharpening. The bang of hammers and the screech of saws adds to the discord. If I concentrate, could I find a tune in it?

But Ali's words echo in my mind, whirling like a sandstorm, shutting out other sounds and thoughts. I'm not who I was. Does anyone stay the same? I've been noticing a lot of things lately that maybe I ignored before.

The silver bracelet on my left wrist glints as a stray sunbeam penetrates the leafy canopy of the tree. I focus on the circlet, trying to calm my thoughts. Usually I wear the bracelet in a soft leather pouch around my neck hidden under my tunic because Papa doesn't like to see it, doesn't want to be reminded of its magic.

My sister was really upset when the old sorcerer died, which only partly makes sense to me. I understand that she didn't want to be a killer, but when someone threatens you and won't listen to reason, sometimes you have few choices. Besides, he boasted he was responsible for our mother's death. Rowan lost her temper, sure, but she did what she had to. Afterwards she stopped wearing her bracelet, though I'm pretty certain she took it on her journey. I haven't found it anywhere in the house.

I put my bracelet on my wrist after I finished working a little while ago. I was looking for a quiet place to try again to connect with Rowan. But then Ali joined me. She noticed the silver circlet and asked if I was going to practise making breezes using it and Papa's soprano wooden flute. The two of us did that once not long after I first found the bracelet. I could always make wind blow, but Ali couldn't do it at all. I run a finger along the linked ivy leaves. The silver feels slightly warm. Everything started to change after I found it, some good, some not so good. I take the bracelet off and tuck it into its pouch.

Ali has given up trying to get me to talk. She's watching one of the great guardian eagles of Aquila soar over the river. The Captain of Eagles had to negotiate with the birds so that they'd let the construction go ahead here. This is one of the birds' nesting and fishing areas after all.

Ali picks up a stick and starts scratching in the dirt, leaning over so I can't see what she's drawing. Probably sketching the eagle or something else that's got her attention, could be anything. Alizarine is her full name. The rise and fall and flow of it is like a fragment of song that keeps nudging at me. I haven't been able to find the rest of the notes to complete the music. Her parents, Mère and Père, named all three of their daughters after colours. Lots of people think Ali was named after a shade of crimson that comes from the madder plant. Actually, Ali's mother picked the name because she'd been given a quilt in shades of navy, also known as alizarin blue. They make that colour from madder as well, though I don't understand the process. It fascinates me that one plant can be used to produce two different colours.

Ali turns back to me. "Her name's Kasma."

"Who?" But then I remember. "Tamtan's new apprentice. How'd you find out?"

"Asked one of the other apprentices working near me earlier. Is Kasma good? On the drums I mean. And why did you forget her name?"

I shrug. "She just started. I didn't pay much attention to her. She was so giggly."

"Girls like you," Ali says

"What?!"

"Come on, you must have noticed! The baker's helper in the market is always making eyes at you. And one of the fruit seller's daughters gives you a cut rate. Kasma's probably sweet on you."

"I don't have time for girls."

Ali shrugs, closing her mouth on whatever she was going to say next. I lean back and gaze up into the rustling leaves. Don't want to think about Ali talking to one of the apprentices or Kasma giggling with another one. The apprentices have never been my friends, or not for a long time. They change periodically, one or two dropping out, new ones starting, but the new ones always join the group that hates Samel. I never thought about it much, just accepted it. After all I had Ali and her sisters as friends, and lots of other people like the drum master, the camel seller, the harpist, and people at the market where I shop. After Rowan left, though it hit me that I didn't have many friends my own age. And I don't want girls giggling at me. Ali and her sisters don't giggle.

Green leaves and dappled sunlight, clouds drifting above. I glimpse a speck in the blue, another eagle. Wish I could be way up there away from all my problems, soaring on the wind, listening to the music of clouds. What do they whisper to each other up there?

"Samel, tell me what's really wrong."

Ali's voice brings me back to the ground and I sigh because I hoped she'd forget about questioning me, but Ali is stubborn. I turn the corners of my lips up in a smile to suggest that everything's fine, but it's not real and Ali knows that because she thumps me in the left shoulder with a fist. I rub my arm and take a deep breath, trying to decide what to tell her.

She starts talking before I can. "You seemed so happy when you first got back from the castle. You found your sister and escaped. Remember all of us in our garden? Cooking the meal, eating, laughing."

I shake my head. "Except Rowan was so quiet. Too quiet probably."

My voice rises and squeaks the way it does now and again. Embarrassing. Papa says it happens as boys grow. Dismissed it, didn't ask how I felt. Typical these days. I take a breath to settle my voice.

"Papa and I should have paid more attention to how Rowan felt. Maybe that's why she took off again."

Ali taps my knee. "Maybe your sister is just a quieter person. Some people are like that. She and her mother did live alone in the forest for most of her life. Rowan's probably not used to a lot of people around."

A lump forms in my throat. "That was *my* mother, too, who died." I turn my head away so that Ali won't see the wetness in my eyes. "I never knew her." I clamp my lips to stop them quivering. I'm too old to cry over something that's been over and done with for a year or more.

"I'm sorry. I know it's been really hard for you." She clears her throat. "Maybe you haven't had enough time to get over it."

A few workers are cutting grass and brush near the old guard tower. Papa is somewhere there. I was really hoping that today he'd find work we could share, make time to talk. I'm not sure what he's doing – not cutting grass. I saw him chatting to a couple of men I didn't recognize. They were pointing here and there and waving their arms. Maybe discussing the building of an addition.

I don't know why Papa insists that he needs me here. Maybe he just wants me under his eyes. Yes, I can haul rocks or run errands, but there's enough other people to do those things. Am I just a chore boy to him? If he really wants me here, why can't he let me have more responsibility? He could show me the plans for the school, talk over problems, ask for suggestions. Once he would have.

Ali lets out a huge sigh and I realize I'm ignoring her. I'm as bad as Papa. At least Ali talks to me and listens.

"Papa just goes on every day as if nothing has changed even though Rowan's gone," I say as a sort of apology. "I miss her. He must miss her, too, but he doesn't say anything about it."

"Parents get like that at times," Ali offers. "I said before that it's not the first time your Papa got absorbed in his work."

"Yes, but you've got two parents and two sisters. It's always been different with Papa and me. I grew up without a mother. I thought it was no one's fault, and it seemed normal. I still had Papa and we were close, understood each other. But he's different now. Since Rowan came? Or maybe it's me. I really wanted to go with Rowan and he wouldn't even consider it. I'm fourteen! Old enough to know what I want. Doesn't he see that? Some days I can hardly stand to be in the same room with him. Can't he see how angry I am that he wouldn't let me go; does he even care?"

Light and shadows dance across Ali's blue tunic like notes made visible. I can almost hear the tune. She leans through the music and grasps my left wrist. "If you don't like what's happening, why don't you change it?" she snaps. The music stops with the clash of her voice. "Explain to your father or do something else. It isn't like you to be so unhappy all the time. And it's hard on your friends."

I glare at her. "Rowan's had two journeys and I've had none. Well, I did come with Papa to Aquila, but that's when I was a baby and too young to remember."

Ali stands, puts her hands on her hips and frowns down at me. "Aquila is an amazing city – music and art, crafts and traders, the palace, the river, the desert, the eagles."

"I know that!"

She interrupts, "But if you really want to get away that badly, just do it."

"Why don't you go?" I shout, my voice cracking. I leap up to face her head on.

She takes a step away. "I'm not the one with the travelling itch!" she yells.

"No, you're an old tree, roots curling around rocks deep in the ground."

"Even trees change with the seasons."

"Oh, I can't talk to you anymore."

I've turned my back when she says, "Fine." And I hear her steps thumping off. I don't try to stop her, fling myself to the ground under the tree.

The morning Rowan left I pretended that I was too sleepy to see her off. I lay in bed thinking about packing and taking a journey of my own, but in the end, I decided to go visit Mustafa, the camel seller. I argued with myself about whether to leave a note for Papa. Serve him right if he came home from taking Rowan to the caravan and I was just gone. But decided I couldn't do that, so wrote: "Off for a walk."

Mustafa has been keeping my camel, Izmeer, for me. Papa and I never actually bought the two camels we picked out to go searching for Rowan last year, because we were transported to her by magic. Mustafa has promised not to sell Izmeer to anyone else. I'm paying for him by working for the camel seller, though Papa doesn't know that.

It would be more fun being with Mustafa and the camels than wandering around at the school site, waiting for someone to give me another task. Like fetching a tool someone's forgotten. At least when I'm with the camels I feel as if I'm truly necessary to them – feeding and watering, exercising or brushing, discussing their latest tricks.

And Mustafa tells good stories. The day Rowan left he told me about his first caravan journey. He ran away and joined when he was just ten years old. Headed south to trade along the river. He saw so much – swamps and plains, forests and waterfalls, new towns. I said that's what I wanted to do. I saw his frown, and added, "I'm older than you were."

Mustafa shook his head and looked stern. "It's not as much fun as you might think, lots of hard work. And it can be dangerous. Besides, your father would miss you and be sad and hurt. You don't want to do that to him."

I thought about it for a while that day as I raked Izmeer. Did he have a father and mother among the camels? Brothers and sisters? Do camels recognize members of their own family? I didn't ask. Maybe Mustafa was sorry that he'd run away from home.

Rowan said that Papa and our mother were wrong to separate us and try to hide the bracelets from us. None of that worked anyway. They should have found another way, studied the bracelets to find out what they were about. That's what I've been trying to do. It would be better if Rowan were here to help me do that. Papa won't talk about any of it.

I used to think that life could make sense. You did what you needed to do and things turned out right.

One of the men working at the old barracks is waving at another. He needs help moving a rock. Why move the rock? What if it has a reason for being there? There's a grey stone with a white line through it next to my right foot. The stone is smooth, as if tumbled and tossed in a river bottom full of other stones. Papa and I used to come here when I was little, and I'd gather pebbles from the edge of the river or look for clam shells. I had a whole collection. Not sure what happened to them. Papa probably threw them out.

There's a spot where the river bank isn't so steep, and when the water's low there's a narrow beach. I could easily find it again. I know this city so well – the colourful street of carpet sellers, the reeking tanning quarter, the noisy metal smiths' alley, the edge of the city where carpenters live near yards filled with lumber from many lands. My drum teacher, Tamtan, took me to the timber yards once to find just the right wood for a special drum he wanted to make.

And I remember the inn, The Eagle's Nest, where Papa and I lived for a while when we first came to this city. My first friend in Aquila lived there. Maxim. We were almost the same age and we played together all the time. That's what Papa told me, though I don't remember much of those earliest days. I haven't thought of Maxim in a long time or been to the inn. It's on the east edge of the city and I never go there.

I pick up a thin green twig and tap on the grey and white stone. It doesn't make much of a sound. Another stone to tap with would be better. I drop the twig. Tamtan has been working here at the arts school, too, but I haven't seen him today. I've hung around here long enough and Papa won't even notice if I go. My stomach grumbles. I ate all my nuts and dried figs earlier, so could go get something to eat from the food tent, but my stomach can wait a while.

It's easy to slip away. I let my hat hang by its string down my back and pull the folded cowl of my tunic up over my head. I keep my head ducked as I walk. Too many people know me and I don't feel like answering questions. So I take short cuts along narrow streets, avoiding busy thoroughfares.

The drum teacher's house and workshop are quiet today and the doors to both the house and yard are shut. No students or apprentices, I hope, especially not Kasma. What is it with some girls anyway? It's enough to make me throw up. Ali doesn't bleat like a lovesick camel. I knock at the side door. It opens a crack and dark eyes peer out.

"Samel!" Tamtan's plump wife opens the door wider and pulls me inside. "Is something wrong? I thought you'd be helping at the school."

"Could I see Tamtan? Is he here?"

"Come." She leads the way to a distant corner, a door I haven't entered before. Knocks, sticks her head in. "Samel's here."

"Enter," the drummer's voice growls.

I sidle in. Tamtan can be very grouchy if he's disturbed at the wrong time. But maybe there's something in my face that lets him know I'm upset for he clears scrolls off a stool and sets it by a small table. Pours me a goblet of water, moves a plate of fried pastry balls drizzled with honey near me. My stomach rumbles so I take a sip of water.

Neither of us says anything. Tamtan begins to scribble on a scrap of old parchment. I can't see what he's writing, but he seems busy. I should just go.

"I'm working on a piece of music for the school opening," Tamtan says, looking at me. "Do you want to play in the youth group for that?"

"I'm not sure." Tamtan has asked me before to play in his youth drum ensemble. It's a great honour that he thinks I could be good enough. I might not have the discipline to practise as hard as they do. And I don't really know any of the others very well. Maybe that's what I need to distract me, though.

"I'll give you a copy of the music," Tamtan says. "Try it out and let me know in a few days." He nudges the plate of pastry. "Sure you don't want to take a couple?"

I pop one in my mouth, lick my fingers, dry them on my trousers, and take the sheet of music Tamtan hands me. He turns back to his table and I know I'm dismissed. I linger to eat another honey ball. Tamtan and Papa have been friends a long time; they play concerts together. Maybe my drum teacher could tell me what to do or say to Papa to really make him see me, talk to me, but Tamtan keeps scribbling and I don't want to disturb him any longer. Anyway, he doesn't have any children of his own, so maybe he wouldn't understand.

At home I get out my two drums. One is small and can be tied to your waist. I made that one myself. The other is larger, an old one that Tamtan showed me how to repair. He said I did a good job and gave it to me as a gift. It has a deep rumbly tone. For a while I practise the piece Tamtan gave me, losing myself in the music. Then try out different beats and tempos, looking for the tune that nudged at me when I watched shadows move across Ali's tunic.

Music has a magic all its own. I don't dare talk to Papa about Ali's idea that Hrashak, the old sorcerer in the castle, might have cast a spell on me. There's no way I can think of to figure out if it could be so, and Papa is the last person I'd ask about it right now. I know that Ali will keep her suspicions to herself; she's that kind of friend. If Rowan were here I might talk to her. I wish I'd been nicer to her before she left.

I set the drums aside and pull out the silver circlet; the ivy leaves seem to quiver in my hands. Rowan might still be afraid of using hers. Please let her sense that I want to talk to her.

Sometimes the bracelets have answered right away; other times like today it's been harder to get them to respond. Moonlight gives the most power, but daylight will work, too. I hold the bracelet loosely in cupped hands. My eyes are closed and it's quiet. I can't even hear anyone passing in the cobblestone street. Concentrate! I mustn't think of anything except my sister.

Nothing happens. I want to scratch or yawn. Feel the weight of the circlet in my cupped hands and try to picture Rowan. So much of the time this last year she had a very sad look on her face. I hope that she's found reasons to smile on her journey. I take several deep breaths.

Colours swirl behind my eyelids. Somewhere the sun is moving toward setting. Not here in Aquila, but I can see it in my mind. I smell dusty grass; I've never had smells with visions before. Does that mean

I'm getting better or that the power of the circlet is getting stronger? Then, there's Rowan sitting cross-legged on the ground beside a large black rock. I'm about to speak when a shadow moves between us. No matter how much longer I try, I can't get my sister's image back.

Chapter III
Visitors

In the next several days Papa and I have few words to say to each other. One evening though, he does tell me that the Lady Domatilla has that day announced she'll give money so that they can include rooms and teachers for singing instruction in the school. She herself was a singer before she married Lord Davus, the ruler of Aquila. I used to like singing for fun, but since my voice became treacherous, I haven't tried.

"That's good about the money," I say to Papa. Why aren't you happier about it?"

He frowns. "It's complicated. This whole project is a mess of politics. Yes, some of the Lady's money will be allocated to the singers, teachers of singing, and singing rooms. What about instrumental music? How do we decide how many teachers and which instruments? Artisans like the weavers have complained that they're left out of the school. Everybody's clamouring for their share. And some in the Lord's Militia are still not happy that we're even building a school. They wanted to refurbish the old barracks for themselves, though none of them ever raised any money. There's also a couple of cousins of the Lord who want to build villas along the river. They keep whining that the school is taking up too much land." Papa sighs and downs half a goblet of wine.

"Oh," I say. "I didn't know. Why haven't you talked about this before?"

Papa wipes his mouth with the back of his hand. "What could you do about it?" He shakes his head and stands. "I'm tired. Going to bed."

I stay there for a while, musing about complications. I wish Papa had told me sooner about all the problems. Maybe he's been so involved with all that he hasn't had much time to think of me or Rowan. And there's the complications of our family. If our parents hadn't had the bracelets made and discovered their power, we might still be together living in a northern forest. Hrashak wouldn't have wanted anything to do with us, even if he and Papa were relatives. If our mother hadn't drowned Rowan might never have discovered that her father was still alive and that she had a brother. I never used to think about how difficult lives can be. I was too young to see these things, much less understand them. I still don't see all the parts making sense, but at least I comprehend that there are many choices and many ways of doing things. Knowing that doesn't make my life any easier or me any happier, though.

So, I still spend time at the school when I'm not apprenticing. I try not to mind the work – delivering a message now and then, sorting lumber and stones for building – though I'd rather be making music. Working with wood is not bad; it reminds me of Tamtan's yard where fine wood for drums is kept. My mind wanders back to what Papa told me about the politics of building the school. I listen carefully to any conversations I can overhear, but they're mostly about dull things like where the sack of nails has got to or why we haven't enough mortar. There's a lot of sitting and waiting time so now and then I take my small drum or Papa's soprano flute to play. It's fun to try and work in the rhythms of various workers: the staccato of hammers, the drone of saws, the swish of scythes cutting grass. Occasionally I attempt to see or talk with Rowan and manage to have brief visions of her – riding through desert, sitting by a fire, walking through a market, but I don't succeed in speaking to her.

One morning I'm playing my drum in my room. Papa's not at home and he hasn't insisted that I go to the school today. Maybe he's realized that I need time for other things. All at once there's a warm spot at my chest where the pouch with the bracelet hangs. Immediately I stop playing and snag the silver circlet.

"Rowan?" I ask.

"Samel?" There's only her voice, nothing to see.

 "Yes, who else would it be? Are you all right? Where are you?"

"I'm with Grandmother Wisdom and her people. We found the lost children. I'm fine. How are you and Father?"

"All right, but he's awfully busy with building the school."

"Wasn't he going to spend more time with you?"

"With us. But you left. The work on the school is taking so long. How can I keep up my studies as an apprentice if none of my teachers has much time for me?"

"I'm sorry. You know I had to go. Father . . ."

"Yes, I've heard it all before."

"Can't you practise music on your own? Or visit Ali?"

"I have but . . ."

And then I know that I've lost the link. I throw the bracelet across the room. A clang as it hits the wall, rolls back to me. I pick it up. There's no damage. Polish it and put it away, quick. I can't stay in the house another minute.

Outside, the sun blazes heating up narrow streets. I've brought the flute and now and then I blow a short tune, which brings a slight breeze. I wander the streets, glancing at shops and outdoor displays, never stopping anywhere for long. People wave to me or smile. I return their greetings but keep moving. A few urchins who follow me run away when I stop playing and growl at them. I want to find someplace new, but I've lived here so long that I know it all.

I've been heading west without really thinking about it, but when I see the inn I realize that I meant to come here all along. The wooden sign with a painting of an eagle standing by the side of its twiggy nest still hangs above the door, but it's faded and weathered. I stop across the street and watch as a young man comes out and starts sweeping in front of the door. He's about my age, the age Maxim would be if he hadn't been killed by a runaway horse. I wasn't there to see, and I don't like to think about it. What if it hadn't happened? Would he and I still be friends?

I don't know the sweeper. There's nothing for me here. I don't even want to see if any of his family still owns or works the inn. What would I say to them? They probably wouldn't even recognize me. I turn away and wander off again.

Finally, because I can't think where else to go, I end up at the school, plopping down under a tree near the river bank. I don't want to keep living like this, at other people's beck and call, aimless. I don't have coin to live on my own, but maybe I could be an itinerant musician. Am I good enough? Would people pay for my playing? Would Papa and my other teachers agree to let me do it? Lots of questions that I don't have answers to yet. I'll have to think about how I might get support for the idea.

I begin gathering twigs, leaves, pebbles, and bark. Arrange them in patterns, meaningless marks in the dirt and dry grass, but maybe they'll help me find sense in my muddled thoughts. It's like composing music in a way. You play some notes or hear them in your head, try others, find sounds that play off each other or go together. A curved twig might look well beside a straighter one, a scatter of pebbles set off the colours in a handful of leaves. Does Ali play this way with paint? I've never asked her.

"What are you doing?"

I recognize the sandals first – dusty red – and then the feet – dusty also, with toenails painted dark blue. Raise my head to Ali's frowning face.

"Nothing much."

She thumps down beside me. "I've hardly seen you for days."

"Been busy." I place a pebble between two twigs. In my head I hear the twang of a lute.

"Doesn't look like it."

"I have to be here if someone needs me." That's kind of a lie. No one asked me to come today and no one's wanted my help since I've been here.

"For what? To gather stones and twigs?"

A huge breath whooshes out of me. "Might as well be doing that."

"Samel, you have to get over yourself!"

"Don't pick a fight now, please?"

Silence. Then a small sigh, and a soft voice, "Sorry. Actually, I came to tell you that someone was at your house."

Not Rowan back, of course not, she's with Grandmother Wisdom. I turn to face Ali. Raise an eyebrow.

"She showed up at our door, a woman with two little boys. The first thing she said was, 'Do you know Rowan?'"

I leap to my feet. "It must be Thea! Our cousin or really our mother's cousin. Why didn't you tell me right away?"

She shrugs. "Anyway, they're at our house for now."

I start to run, pounding toward the nearest street, blurring past the carpet sellers, the musician's lane, and the market. Ali keeps up with me all the way. People see us coming and scatter. I pay them hardly any attention.

Now and then Ali gasps something at me. "They're not going to run away!" or "Slow down a little?"

I ignore her and keep hurrying until we reach Ali's front door. I stop there and wait for her to catch up. Ali stands beside me, panting.

"So open the door already," I say.

She glowers. "Why?" Is paying me back for making her run so hard.

I sigh and knock. Ali's younger sister Ivoire opens it. "Ali? Why did you knock?"

Ali shakes her head.

"Are they here?" I say, stepping in and looking around. "Can I see them?"

Straight down the hall the door to the courtyard is open. Someone stands silhouetted there. With the sunlight behind, I can't tell who it is.

"Where's Rowan?" a woman's voice asks.

"Not here," Ali says, "I told you." She pushes me gently forward and closes the door behind us.

"Thea?" I ask.

She walks closer. "You're Samel?"

"Yes."

"I wanted Rowan."

Great, even a cousin I've never seen isn't interested in me. Maybe I should move in with Mustafa and become his camel assistant permanently. There's a scrabbling of quick feet on tiles and two small children are clasping Thea's legs below the knees. I walk closer and two identical dark-haired boys stare up at me with wide blue eyes.

"Well, Rowan's not here," I say. "Gone off on a journey. You'll have to make do with me and my Papa."

Thea looks at me, then at Ali. She pats the children on the head. Sighs. "Can we go to your house? These boys need to sleep."

I carry one of the boys, Thea the other. I've lifted little ones before – Xylea the harpist has very young apprentices, but never any as small as this, two or three years. The boy I'm carrying is surprisingly heavy for his size. His little arms drape around my neck and he hides his face on my shoulder. We put them in my bed, where they close their eyes immediately.

In the kitchen I offer Thea tisane, wine, water, food. She sinks into a chair.

"I'm tired, too, but a tisane would be good. It's been too many days since we left the north. A wagon train. I leased Rowan's property to a neighbour. I hope she doesn't mind. I brought the money and her leather book."

I don't know what to say so just murmur "hmm" or shrug.

Thea sips the tisane and leans her head on her arm. I can see she's exhausted, so don't trouble her with questions, though I have many. Papa arrives home as I'm heating up a chicken stew. I hear his steps and turn as he stops in the kitchen doorway. His mouth opens but he doesn't speak.

Thea lurches to her feet. "Yarvan."

"Thea? When did you arrive? Is something wrong?"

"Stew, bread and fruit in a few minutes," I say.

They both sit. I put out bowls and plates, cutlery, goblets. Papa and Thea stare at each other. It seems strange that they're not talking more. What are they thinking? I don't know if they ever met; if they have, it must have been long ago before I was born.

Thea speaks first. "Nothing's wrong. I need to go to Schönspitze in the mountains. Had a message that there's family business to conduct. I thought Rowan might want to come along, see the place where her mother was born."

"Rowan's not here," Papa says.

"Samel told me. Will she be back soon?"

"I don't know," Papa says. "Perhaps in a week or ten days? I'm not sure exactly where she is right now."

I could tell them that I talked to Rowan at Grandmother Wisdom's, but Papa doesn't like us using the bracelets. And anyway, I don't know when my sister will start back. If she does. What if she decides she doesn't want to live with us after all?

"Could the boys and I stay for a few days? In case she comes back. Anyway, I could use a rest." Thea yawns.

"The boys," Papa says. "Where are they?"

"Asleep in my bed," I say.

"How old are they now?" Papa continues. "And what are their names?"

"Kosto and Pello. They're three and a half."

I set the food on the table and there's no more talk for a while. Papa glances at Thea now and then. Does she look like Mother? Her hair is brown and her eyes are blue. Not the same colouring as Mother's the way Rowan described her. But perhaps there's a similar look in the face? The shape of a nose or chin. I wouldn't know.

Papa cleans his bowl with a wedge of bread. Chews, swallows. "You and the boys are welcome to stay," he says. "You can have my bedroom. That bed is bigger than Samel's. We are building an addition for Rowan's bedroom, but it's barely begun."

"Thank you. I should look in on the boys."

After Thea has gone upstairs, Papa clears the table. He touches my shoulder on his way by. "Thank you for making the meal."

"Mountains," I say slowly. "I'd like to see the place where Mother was born."

"Don't," Papa says. "I want you here."

This time I don't argue, just start washing dishes. Papa dries. Then he goes off to see if Thea and her twins need anything.

Before going to bed I think about attempting to talk to Rowan again. I should let her know that Thea is here, that she wants Rowan to travel to the mountains with her. But I don't feel like trying right now.

***

The next morning I'm woken by two little hands patting my cheeks, and two small faces with blue eyes staring at me. It's way too early. I groan and sit up in bed. The boys fall back onto their bums.

"Did I scare you? Sorry."

They just hunker there blinking at me. One of them sticks a thumb in his mouth. I don't know how to tell them apart, though it probably doesn't matter.

"Pello and Kosto," I say.

The other one sticks his thumb in his mouth. Can they talk? Not with thumbs in their mouths.

"Hungry?" I ask. "Thirsty? Eat?"

The last word brings a change. They both take their thumbs out of their mouths and look at me with mouths open. One of them babbles to the other, not real words, maybe a different language; anyway, I can't understand it. I slide out of bed and pull on the robe lying on the floor nearby.

"Come on. Food's downstairs. Eat!"

They toddle after me. At the head of the stairs they stop and sit. Yesterday Thea carried them up. Probably they don't know how to do stairs. Can't carry them both at once. If I carry one, will the other stay and wait?

"Show them how to crawl down backwards," Papa says. He's at the bottom of the stairs. "That's what you did at their age."

The boys catch on quickly, scrambling down and then each grabbing one of Papa's legs. He bends, picks them up, one for each arm. In the kitchen he sets them on the floor, hands them each a crust of bread.

"We need more food," Papa says. "If I make a list, can you go? I'll stay home today. Sent a message to the builder to come and work on the addition. Might as well make some progress on the extra bedroom."

He didn't say 'Rowan's room.' Maybe he has doubts that she'll come back. I'll think about that later. I help him feed the boys and manage to get down some food for myself. Was Papa with me like he is with the twins when I was small? Grinning at them, tickling them, making faces. The boys giggle, and prattle more meaningless sounds.

Thea comes down and the boys smile broadly, waving their bread and drumming their heels on the floor. She squats beside them. "Up early, as usual." She glances at me and Papa. "I hope you don't mind?"

"I'm always up early," Papa says. "But what do they like to eat? And why don't they talk? You said they're three years old? Are they just shy because they don't know us?"

Thea stands and faces Papa. "It's a long story. But partly it's because they're twins. They have their own talk between themselves and they don't need to talk much to the rest of us."

"Are you sure?" Papa sounds skeptical.

"Yes," Thea snaps. "There were twins in Schönspitze when Zarmine and I were girls. They took a while to talk, too." She shrugs one shoulder. "And I had to keep the boys as goats most of the time for the first couple of years. That probably didn't help."

"Rowan told us about that. I'm sorry." Papa wipes crumbs off the table. "What do they like to eat? Samel's going to the market shortly."

At the market I take time choosing food – three varieties of fruit, cheeses, bread, pastries, a bag of groats for gruel, two chickens for roasting. I chat with sellers, other people I know. I've lived in this city most of my life, don't remember any other home. I do like it here and I wish my sister had liked it as much as I do. I hope she'll come back some time. But don't I deserve a trip, a chance to see other places?

Chapter IV
Decision

The house fills with the sounds and activities of a woman and two small boys – babbling voices, unfamiliar cooking smells, more movement than I'm used to. Papa goes back to work at the construction site after a couple of days, but he doesn't ask me to go along. At first the noise and extra people in the house are annoying, but the boys take naps and that helps. It's like suddenly having two little brothers. In the morning I wake to small hands on my face and giggling. At meals their smiles at the sight of food makes me chuckle. Thea and I take turns cooking. She teaches me how to make pan bread, I show her my chicken stew. It's almost like having a mother.

The extra bedroom gets closed in and though it's not completely finished inside, Thea and the twins move there. I guess Papa's glad to have his room back, though he doesn't say anything about it. I don't get woken up by touch anymore, but by voices calling, "Sam, Sam!" They've learned to say that, at least. I hurry down the stairs to find the boys because they're easily distracted. They may have called me but then they stop to chew on chair legs, bounce on pillows, investigate bits of fluff. I'm always afraid that they will hurt themselves or eat things that aren't food. Thea doesn't seem to worry about it.

We have moved a lot of things out of the twins' reach as one of the easier ways to keep them safe. But it's not all worry. Pello and Kosto like being tickled and playing peek behind the hands. And they love food – bananas (which Thea says they've not seen before), crusts of bread, shreds of chicken. When I play Papa's soprano flute they bounce and dance.

"You're good with that," Thea says.

I can't remember the last time Papa praised my playing.

Thea is restless, going every day to check when caravans might be leaving to head to the mountains. Soon, she's told, but no fixed date yet. She asks me often if I have any idea when Rowan might return. How much does Thea know about what the bracelets can do? I haven't tried to connect with my sister again.

One day when Papa isn't home Thea asks, "Did Rowan show you the bracelet she found? She thought it gave her visions of you and your father before she knew where you were."

"Hmmm," I say. "I know about that."

"So, have you had any visions of her?"

"Umm," I say, "Papa doesn't like . . ."

"I don't care what Yarvan likes or doesn't!" she interrupts. "Do you know more about Rowan's return than he does? Is she coming back?"

"I've seen her," I say. "A sort of vision. She was with the Grasslands People. I have no idea when she's coming back. I haven't really been able to talk with her."

Thea sighs. "I can't wait much longer."

I could make more of an effort to connect with Rowan, find out if she's coming back and when, tell her there's a chance for more travel. But I'm reluctant. The twins like me and I get along with Thea. I could help on their journey to Schönspitze. Besides, maybe Rowan will be tired of travelling. I need to think about how best to persuade Thea that I'll make a good substitute for my sister. Though Papa's not likely to let me go.

The next afternoon I return from a walk, opening the door quietly in case the boys are napping. From just inside I hear voices in the living room – Papa and Thea.

"I wish you hadn't come." It shocks me to hear Papa be so rude. "You're putting temptation in Samel's way."

I want to know what else they have to say, so I stay silent by the door.

"I came for Rowan. I've already told you that."

"But she's not here and won't be coming back any time soon as far as I know. So why are you still staying?"

"This is the way you treat your wife's relatives? No wonder she sent you away if you were this cruel to her! And I can't believe you let Rowan go off again on another dangerous journey!"

"Rowan is travelling safely with a caravan. Better than when you let her leave home alone from the north! And Zarmine didn't send me away; we made the decision together. The children and the bracelets had to be separated."

"So you say."

"Well, you wouldn't know, would you? Zarmine didn't trust you enough to confide in you."

"She asked me to come and stay with her."

A deep sigh. I think it's from Papa. "It's useless to argue over the past. It's the present I'm worried about. I'm sure Samel wants to come to the mountains with you."

"Of course he does. Anyone would want to get away from you."

Thea can be rude, too. There's the sound of a door closing. I wait a moment and then clear my throat. Papa appears. He's frowning.

"How much of that did you hear?"

"Can't you let me go? You don't really need me right now and I'd like to find out about the rest of my family."

"That's what Rowan wanted, and it didn't work did it? Do you see her here?"

His face is so sad that I suddenly understand. "You're afraid I won't come back."

Papa turns and walks into the kitchen. I follow. He stops by the table and just stares at me.

"Aquila is my home, but I want to see more of the world. Can't you let me do that? Please? I'm old enough. And I promise to come back."

I think he's not going to answer at all, will just turn around, walk away and then I'll have to decide what to do. But a big breath whooshes out of him like a gust of wind. His shoulders sag and he shakes himself.

"I do understand. Didn't I leave your mother and sister? I convinced myself that I had to do that to keep them safe. And now, after all this time, I think maybe I was wrong, shouldn't have left. I've been worried because you don't seem to have many friends your age. Has it always been like that?"

"Ali and her sisters are my friends." I hesitate, then curiosity makes me continue. "There was Maxim, too. I don't remember much about him. I was only seven or so when he died, wasn't I?"

Papa's face grows even sadder looking. "You and Maxim were inseparable. I thought you'd forgotten about him."

"It was a runaway horse, wasn't it? That killed him."

"Yes, at his father's inn. The family never got over it. They left within a year."

"I didn't know that. I went by the inn the other day but didn't see anyone I remembered."

Papa shakes his head. "Lots of memories from the past coming back since Rowan returned. But there's no way to fix some things."

"I know, but that doesn't mean we can't find new ways to go on. We should follow our hearts. That's what you've told me more than once. And I need to make my own mistakes. Please let me go with Thea, Papa, even if you think it's wrong."

He sinks into a kitchen chair and rests his head in his hands. I just stand and wait. What else can I say to convince him? Am I wrong to try?

Finally, he raises his head. "I won't stop you."

I grin. He doesn't smile back. I want to cheer and jump up and down, but I do none of that to spare his feelings. Instead, I give him a quick hug.

"Thank you. Now I have to go talk to Thea."

"I don't think she'll be hard to convince," Papa's mumble follows me.

I knock softly on the door to the new bedroom, then open it a crack. Thea is folding clothes into a bag. The boys are asleep in the middle of the new bed.

"Can I talk to you?" She waves me in.

"I don't want to wake the boys," I whisper.

"They sleep through thunderstorms. What is it?"

"Could I come to Schönspitze with you instead of Rowan?"

She folds one more set of small breeches. Puts her hands on her hips and stares at me. "Have you discussed this with your father?"

"Yes. He's agreed to let me go if you're willing."

"Really?" Thea frowns, picks up a tiny tunic. "He said that?"

"Yes." Quickly I add, "I know you prefer Rowan, but who knows when she'll get back. Won't I do?"

"How soon can you be ready to leave? There's a caravan heading to the mountains in two days."

That's when I realize that Thea has been seriously packing.

Chapter V
Memento

I'm sorting through a pile of clothes on my bed trying to think of all the things I might need. What will the weather be like on the journey? What might we be doing besides riding? Papa said I can take the soprano flute, but I don't think I'll have room for even a small drum so I'm mostly thinking about clothes to take.

I had to let Tamtan know that I can't play for the school opening; one of the hardest things I've ever done. It's such an honour to be asked, but I might not be here and even if I'm back in time, I won't have put in the practise needed. I could see the disappointment on Tamtan's face. It almost made me change my mind, but this is my chance to travel. I might not get that again. Anyway, the drum teacher wished me well.

He even offered me tisane and a honey cake, but I said I had to hurry home.

I glare at the two saddle bags I'm allowed. They're not very big. I've packed twice already and both times decided I had too much stuff. One more try. I keep getting distracted by thoughts of the caravan and what it will be like to travel, worries about Rowan, guilt about leaving Papa. But the need to go is stronger than any of these.

I've watched caravans come and go in the City of Eagles since I was a small boy. Because we live on the edge of a desert, we don't have space to grow as much food as we need, and there's no huge forest nearby for hunting, nor enough grazing space for meat animals to feed the whole city. We have to bring in a lot. But we have musicians and artists, as well as other craftspeople who have goods and talents to sell and trade. Our carpets are famous and get good prices; our metal work is sought after. There's camel breeders and sellers, of course, and a couple of horse breeders, too, as well as a few sheep and goat farmers.

I've never travelled with a caravan, though. When Papa, Rowan and I came back from Hrashak's castle it was just the three of us in a wagon pulled by two oxen. And I was too worried about Rowan, who slept a lot, to pay much attention to the journey home.

There's a rattle of wheels and hoofbeats outside. I glance from the window to catch sight of the back of a donkey and loaded cart. Heading up to the palace maybe. The artists' house across from ours is quiet.

I can see into their courtyard because their house is only one-storey. No one's there.

I haven't seen Ali for days. I'm not sure whether it's because she's avoiding me or I'm avoiding her. Maybe we're avoiding each other because we haven't been getting along lately. Now that I'm leaving, though, I've got to at least say good-bye. I cram a last tunic into a bag and glare at the heap of clothes on my bed. I'll leave the rest behind. A few are too small for me anyway. The bottom of the wooden chest that usually holds my clothes is mostly empty, dusty with scraps of leather and a few crumples of parchment.

There's also a black stone, small enough to hold in my hand. A memento from the old man's castle: I pried it out of the dungeon wall and kept it. Hesitantly I pick it up and polish it on my tunic. It's shiny enough to dimly reflect one of my eyes.

I shiver as I remember the darkness of Hrashak's dungeon, completely impenetrable. Rowan and I were able to make light using the bracelets, and that's when I found the stone. It made me think of the arrow heads from the Lord's Militia, a reminder of home. I stuff the stone into my belt pouch next to the bracelet wrapped in a bit of silk. I know what I want to do.

After the cook lets me into the artists' house, I cross the courtyard and rap gently on the door to Ali's room. There is no answer. I push down the latch and open it slowly. The room is empty except for a bed, a wooden chest, a set of shelves holding paint brushes, paint pots, a mortar and pestle and other things I don't know the use of. There's also a small table and a chair. The walls are white. I haven't been in Ali's room for a long time and it shocks me to see it look so normal. I'd certainly expected murals on the walls, paints and brushes scattered about rather than neatly stowed. There aren't even any painty rags or clothes. Has Ali stopped painting altogether? Is that my fault?

I back out and close the door. The cook has disappeared, back to the kitchen probably. Should I go wandering about looking for Ali? It's not good manners.

"Samel." Ali stands behind me. "I'm surprised to see you. Been busy with your cousins?"

"Yes. Sorry, I should have stopped by before now." I follow her out into the courtyard.

"What's happened?" she asks.

"Nothing. I mean …" I don't know how to say it.

Ali doesn't speak, merely stands waiting. With the sun behind her and the shadow of the fig tree over her face, I can't see her expression.

I clear my throat. "I, um, actually leaving tomorrow, and I wanted to talk to you before I go to the mountains with Thea," I say in a rush. "Came to give you something, too." I reach into my belt pouch, feel the smoothness that fits so perfectly into my hand. Pull it out. "Here."

She just stands there for a couple of moments. Shakes her head slightly. "The stone you found in Hrashak's castle?"

"I want you to have it." My voice squeaks and I scowl.

Ali puts both her hands behind her back and shakes her head. "Why would I want that?"

"You like stones, grind colours from rock and earth. I thought you might have it to remember me by. It's obsidian."

"From that wicked old magician's dungeon? No. What if he put a spell on it? Have you been carrying it ever since? What if that's why you're so restless. He wants you back in the mountains."

"Ali, he's dead! I saw his body myself. And I really don't think this stone is bad. When we found it, it made me think of home. The arrow heads of the Lord's Guard are made of obsidian."

"So? That doesn't mean the stone hasn't been put to evil use."

I look at the black rounded triangle in my hand. Could Ali be right? If I stare at it long enough it feels as if I might be able to see through it to somewhere else. I've tried that before but haven't managed to discern anything except the stone. When I was with Hrashak once, the stone turned warm under my fingers along with the silver bracelet. As if the two things were in tune, like a flute and a drum harmonizing together. Maybe there's a different way to find the stone's power, if it has any. Music?

"Samel?"

Two notes, D and G maybe. Or C and E flat from the minor scale could be more fitting. There's no time to test it, though. I blink and find Ali right in front of me, one finger on the stone.

"It feels cool," she says, then hesitates. "Wait, no, warm."

"Make up your mind!" I lean forward. "I'm sure it's not evil. It has a good feeling to me. Will you keep it while I'm gone? Think of me when you hold it and I'll think of you. Um, maybe just before we go to sleep each night. It will be a way to keep connected."

"Like you and Rowan with the bracelets? Are you thinking we might see or speak to each other?"

I shrug. "Who knows? We can try. Please?"

Ali smiles just a little as she takes the stone, holds it in a cupped hand. "It sounds as if you might miss me."

I step back. "Of course I'll miss you! I'm not running away from you." I feel my cheeks heat and am sure that my face is turning red.

"I'll miss you, too, Samel," Ali says softly. "And I will think of you when I hold the stone." She closes her fingers over it.

Chapter VI
Departure

The sun barely peeks over the distant edge of the desert, turning everything the colour of peach roses as we pass through the city gates. It's one of the longest caravans I've ever seen, with camels, horses, wagons and ox carts. Even Papa, when he came to see us off, said that it was more impressive than any he could recall. That's probably because Lord Davus, the ruler of Aquila, has provided funds and other support for it. A half dozen militia ride along as guards, and one of the large wagons is rumoured to hold special gifts from the Lord to some leader in the mountains. I wonder what those gifts are. We've traded with mountain people before, but it's always been informal, small caravans got together by merchants. This time it seems there's more at stake, though when I tried to question Papa, he only shook his head.

Maybe Papa put me off because we were out in the open when I asked, standing near the city gates. Anyone could have heard. Or maybe it's more like the complications about the school, though I don't see how that could be. I've grown up with the currents of power in the City of Aquila, heard much from Papa about diplomacy and politics. Even a musician like Papa has to know enough to keep out of trouble. The last time someone tried to manipulate power, Papa, Rowan and I ended up prisoners in Hrashak's castle. But the old sorcerer is safely dead, and his castle is taken over by his former wife and his daughter. I've heard no rumours about them, and though Hrashak's daughter wasn't friendly to us, she didn't stop us leaving after Rowan killed her father.

My camel, Izmeer, ambles along swaying from side to side. He raises his head and bellows as he catches a whiff of open desert. I lift my head and smile; I'm on my way!

Spiny plants line the road which is packed sand and stones. I know this road was made long ago when the first lord started building the city. Soldiers used it then. Now it's mostly caravans and a few lone traders. But as far as the names of plants go, I've no idea, unlike my sister. Ali might know because her family uses plants, ground rock and similar things to make pigments. Maybe there's someone in the caravan who knows about plants. What new things will I learn on this journey?

The sun beats down. Ali gave me a new broad-brimmed hat which shades me nicely; she said my old one was too tattered. I'm wearing the loose cotton robes of experienced caravanners. These protect against the unshaded sun and keep me cool at the same time. Once Papa agreed, however half-heartedly, that I could go on this journey he was generous in outfitting me. Though Papa looked sad this morning, he didn't complain about my going.

Thea has been grumpy ever since we got up and now she frowns. She's probably wishing Rowan were here instead of me. And maybe my sister would be better at helping to look after the boys, even though they seem to like me. Thea had a hard time getting them into the wagon. They kept trying to run away; maybe they have bad memories of the trip from the north. It can't be very comfortable riding in an open wagon for days under sun or rain, heat and cold. Papa and I helped chase the boys down, but even after we got them into the wagon they kept trying to climb out. Thea tied them in with soft strips of cloth. It seemed wrong to me, but I didn't have any better suggestions.

Papa waved for a long time as we set off. An eagle followed us for a while, but it's gone now; it's odd not to have an eagle or two in the sky somewhere. I'm riding close to the wagon holding Thea and the twins; we're at the end of the line with only two militia riders behind us. The boys sit quietly now, looking at me. Thea has her eyes closed. One of the boys pulls at the knot of the scarf at his waist. It doesn't come undone, though it loosens.

I reach into my tunic and pull out the wooden flute in its cloth bag. Papa gave it to me for the journey so I could keep doing at least some music. Izmeer will walk happily following the rest of the caravan even if I'm not holding the reins, so I start playing a simple tune.

A small puff of dust rises from the road in front of us, whirls away across the flat scrub surrounding us. I still have the ability to make wind, which might come in useful at some point, though right now I can't imagine how. Strands of Thea's hair rise from her head. The boys grin and bounce a little. The ends of the cloths tying them dance in the breeze, the knots loosen more. Not a good thing. I stop playing and the breeze does, too. The boys' mouths turn down and one of them whimpers.

Thea opens her eyes. "What's the matter now?"

Quickly I put the flute away. "Just feeling restless I guess."

Thea inspects the knots. "Coming undone," she mumbles. She tightens the scarves.

"Do they have to be tied?" I ask. "If it was me, I'd hate it."

"I don't want them falling out," she says shortly. The boys are wriggling like worms on hooks.

"It's horrible," I say. "Let them loose."

Thea ignores me.

One of the boys has got himself undone and is scrambling for Thea's lap, hindering her. The other bursts into a babbling song. Thea grabs for an arm of each but the boys slip to the side and stand looking out.

"Kosto! Pello! Both of you sit down," Thea shouts.

"Do you need help?" I ask.

"No it's fine. Boys, sit or no bananas!"

The mention of food always settles the twins. It's a wonder they're not as round as melons, the amount they eat. Was I like them when I was small? Was Rowan? Why can't I remember those early days? Will these boys remember anything of this journey? Papa used to tell me stories about my childhood, but I wish I knew more.

Thea leaves the boys loose as they eat. My own stomach grumbles softly, reminding me that breakfast was extra early. There's nuts, dried grapes and a bit of hard cheese in my saddle pouch, so I munch happily. The caravan continues moving slowly, only the mounted militia showing any speed. Most ride horses, but a couple have camels. How did they decide about that? It must take a lot of planning and work to organize a caravan. Could I do something like this when I get older? Would I want to? Has there ever been a caravan of musicians?

Everyone I know seems to take it for granted that my work will be something to do with music – I may play in an orchestra, teach or compose. But is that

what I want to do? I used to think so, but I'm not
sure anymore. Maybe this journey will help me decide.

The riders take it in turns to gallop along the line
of wagons, heads swivelling, eyes here, there and everywhere. This close to Aquila there's not likely to be
any bandits, but it's good to know our guards are on
the job. The sun rises higher and sweat trickles down
my neck.

"Samel!" Thea calls. "Can you help me raise this
leather sun protector?"

The caravan moves slowly enough that I can stop,
tie Izmeer to the wagon and join Thea and the boys.
Designs of intertwined knots in silver and gold are
painted on the outside of the cart. Inside it's compact,
but large enough for the three of them to sleep in.
Thea has stocked it with food, water and a couple of
soft toys for the boys – a camel and a horse. At each
corner of the wagon a long piece of wood sticks up.
Thea has a large piece of rolled leather with narrow
ties. She starts to fasten it to the first post. The ox,
left to itself, saunters along contentedly following the
wagon in front. We get the leather sun protector tied
down quite easily. The boys are curled in one corner
of the wagon, eyes nearly closed, mouths and cheeks
crusted with banana.

"I should wipe their faces," Thea whispers, "but
I'll wait until after their naps. Thanks for helping. Go
on, get back on Izmeer again. It's crowded in here."

"Want to trade places for a while? I don't mind
staying in the cart to watch the boys."

"I've never ridden a camel."

"It's not hard," I say. "I could get Izmeer to kneel, but we're moving so slowly and he's close to the cart. Let me help you climb on."

We manage it without too much trouble. At first Thea holds herself stiffly and grasps the reins tightly. She keeps shifting her legs, which are hanging down on either side.

"Relax," I say. "Izmeer won't throw you off. Curl your legs up by the saddle post. Remember the way I was riding? Sway with his movement. And don't try to control him the way you would a horse. He'll follow the wagon."

The cart rumbles and jostles on the bumpy dirt track. It's not as comfortable as riding a camel. I think about how carts are fashioned, consider whether they could be made easier to ride in. An extra mattress or more blankets under us would help. Maybe there is a way the wheels and the pole that holds the wheels could be put together not to bounce so much. Who would know about that? There must be wagon and cart builders in Aquila. So many things I've never thought about.

We're surrounded by sand, low hills and shallow valleys. Traders' Road will wind through this until it reaches the first oasis. I remember that from when Papa, Rowan and I came back from Hrashak's castle. This caravan will probably get to the oasis by lunch time.

Papa and I used to walk in the desert close to the city, especially on clear, cool evenings when the days had been extra hot. The militia leaves the gates open late then, builds watch fires outside the walls and it becomes a party. Food vendors set up booths, itinerant performers dance, drum, and sing.

On such nights the silhouettes of the Lord's Stargazers can be seen on the ramparts of the highest towers studying the sky, particularly if a celestial phenomenon is expected. Late summer is really popular for sky watching because each year there are falling stars, streaks of light sparking across the darkness.

A long time ago, it's said, people feared this time thinking that the stars would fall on houses and inhabitants, setting them on fire, perhaps burning the whole land. But mostly this never happened. A Stargazer or two speculated that just like people, stars could die. This made many sad because they thought that eventually there would be no more stars. The Stargazers explained that new stars would be born. I've often wondered how that works and how the Stargazers get their knowledge.

Staring up into the dark sky I'd imagine cities of stars, villages, isolated farms. You can see how in some places the stars cluster together and in other parts of the sky there are fewer. What do they look like close up to shine so bright? Perhaps the falling stars are wanderers, travellers that have strayed too far and fallen off the path. Stargazers have stories, too, about star gods and goddesses, even giving names to certain groups – the chariot, the bear, the eagle. Maybe someday people will find a way to travel to see those places in the sky. Right now, though, it's mid-morning and already getting hotter.

"I don't know how you can stand it here," Thea says, fiddling with her hat. "The heat and the sand, no trees or water. I prefer the cooler mountains or the northern forests."

I smile. "Aquila's not as hot or dry as this and that's where we live. But I like the desert and there's a lot more of it before we reach the mountains. Look at the beauty here. Shifting sands, shadows and light, tiny plants. Though if you're too hot I'll trade back."

Thea shakes her head. "Not yet."

I can see that she's taking in the scenery, perhaps with more generous eyes. We're passing a huge red-dish-brown boulder. There are no other rocks or out-croppings nearby and I wonder how that single rock got here. There are many mysteries in the desert.

Izmeer farts loudly and I hold my nose at the stench. Thea pulls her cotton scarf over her mouth and nose. Camels seem to enjoy farting and belching; unlike us, they don't think about being polite. I hope that Izmeer doesn't decide to pee. That can stink bad enough to make your eyes water. Thankfully, we're moving and can leave the smell behind.

In the cart I lean against a roll of bedding while keeping an eye on Thea and Izmeer, but my eyelids droop. The squeak of the wheels reminds me of a lullaby Papa used to sing to me. A clatter and rumble like many hooves running along a cobblestone street jerks me awake. It must be just the wheels of the cart rumbling over scattered stones. Some streets in Aquila are packed sand, but near the palace and the market lie cobblestone lanes that I like to stroll in. I turn a corner and am suddenly surrounded by bleating goats. They rub against me and my skin starts to itch.

"Samel! Wake up! Get me off this camel. Kosto, Pello, not now!"

A goat butts me in the side. I open my eyes and, talons, it's real! Instead of two little boys, there are a couple of small goats. Thea has managed to scramble off Izmeer and is in the cart, squashing me up against one side.

An elbow slams into my chin. "Ow! You made me bite my tongue."

"Got to get out the potion."

She pulls a pottery flask from her belt pouch, uncorks it and pours a slug down the throat of one goat, then the other. The goats bleat and shiver, then start to cry as they change back into little boys.

"Good thing we've got the sun shade up," Thea says. "I don't think anyone noticed."

"You're sitting on my foot," I complain.

"Sorry." She shifts. "Will your camel be all right without a rider? I think I should stay in the cart."

Izmeer trudges beside the wagon, looking rather mournful. I give him a shrug, meaning to say, what can you do? Izmeer's head moves up and down.

"He's fine. But," I say quietly, "I've never seen the boys change before. Rowan told me they can become goats, like you, and I remember you saying they stayed that way for a long time. Do they change back often?"

"Mainly when they get too agitated or overtired. And I thought I had it under control. There's spelled protections painted on the cart that help, but I forgot to give them their potion this morning. They're not old enough to have the control on their own, so they change any old time if I'm not careful. It's probably because I kept them in goat shape for so long when they were first born."

"Does it matter if people see them change?"

"Of course! I don't want them hurt by those who fear them."

"There have always been rumours of shape shifters. Some of these people may even have seen one or two before."

"Kosto and Pello are small boys," she says coldly. "They can't protect themselves."

One of the boys kicks me in the stomach. I don't know if it's an accident or meant. "It's too crowded in here. Guess I'll get back on Izmeer."

"That would be best."

Thea sounds cranky, but it's not my fault that the boys changed. Even if I'd been awake, I wouldn't have been able to stop them. Both are crying again and throwing themselves against the sides of the wagon.

"Why not let them run for a bit," I say. "The caravan's not moving very fast. I'll get off Izmeer and keep them safe."

Thea grumbles, but one boy is already trying to climb out of the cart; he probably understood what I said. I slide off Izmeer quickly and grab the boy, set him on the ground. Thea hands me the other. The boys toddle ahead, nearly colliding with the wheel of the next wagon. I sprint after them and hoist one under each arm.

"Watch it, boys. See where you're going."

I don't know how much they understand even yet, or whether they choose to pretend not to understand. When someone doesn't talk much it's hard to know what's going on in their heads. I carry the boys to the side of the road where they can run without getting near wheels or hooves. Izmeer follows along behind. I consider tying him to the wagon, but I'd rather let him walk free.

"Come on, boys, let's play a game. Do what I do."

They stop and look at me. I speak and suit action to words. The boys giggle and follow.

"Walk, walk, walk. Hop, hop, hop.

"Run, run, run. Now we stop."

They try to follow my actions, stumbling now and then. I have to be ready to catch them if they fall. One of them does land flat on his front but doesn't cry. Eventually I put the boys back in the wagon and they go to sleep.

Chapter VII
Stories

B y mid-day when we reach the first oasis, I'm pooped, so after watering Izmeer, and eating a bit of bread, dried meat, and fruit I stretch out in the wagon. Thea takes the boys for a walk to splash and cool off at the spring. I'm amazed they're on their feet again after all the exercise earlier. I can't get comfortable because the wagon is nothing but lumps, so I decide to reorganize it. Papa has taught me how to be neat and orderly, though I often ignore those lessons.

Under a blanket I find a worn leather-covered book. It's heavy as a sun-dried brick and much the same colour. Is this the book Rowan always talked about? I don't remember ever seeing it, but I was so small when Papa and I left the north. Maybe Mother read stories from it to both Rowan and me.

Between the covers the pages are thin, fine parchment. I worry that I might damage them, but they
turn smoothly and seem strong. A faint glow comes
from the book or perhaps a stray sunbeam reflects off
pale pages. The writing is curlicue and dark, not faded as I would have expected in an old book that may
have been in our family and Mother's for more years
than my age.

Here and there pictures in coloured inks stop my
breath. A black dragon rearing above a mountain
path; a man with red, green and blue ribbons swirling
about his clothes; and an eagle soaring in blue sky
over a mountain peak. I wish I'd known about this
book when we were still in Aquila. Ali would have
loved to see these illustrations. I study the eagle the
longest, have always been fascinated by the great eagles of Aquila, even more when I found out that Papa
could speak to at least one of them. I begin to read
the story called 'Kingdom of Eagles.'

*When the world was much younger than it is now, when
dragons still roamed, and animals could speak like people, when
many folk could take the shape of animals, there existed in
distant mountains a Kingdom of Eagles. There were old eagles
and young eagles, males and females, bald eagles, golden eagles,
and many others.*

*The kingdom covered a huge territory for eagles do not gen-
erally like to gather in flocks except under special circumstances.
When they are roosting in trees by a river or sea and waiting
to dive for fish, for example. And different sorts of eagles don't
usually congregate together. The eagles were much mightier than*

those seen nowadays, even larger than the guardian eagles of the great trading city of Aquila.

How amazing that Aquila is mentioned in such a book. I'm not sure how old the city is, but I guess it was founded before the book was written. Ali and I have talked about the first Lord of the city and how the eagles came to be the guardians. Perhaps there'll be something in the story about that.

Few people lived in this mountain refuge for the eagles took turns guarding the borders of their kingdom, and people feared the talons and beaks that could capture and rend. The great birds flew anywhere they wished, sailing on the winds, gliding on rivers of moving air. They watched over all that occurred in their land and along its borders.

Though the eagles mostly lived spread out in their territory quarrels did occur now and then, particularly among the different groups. A bald eagle doesn't necessarily want to give way to a golden and vice versa. However, any disputes that arose were settled by the king and his small group of advisors. Still, young eagles need to stretch their wings and at times this resulted in challenges to authority. The king and his counsellors had a way to deal with that as well.

Once a year in summer eagles gathered for a tournament in a hidden valley. This was very unusual among eagles, but the king, who was old and wise, had established the custom years before and it had become accepted. They held flying races and acrobatic competitions as well as demonstrations of soaring, diving and swimming. Yes, eagles can swim. They kick with their legs and row with their wings. All the eagles enjoyed these contests; those who won preened and shrieked their victories.

One year a very small eagle took part in the contests. No one expected her to do well, and it was true that she couldn't dive as fast or swim as well as the others, but during the cross-country flight this smallest of eagles surprised everyone. Somehow, she caught a wind current that circled up and up, which carried her higher than anyone else. The young eagle discovered that she could ride the winds at the tops of certain clouds.

The rest of the eagles lost sight of the juvenile. Even the swiftest couldn't find the smallest one. As the day waned all thought that the young eagle had been blown far away and they would never see her again.

The adventurer kept finding more currents to follow. Eventually she realized that she hadn't seen another eagle for a very long time. She was far from home, but how far? Hunger and thirst began to plague her. She cast about among the wind rivers and found a down draft. She landed in a narrow valley with a stream winding through it and slaked her thirst. The stream had only tiny fish, however, so the eagle took to the skies again in search of more substantial food.

She hoped for a rabbit or similar-sized creature that could be easily killed. And soon she spied a plump grey animal with rounded ears and no tail. Quickly the eagle dove, but the pika scampered into a thorny thicket, and unfortunately the eagle followed. The pika escaped but the eagle was held fast in the bush, pricked by thorns, tangled in branches. Shrieks and struggles came to nothing. No help appeared and the eagle could not get loose. She spent a very cold, hungry and lonely night.

With the morning came both fear and hope. It began with chiming and the sound of feet. The eagle crouched as low as *possible hoping she was hidden from whatever danger came. She couldn't stop herself from peeking, however, and saw a group of four-legged creatures and a two-legged one. Two-legs had no wings and though the eagle had heard stories of people, she'd never seen any before. The four-legged ones reminded her of the wild sheep that lived on high crags. The creatures in front of her, however, were much smaller than the wild sheep. They also had shiny things around their necks that made the singing sounds. The sheep browsed, stopping now and then to eat grass and leaves. The eagle thought that if she could get free, she just might be able to kill and eat one of these four-legs. But two-legs had a long stick that it used for walking and directing the sheep. It could be used as a weapon. After a while the two-legged being sat on a large flat rock and brought out food and began to eat.*

An involuntary faint shriek of hunger escaped the young eagle's beak. The sheep backed away from the bushes and huddled together. Two-legs came boldly forward and poked at the bushes with its stick.

"Bird! What are you doing there? Are you stuck?"

The eagle tried to shrink away from the stick, and then felt ashamed of being thought cowardly. She raised her head, opened her beak and screamed defiance.

The two-legged creature took a step back. "I don't want to hurt you. If you're trapped, maybe I can help."

Strange, the eagle thought, I can understand what this creature means. She had thought it an enemy, but perhaps that wasn't true.

The eagle clattered her beak. Two-legs seemed to take encouragement from the sound for it moved forward, bent down and reached out slowly. The eagle closed her beak and waited. The stick poked, the being moved, and the young eagle felt unfamiliar but gentle touches across her feathers. She ruffled pinions, stretched a wing and was lose from the thorns. A step into a gap, a hop and she was free.

Two-legs stood back.

The eagle tipped her head to look first at two-legs and then at the cluster of four-legs. She would not feed here, owed a debt of thanks. Spreading wings, she leaned forward, leapt and launched into air.

Below, the two-legged creature made noises that sounded pleased. The young eagle circled a few times, shrieking thanks. The sheep scattered and two-legs ran to gather them together. The young eagle headed for home. She had quite a story to tell.

"You found the book."

I jerk guiltily and close the covers. Thea and the twins are standing beside the wagon. "Sorry. I was just cleaning up a little and . . ."

"I brought it for Rowan. The book, I mean. Your mother had it. It belongs to both you and your sister."

The twins are thumping on the side of the wagon. "Up," they shout. "Up."

"Maybe they'll nap again," Thea says. "Then you and I can talk. There's things I haven't told you."

"The caravan might be moving out soon. I should get Izmeer ready."

"I spoke to the leader, Primarius, he calls himself. He said we'd be here a while yet. He wants everyone and the animals to have a rest during the hottest part of the day."

When the twins are asleep, which doesn't take long, Thea and I sit tailor fashion on a folded blanket beside the wagon. She holds the book and strokes it gently. Her head is raised, though, and her eyes look past me into the desert or ahead to the mountains.

After a while, Thea turns her eyes to me. "You haven't asked me any questions about this journey or about your mother."

"Well, you told us you'd had a message there were things to settle in the mountains. I was, am, curious, but it didn't seem polite to ask."

"And you're always polite?"

I shrug. "No."

Thea chuckles softly. "I didn't think so, and you have a right to know. My story starts before you were born. I don't know how much Rowan told you." She stops and I respond with a shrug. "Anyway, your mother and I grew up with two sets of grandparents, in Schönspitze in the mountains. The parents of both of us had died when we were young – a fever that swept through. We lived in a big house and despite the tragedy, had a good childhood. One grandmother taught Zarmine, your mother, about herbs and healing. The other grandmother taught me some small magics – changing a walnut into a beetle and a twig into a worm. Then, when we were grown, your mother met your father, a travelling musician, and she left with him. One pair of grandparents died soon after so there were only three of us left in the big house.

"Zarmine wrote to me now and then for about a year, but then the letters stopped. Five or so years after she left, your mother sent a message asking me to come to her in the northern forest. Our last living grandmother had died recently, and our grandfather had disappeared, so I was alone.

"When I joined your mother, I found her living with just your sister, Rowan. Zarmine wouldn't talk about what had happened between her and your father. Didn't tell me she had a son as well.

"Your mother persuaded me to develop my shape-shifting. I learned to become a goat and spent much of my time that way because supposedly there was danger from an unspecified source. Zarmine didn't want anyone to know I was there. Thinking about it now, it all seems very odd. Why did I give in to her? I did wonder at the time if your father was the danger, and asked why we couldn't leave, find a safer place. Zarmine wouldn't consider it and gave me no reasons. So I just did what she wanted."

"Why a goat?" I ask. "You could have chosen some other animal, couldn't you?"

Thea smiles and looks out over the desert toward the west. "I was named after a legend. Amalthea, a goat who saved a child from being killed by secreting him in a mountain cave."

"Who was the child?"

"The son of a wizard who feared the child's power. There'd been prophecies. I don't remember all the details now. In the end it was the wizard who died."

Thea sighs. "I wish I could have done something to prevent Zarmine's death."

"But that was Hrashak's fault, the old sorcerer. We found that out later."

"Hmm." She's staring off into distance again, frowning. "Did Rowan tell you that your mother fed her a tisane regularly to make her forget about you and your father? I wonder if she did something similar to make me agree with her. It didn't occur to me at the time."

"Really? Rowan didn't tell me that. How could a mother do that?"

Thea sighs. "She must have thought it was for the best. She didn't want Rowan to face the pain of missing you."

"It was hard when I found out I had a sister still alive and a mother who'd just died. I don't think it was right what our parents did."

"Parents do strange things at times."

"Like you taking your boys away from their father? Who was he?"

"Ah, politeness is over." Thea shakes herself and looks at me. "I didn't take them away from him. He never knew them, was a peddler, someone I met in my wanderings in the forest near your mother's cottage. Mostly I stayed in goat shape because your mother insisted, but at times I wanted to be myself again. Anyway, he didn't know I was with child, was long gone when the twins were born." Thea looks down at the book she is still holding.

"He's not mentioned in there is he?" I ask.

"What? No! At least I don't think so. Still, this book is strange. Sometimes I read a story in it and later I can't find it again."

"Speaking of not finding again, didn't the peddler ever return?"

"Well," Thea clears her throat, "as a matter of fact, he was the one who brought the message, a letter from an advocate who worked for my family in Schönspitze, telling me that there was family business to do."

"So he did meet the boys!"

"No. I was in the village alone and he found me there. I'd left the boys with a neighbour."

"But you told their father about them."

"No."

I stare at Thea, shake my head. "I don't believe this. You, Papa, our mother. How could you do these things? My friend Ali's parents wouldn't dream of abandoning any of their children, I'm sure!"

"I didn't abandon . . ."

The shouts of the caravan leader interrupt us. It's time to start off again. Gladly I jump up to find Izmeer. I've had enough of Thea. I check my saddle and harness to make sure all is secure. Out of the corner of my eye I see that someone is helping Thea with the ox and the wagon, which is good because I can't be anywhere near her right now. All the words I could say are rolling around in my head like stones in a rushing creek.

Once I'm mounted on Izmeer I leave the wagon holding Thea and the boys behind. There's plenty to see in this caravan, lots of other people to meet. Two women drive one of the wagons. I nod at them as I pass, and they smile back. A burly lone driver waves me over and asks if I'd like a drink.

"Hot out here," he says handing over a ceramic flask.

I take a swallow, expecting water and nearly spill the flask with my coughing.

The driver grins. "Distilled wine," he says. "Some call it brandy. Never tasted it before?"

I shake my head, still unable to talk and hand the flask back. I ride beside his wagon thinking about my earlier ideas for softer rides. Study the wheels of this wagon to see how they're fastened.

"What's wrong?" the wagoner calls to me. "Is something wrong with the wheels?"

"I don't think so. I'm just trying to figure out how the wheels stay on and how they turn. I tried to make a toy wagon once and I could never get the wheels to turn properly."

"That's a wheelwright's business," the man snaps. "Just because I gave you drink you're not used to, don't be giving me the evil eye!"

He scowls and I decide to ride on. Why did he say that to me? What does he know or guess? I don't know how to find out except to pay more attention to the other people in the caravan.

Izmeer glides along so smoothly it almost feels as if we're gently flying. Too bad wagons don't ride as easily as camels. One of the guards who is also riding a camel stops me near the middle of the line.

"Off somewhere?" he asks.

"I just want to give my camel more exercise."

Does this guard think like the wagon driver? Will he make me go back to my former place in the caravan?

"Now that is a good idea!" He grins. "I'm Distans. What's your name?"

"Samel."

"You up for a race?"

I nod, relieved that he's friendly.

He points ahead. "That boulder. First one there wins a sliver coin. Agreed?"

"Yes."

We line up our camels and the guard yells, "Go!"

His camel is larger than Izmeer and older. That might be good or bad, but I have no time to think. Izmeer stretches his neck and is off. I've never tried racing with him, and his usual speed is a slow walk or a relaxed lope. Now he's skimming over the road like a dust devil before the wind. The other camel thumps along at my side, but a touch back. I want to lean forward but am afraid of falling off. I'm hanging onto the reins with both hands as well as to the front of my saddle. There's slack in the reins; don't know if that's the right way to ride in a race or not. In my head I hear Mustafa's voice: "Fool boy! What are you up to now?" Cheers rise from the caravan as we surge past. We're providing a little excitement on a dull day. I hear the guard yelling at his camel and then Izmeer and I have reached the boulder. I pull back on the reigns, slowing Izmeer gradually. Once we've stopped, I mop sweat from my face.

The guard rides up beside me grinning. "Well raced!" He pats Izmeer. "Talk to you again later. Now I've got to get back to my work."

I watch him as his camel walks off. The wagoner beside me waves to get my attention. I bring Izmeer closer.

The wagoner holds out a skin bag. "Have a drink."

"Is it water or something else?"

"Just water," he says, then grins. "Ah, you've met Ganeo?" Waves a hand to the rear. "He never carries water."

"Thanks." I take a deep drink and hand back the skin.

Chapter VIII
Oasis

We reach the second oasis by midafternoon – a bubbling spring, a few palm trees and clumps of striped grass. Primarius, the caravan leader, tells everyone that he wants to get to the hostelry by nightfall so we're stopping only briefly. I've avoided speaking to Thea for a while, left her to handle the boys on her own. It's not right, I know, especially since I'm not angry at the twins and I like them. I noticed, though, that Distans started riding close to Thea's wagon. The two of them seemed to be having a long conversation at one point. None of my business, really.

As I'm giving Izmeer a rub down under a palm tree, I hear small voices.

"Sam. Sam!"

The twins are running ahead of their mother, arms out, grinning. My mouth stretches to match their smile. I look around for Distans, but don't see him nearby. I give Izmeer an apple to crunch and a pat. Then I crouch to the boys.

"Hey, what's going on?"

Together the boys smack into my chest, nearly knocking me down.

"They've missed you," Thea says.

I sit on the ground and let the boys crawl over me. They tug on my hair, investigate my ears, pull at my tunic. Thea hunkers beside us.

"Do you think they'll start talking more soon?" I ask, not looking at Thea, as I pull a chunk of travel bread out of my pouch and break off a bit for each of them.

Thea shrugs as the boys sit and begin to chew. "Probably. But even now they can make themselves understood."

"Especially when it comes to food." I break off more bread for them.

Thea taps my knee. "Look," she says, "I'm sorry about being so grouchy before . . ."

"No, it was my fault. I wasn't there, have no idea what things were like when you lived with my mother. Don't even know what my mother was like. She could have been horrible for all I know."

"Didn't Rowan or your father talk about her?"

"Sure, they told me stuff, but it's not the same as knowing for sure or remembering."

Thea nods. "The way she tilted her head like you're doing now. How her eyes crinkled like yours do when you're happy."

A lump in my throat stops words and I just shake my head.

"Life isn't always easy," Thea says. "And we don't have to be perfect. After Rowan left to find you and your father I wanted to pack up and go after her, even though she didn't want me to. I spent a lot of time chopping wood, pulling weeds, yelling at the moon."

I choke off a laugh. "Did it help?"

"A bit. Then when I got the message about Schönspitze I was relieved. I wouldn't have to stay there anymore, and I had a good excuse to come see Rowan."

"But she wasn't there."

"Hmm. And the twins were a handful. At times on the way down from the cottage I was ready to give them away."

"Not seriously."

"No, not really. I love them." Thea pats her sons on the head. One of them grabs for her hand.

"How do you tell them apart?"

"A mother always knows."

"What about the rest of us?"

She smiles slightly. "Take a look at this one's eyes. The right is a little bigger than the left and that eyelid droops a bit. That's Kosto."

I bend my head to study the boys who are just finishing their bread. I've known them for some weeks now and didn't look at them very closely. Pello's cheeks are plumper and his nose is smaller.

"Mount up!" Primarius' shout is picked up by the guards.

"Help me get the boys in the wagon?" Thea asks. "And by the way, your voice seems to be settling down."

She smiles at me and I feel my face heat. She noticed my squeaking? I duck to lift the boys. They're heavier than I remember; could they have gained weight in just a few hours? I don't know much about little boys or girls. Or even about people my own age, I guess. Has my voice really stopped cracking? I can't remember being bothered by it recently. I find the soft camel and horse toys, hand them to the boys, and they snuggle together. They'll probably sleep for a while again. Izmeer kneels for me and I'm up and riding beside the wagon.

Thea leans over. "I've been thinking about everything you said. The more I ruminate about it, the more it seems strange that I let your mother persuade me to stay as a goat so much." She slaps the reigns on the ox's back.

"And not telling the peddler that he was a father? Was that my mother's fault, too?"

Thea shrugs one shoulder and urges the ox on. I watch the wagon pull away and decide it's not worth arguing with her anymore. The past can't be changed. I ride along through the late afternoon looking across the desert, but not really seeing it. I'm musing about my mother, recalling some of the things Rowan told me about her. Rowan wasn't sure whether it was our mother who persuaded our father that the two of us should be separated or the other way around. They could have made the decision together. Because they were afraid of what the bracelets could do, especially jointly.

There was that incident in the forest that neither of us remembers, but that Papa wrote about in a letter to our mother. A wolf threatened us and somehow we had the bracelets and the wolf backed off. Papa worried about the intentions of his uncle, Hrashak who he didn't like. We later found out Hrashak was responsible for our mother's death. He had been watching all of us and the wolf could have been him for he was a shape shifter, too. So, Mother had been right that there was danger, but did that give her a reason to ask Thea to stay in goat shape? What kind of a grown-up will I be? Too many questions without answers. I don't know enough about my family. Maybe I'll learn more in Schönspitze. I'll have to ask Thea to tell me as much as she remembers about my mother, if she's willing.

Chapter IX
Changes

At dusk we reach the hostelry in the only village between Aquila and the mountains. I vaguely remember it from when Papa, Rowan and I escaped from Hraschak's castle. We were both worried about my sister then, so I don't remember many details about this village. It's a small place with one street, various huts and cottages scattered along it. In the centre stands a two-storey mud brick building with timbered uprights and cross pieces. The caravan enters the enclosing wall of the yard through a double gate standing open. With stables and other outbuildings there is barely room for all the wagons, horses and camels. I doubt that the main hostelry building will have bedrooms enough for us all.

"Most will want to sleep with their wagons," Primarius shouts. "I've a room on the second floor. The hostel keeper will direct you if you need me."

Primarius clamps an arm around a rotund, short man with straggly black hair. The man grins and waves a hand, then the two of them walk off. A couple of skinny boys come running to sort out the confusion, bring fodder for the animals, point out the well, and arrange stable space for those who insist upon it for their horses.

"I guess we'll sleep in our wagon," Thea says. "I'd been hoping for a bed, but I think I'd rather keep watch over our things."

"I could sleep in the wagon if you want to get a room for you and the twins," I offer.

"No, I'll stay out here. It looks like it will be a fine night. I hope we can buy a bowl of stew or something like that, though."

"Roast chicken and vegetables in the kitchen," a man holding a bowl says. "Not bad."

As I'm grooming Izmeer one of the stable hands sidles next to me. "Nice camel. You heading to the mountains? Best leave your camel here and take one of our horses. Straight trade and switch back when you return. We'll take good care of him."

"No," I say shortly, and lead Izmeer to the water trough.

The stable hand shrugs and wanders off.

Thea, hanging onto a boy with each hand follows me. "The man had a point," she says.

"I don't want to leave Izmeer here. I don't know these people. How can I trust them to take care of him?"

Thea sighs. "Samel, he can't go into the mountains. It's not camel country."

"But no one said anything about this before!"

"I guess everyone else in the caravan assumed you knew."

"I'm just supposed to leave him here and ride in the ox cart with you and the twins the rest of the way? There's barely room for the three of you."

"We'll manage. Or you could trade as he suggested."

"I don't trust the stable hands. They both look shifty. What if they sell Izmeer once we're gone? Or forget to feed him properly?"

Thea glances around. There is a great deal of bustle and commotion in the inn yard. Wagons are moved into position, horses and oxen stabled. The boys splash in the water trough, the ox munches on a handful of hay. Izmeer stands beside me waiting for his fate.

"There's another possibility," Thea says so quietly that I can barely hear her. "A way you can keep Izmeer, but if it works, you can't tell anyone."

"How?" I whisper back. "Tell me."

Thea moves so that our shoulders touch. "You know that I can shapeshift."

"Yes."

"I've gotten even better than your sister knew.

Didn't have much to do on those winter nights last year in the north woods, just me and the boys, and the animals."

"So?"

"Chickens into turkeys, donkeys into dogs. And back again."

"Can you change Izmeer? Into a horse maybe?"

"I think so. But people would be suspicious if Izmeer just disappeared and you suddenly had a horse. We'd need a plan."

"What if I said that I'd sold Izmeer and bought a horse?"

"How, where?"

"There's a lot of people staying here. How would anyone know that I hadn't met someone and did the deal?"

"Let me think about it," Thea says "We're not leaving until tomorrow morning. Maybe we could do something late tonight. After we've had something to eat and I have put the boys to bed."

Much later the stars are out; I'm wrapped in a blanket propped up against the wheel of Thea's ox cart, dozing. The boys sleep soundly inside the cart. Thea has gone off somewhere.

"Evening."

I lift my head to see a man standing in front of me, cloak and hood on, head ducked. He looks vaguely familiar, but I don't recall seeing him in the caravan. He could be one of the other guests staying at the hostelry.

"Heard you was in the market for a horse," he says in a low voice. "And want to trade a camel. Me, I'm heading into the desert later, so could use a camel."

"Sorry, I'm not selling." I straighten and unwrap from the blanket.

"Your friend, she told me," the man adds.

"Thea?"

"Said she'd meet us outside the wall. Told me to tell you, bring your camel."

He starts to walk away. Has Thea actually made a deal with him to sell Izmeer? That's not what we agreed. But if it's to help us change my camel, why didn't she warn me? I glance at the boys. They are solidly asleep. I could go and see what Thea wants. Distans is lounging against a nearby wall.

"Can you watch the wagon and the boys for a little while? I need to go do something."

He probably thinks I'm heading for the privy. I untie Izmeer, check that the rope around his neck isn't too tight. The stranger walks very quickly. I almost have to run to keep up with him. Izmeer ambles along behind me. As I follow the cloaked and hooded man toward the gates it occurs to me, I could be making a mistake. What if he's hurt Thea and is going to rob me? I could ask someone to go with me, but Thea didn't want anyone else to know what we were doing.

I touch my belt knife for reassurance and slow my steps, but the man is heading out of the inn yard and Izmeer nudges me along. I glance along the outer wall. It's rather dark here and I can't see any sign of a horse and there are no other people. What do I do now? I stop and fumble at my belt knife, turn to look back into the yard. Should I yell for help?

"Samel." It's Thea's voice behind me.

When I spin to look, all I see is the stranger who brought me here. I search the shadows but see no one else. Could it be? She is a shape shifter. Could she have learned how to be a man?

"Yes," she whispers, "it's me. Quickly, bring Izmeer here and then if you don't mind, turn your back and walk some distance. It distracts me to be watched when I'm working at this."

"Can you change him back later?" I ask. "He won't be a horse permanently?"

"Of course," Thea says.

I hope that she's telling the truth. She sounds certain, so I do as she asks. There's faint chanting, a few grunts and groans, then more chanting and some stamping. It's hard not to turn and look. There's a tug at my shoulder, then breath in my ear. I swivel to find a small sand-coloured horse with a white mane. Thea stands beside it.

"Izmeer?" I say.

Thea nods and the horse snorts into my shoulder. I grin and pet my friend.

"Sorry it's not as big as the other horses, but this is the best I could do," Thea says. "Let's get back inside the wall. I need to eat again and then sleep. This . . ." She stumbles and I grab her, "takes a lot out of me."

I get her back to the wagon. Distans stares at my horse.

"Thea found someone to trade my camel."

The guard nods. "Not a bad looking horse. The others who had camels have switched them for horses. We've paid a couple of people from the village to take the camels back to Aquila tomorrow." He offers to fetch Thea another bowl of chicken and vegetable from the inn kitchen.

I could have sent Izmeer back if I'd known about this arrangement. Guess I'd better pay more attention to what's going on in the caravan, listen to people talk, ask more questions. Oh well, I'm glad to have Izmeer with me. I fetch a bundle of hay and a handful of oats for him. No one seems to be paying us much attention, busy with their own affairs, eating, feeding animals, getting ready for sleep or already dozing. I realize that I'll have figure out a way to switch my camel saddle and tack for gear to suit a horse.

It's our first night sleeping out as a caravan and I'm not used to it – the snores, the shifting of animals, footsteps, laughter. Are some of these people planning on staying awake all night? If it keeps on like this, I'm likely to tumble off Izmeer tomorrow because I'll fall asleep while riding. And I'm going to have to get used to riding a horse, which is different from riding a camel. I've no experience in that. Why didn't I think more about what I was doing before I set out, talk to a few people? I was in such a hurry to get away.

I'm familiar with the desert, but mountains are quite new to me. I've heard it can be cold there. When we were at Hrashak's castle in the mountains last summer we spent hardly any time outside. It's nearly the end of summer now. I hope I have enough warm clothes. Even out here in the desert it's chilly at night; I pull my blanket closer. At last it's quieter. I can drift off, dream, see Rowan maybe, ask her some of my questions. My eyelids flicker, droop. Rowan's chattering too much for me to get a word in, clucking away with a group of people I don't know. They sound like a bunch of worried chickens.

"Hey!"

I sit up quickly, bump my head on the wheel of the wagon. Torches flare, men run here and there. A rotund man waves his arms. It's the hostel keeper. I get up, approach him. A group gathers round.

"It's all right," the hostel keeper says. "Go back to sleep. A fox or two after the chickens. We've had a bit of trouble that way lately, but we'll catch those beasts eventually."

Chapter X
Mid-Day

Riding a horse is definitely not the same as riding a camel. Thea found me an old saddle and other gear for a horse, making some kind of deal with a merchant at the hostelry early this morning, not someone travelling with the caravan. If any of the wagoners ask about the switch I'll just say it was a spur of the moment thing.

The saddle isn't very comfortable. Even more difficult if the horse was once a camel and tries to act like one. That first morning Izmeer scares himself when he neighs as the Aquilan guards' camels are ridden away, and I nearly slip off his back. He wants to go with them, and he isn't used to the sound of his new voice.

He also doesn't like the clomp, clomp of his hooves on the hard-packed road as we move away from the village. Camel feet are much quieter than horses. And of course, camels move the feet on each side together while horses move their feet crosswise. Poor Izmeer! I didn't think of all these disadvantages when I let Thea change him.

I chat to and pat my horse/camel as we ride, ignoring my legs' tendency to want to curl up by the saddle. A horse isn't made the same way as a camel and your legs have to hang down one on each side and tuck into stirrups.

What if it was just as hard for Rowan to come and live with Papa and me as it is for Izmeer to be what he is not? That just never occurred to me at the time because I was so happy to find my sister. The bracelet lies well wrapped in my belt pouch. Perhaps this evening I can find a quiet and private place to use it and try to reach Rowan. Maybe I should apologize to her for not understanding. Would she forgive me? Or say it wasn't my fault?

Then I remember Ali. I forgot to think of her last night before going to sleep! She's going to be annoyed with me all over again. I imagine her now, sitting under the olive tree in their yard, but of course there's too much distraction around me to get a real vision of her.

Distans, the caravan guard, is riding his magnificent black horse close to the wagon and talking with Thea. I'm trying not to compare Izmeer as a horse with Distans' mount. Thea looks a little nervous, so I wonder if she's worried about the boys changing shape. This morning she gave each of them a good gulp of potion before we set out. Maybe I could do something to relieve her worries.

"Thea, would you like to ride for a while? I can look after the boys."

At the moment Kosto and Pello are playing with a strip of leather, pulling it between them, taking turns chewing on it. Thea nods and we make the exchange. She and Distans ride off toward the front of the caravan. I find a couple of apples and cut pieces for each of the boys and myself. Thea has left them untied today and I'm happy to see it.

When we're finished eating I clap my hands. "Let's play a finger game. This is one my Papa taught me."

"Two little eaglets sitting in a tree (I wave my hands like the branches of a tree);

"One named Brack (I make a fist with my right hand),

"And one named Bree (make a fist with the other hand).

"Fly away Brack (I flutter my right hand and hide it behind my back);

"Fly away Bree (I hide the other hand).

"Come back Brack!

"Come back Bree!"

The twins giggle and clap their hands.

Kosto yells, "Fly!"

Pello shouts, "Back!"

I play this game with them over and over. They never get tired of it and each time they shout a different word. Soon they'll be stringing a bunch of words together. It's starting to get hot and I look for Thea to help me put up the sunshade. Then I realize that we're coming to the edge of the desert. There's a lot more shrubs and tufts of grass growing here and there. The boys have curled up and closed their eyes.

Distans and Thea come galloping. "The river's not far away," Distans says. "We'll stop at a shady spot for mid- day, then follow River Road to the mountains."

"You've come this way before?" Thea asks.

"Oh, yes, many times."

"Will we reach the mountains today?" I ask.

"No, though we'll soon catch sight of them. And then days to go before we get to Schönspitze."

The river, when we arrive at the stopping place, is different than at Aquila. There it's wide and swift, and the banks are steep in most places. Here the stream is narrower and the edges low and grassy. The caravan pulls into a grove of trees that forms a tunnel over the road. To our left, sunlight on water glints through leaves.

As soon as the wagon stops, the twins are awake and both yell, "Out! Out!"

No one wants to take too much time, so we don't build fires or cook meals, but rather eat dried or fresh fruit, nuts, cheese, bread, and dried meat. Animals are watered and allowed to graze a little. I take the boys down to the river because Thea wants to tidy the wagon. There's a narrow strip of sand and the water is shallow, so I let the boys wade.

I lean against a rock and throw bits of branches to Kosto and Pello. They scramble for them, float them in the water, then crawl out to stick them in the sand. As usual, they eventually put the bits of wood in their mouths and chew. Should I stop them? I don't see how this can hurt them even if they swallow bits of branch.

My nose starts to itch and then my arms. Suddenly all I can think of is goats – the way they smell, their sad bleats, two goats butting heads. Quickly I glance at the twins, who are wrestling now. A slight tightness develops between my eyes and then it's as if a knob is developing under my skin above each eye. I reach up a hand, but there's nothing.

"Samel!" It's Thea running up. "You should have called me. The boys are getting too rambunctious."

"They're fine," I growl.

Thea shakes her head and grabs the boys. "Time to go."

When we get back to the wagon Thea makes the boys drink the potion. Were they about to change? I'd have liked to see it, but of course, Thea doesn't want anyone to know that her children can change shape. For a moment or two I felt like a goat. Could I ever learn to change shape? It's never occurred to me that I could and I don't know if I'd really want to. It would cause even more complications in my life.

"Thea," I say, "do the boys always put everything in their mouths? Earlier they were chewing on a strip of leather and by the water they chewed on branches."

She sighs. "I think it's because of them being goats, for so much of their first years. Just keep an eye out and stop them putting things in their mouths if you can."

Chapter XI
River

For the next several days we travel along this road that winds by the water. People need rivers for travel, food, water, and play, but waterways are as different as people. Short or long, narrow or wide, sluggish or quick. Rowan doesn't like rivers, mostly I guess because our mother drowned in a northern one. That was the old sorcerer's fault though, so I don't see why the water should be blamed.

Papa used to take me to the river at Aquila often when I was small, and later I kept going there on my own, to fish, to swim, to hunt for stones and other treasures. This river beside us is part of the same one as at the City of Eagles and yet it has its own character and music. Which may sound odd, but the sounds and shapes of the water make me think at times of flutes, drums, and harps. The width and depth of water vary. Perhaps even the kind of fish, the birds that fly above it, and the animals that come to drink. A person could write a whole series of pieces of music about all that. I should make a few notes so that I have something to show my teachers when I get back home.

We haven't seen many wild animals on our journey so far, though. The caravan is too large and noisy probably, drives wild creatures away. I've seen snakes, a rabbit or two, and the hostel keeper mentioned foxes. Yesterday there were black birds in the distance. I've never seen a raven, though Rowan talked often about her pet raven in the north. The black birds could have been ravens although they seemed rather small.

I haven't seen any of the great eagles since we left Aquila. Last year when Papa and I were talking about finding my sister he sent an eagle to look for her and that bird flew far. It feels odd without an eagle or two in the sky.

I'm getting used to riding a horse, although Izmeer still isn't quite comfortable in this body. Occasionally he stumbles, and once today he tried to eat a spiny plant by the roadside that his camel lips could have handled, but it hurt his horse lips. That's the way I feel sometimes with that growth spurt Papa and I talked about; in the wrong body. Does changing shape make you feel as if you've grown in odd ways? Last evening, I asked Thea what it was like.

She glared at me. "That's not something I want to talk about here."

"But no one is close by."

"I'm taking no chances."

And that was the end of it. Would she be as short with me if I asked more about Mother and her family? Did they always live in Schönspitze? Might I have other relatives? More cousins. I don't even know if Mother was an only child. Families are like rivers in a way, different in many ways and yet similar. And tributaries flow together to make one.

East of Aquila three rivers join, this one and one from the northeast flow into a great waterway that runs south. I've never seen the spot but have heard stories. Mustafa, the camel seller, said that as a young man he once took passage on a large flat-bottomed boat that floated all the way to a great southern sea. Now that would be amazing! Papa travelled with a band of itinerant musicians when he was a young man. Maybe that's something I could do. I don't know where this river begins. Somewhere in the mountains probably.

Where does discontent begin, the need to change one's life? We saw the mountains this morning. Shapes so hazy in the distance that at first I thought they were low clouds.

Thea looked at me and then just laughed. "Of course, there are clouds on the mountains," she said. "But these are mountains themselves. I thought you saw similar landscapes around the old man's castle. Don't you remember?"

"A lot of that is blurred in my mind," I answer. "So much confusion and danger. I spent little time admiring the scenery." It occurs to me that the old sorcerer might have been responsible for the blurring. I don't want to think about that.

"Well, the mountains are my land, the way Aquila and the land of Ameer is yours. It's as familiar to me as the house I lived in all my life."

My life has been familiar for a long time, much the same from one day and year to the next. Yet, the future is as indistinct as those mountains. For now, I am excited to see new places and interested in what other people think about travel, but not all of the people in the caravan have been friendly. Distans, though, has been riding close to us a lot. I think he's sweet on Thea. Anyway, he says that what he likes best about travelling with caravans is not the variety of land, but the assortment of people you get to meet.

I nudge Izmeer forward beside the caravan guard. "So, Distans, how many times have you made this journey?"

He scrunches up his eyes, waves a hand. "More than I remember."

"Where else have you gone?"

"North to Timberton once. East to Vatnborg, south along the great river."

"Did you travel by boat on the river?" I ask.

"No, just by wagon and horse."

"What did you like best?"

He takes a while to reply. "It's hard to find only one thing, even two. We met men who poled rafts down the river, carrying fish and furs to trade. The rafts were large, with little huts built on them. Some of the people – men, women and children – lived all their lives on the river. Then there were the wild cattle on the way to Timberton. We had to stop for a whole day once to let a herd pass. Their movement rumbled like thunder and shook the ground."

"My sister talked about those," I say. "She saw them, too. I hope to make more journeys. So much to see in this land."

"Don't you ever get tired of constantly being on the move?" Thea asks from the wagon. It's as if she's trying to discourage me.

"I don't go with the caravans all the time," Distans says. "I'm part of the Lord's Militia so I work as a City Guard, too. And I own a house in Aquila. It's not huge, but it has a garden with a lemon tree and an olive tree."

"Do you have family living there?" Thea asks.

"Only my old mother and father. But there's room for a wife and children." He smiles at Thea and she looks away.

Ah, this is turning toward courting. I leave them and I ride up the line. Ali's face is suddenly in my mind, the way her hair swings when she runs, how her eyes crinkle when she laughs. I left too suddenly for a proper good-bye; was thinking about myself, not her. We've been friends for so long and I really like her, but I've not been treating her well lately. I've got to try seeing her or talking to her tonight.

Izmeer plods along with his head down. Maybe he's tired. I could give him a rest and then gallop to catch up the caravan later. Trees have closed in and I can't see the mountains anymore. Then I notice that the oxen are plodding more slowly as well. I feel as if I'm carrying a heavy pack, but there's nothing on my back. I think of Hrashak, the old sorcerer. Could we be near his castle? Even though he's no longer there maybe his evil presence remains. I shiver and urge Izmeer on past the front of the line. Then, as I reach to stroke his neck my horse shimmers and briefly is a camel, then a horse again. I almost slip off but manage to hang on. Quickly I glance behind. No one seems to have noticed.

Dark clouds are massing overhead, and that's what people are watching. Some of the wagon drivers pull aside to tighten ropes and covers. Primarius and the guards are busy making sure no one gets into trouble or is straggling too much.

The first sprinkles of rain hit as the road turns slightly away from the river and winds between out-croppings of rock. I pull out my hooded cloak and put it on, then turn back to check on Thea and the boys. They've got the sunshade up, which will serve to protect them somewhat against rain. The caravan speeds up; perhaps there's shelter of some sort ahead. Rain drums against my hood and mist closes in. I feel sorry for Izmeer and the other animals who have no choice but to get wet. I'm keeping a close eye on Izmeer, but he hasn't changed again. Thea never mentioned that something like this might happen. Should I ask her about it? But maybe it was just my imagination, and I don't want to cause any needless upsets.

Soon we are slowing even more because the road is slick with mud. Wetness has begun to penetrate my cloak and a chill sends shivers up my back. Then I see that the wagons are turning to the right, moving under a long overhang of rock. We'll be able to get shelter as long as wind doesn't drive the rain straight at us.

After reaching the overhang I dismount and do my best to dry Izmeer with a blanket. He's shivering slightly. Others are taking care of their animals as well, everyone crowded as close as they can get so that the whole caravan has managed to fit under the overhang. We're on a slight hill overlooking the river. The mist has pulled back though it still obscures the distance.

Rain and clouds tint the land in shades of grey. Ash, dove, flint, iron, mist, pewter, silver, slate. These are ordinary words, but I think of them in terms of paint now because of Ali. I lean against Izmeer, sharing his warmth and thinking of my best friend. It's not likely to be raining in Aquila, so is she sitting in the courtyard of her family's house, sketching? Perhaps she's gone to the market and is buying cheese or roast fowl, bread and fruit for a picnic. There's an ache under my ribs, and it's not because I'm hungry. There's still nuts and dried fruit in my saddle bags. I could get some out.

I keep my eyes closed. Ali's face in my mind is so clear. She's sitting under their lemon tree. In her cupped hands lies the obsidian stone I gave her. She raises her head from looking at the stone and smiles directly into my eyes.

I gasp, "Ali!"

My eyes fly open and her face is gone. Did I really see her, not just imagine? I've never joined with anyone like that except for my sister. And it's the silver bracelets that make that happen. What if the black stone from Hrashak's dungeon really does have powers? I told Ali I thought it might but wasn't sure. My friend may have unusual abilities, too. When I found out about having a sister, Ali dreamt about Rowan and painted murals on her bedroom walls showing things that happened far away. Those murals are gone now, covered over. I never asked her why she did that. What if I can actually talk to Ali no matter how far away we are from each other? I definitely have to try again.

A shout interrupts my thoughts. A couple of the caravan guards are pointing at the river. I can see through the sheets of rain that the river is wider than it was earlier. The water is rising! We've got rock at our backs, no place to go. The road is still clear of water, but for how long?

Our caravan leader has to make a decision. He

moves into a huddle with several guards and drivers. I look past a horse on my left, toward Thea in the wagon with the boys. She stares back at me, eyes wide, with a boy wrapped in each arm. Whatever happens she could survive by turning the boys into goats and herself into a goat or some other creature. They'd be able to swim to safety. Probably most of our horses and oxen can stay alive in the flood too, if they are free. I learned to swim in the shallow parts of the river near Aquila, but I don't know if I'd have the strength to go the distance in a flood. I'm shivering, my teeth chattering. I clamp my lips. Are other people scared and worried?

The guards move along the line talking to people. I manoeuver Izmeer to the side of Thea's wagon. Distans reaches us at the same time.

"We'll be all right here," he says reassuringly. "We're high enough to be safe."

The water is now a wagon length away from the road and I'm not sure that I believe Distans. Thea looks only slightly worried. Distans pats her arm and moves on. Thea gets out a couple of apples for the boys.

"Did you give them any potion recently?" I whisper.

"Not since this morning."

"I don't think you should give them any until we're out of this."

Thea nods. She understands what I'm not saying. I notice that a couple of the wagon drivers have

unhitched their oxen. And so we wait, watching the
river and the rain. Eventually the rain gets less and
less, finally stops. Water laps at the edges of the road
below us, but nowhere has it covered the road. Primarius and the guards, who know the route better
than any of us and should know if there's danger of
flood ahead, urge everyone back into harness and on
our way, as quickly as we can manage.

It's late afternoon and still chilly, thought the mist
has disappeared. I find extra clothes in my saddle
bags. Everyone searches out blankets and other ways
to get warm. We trot, roll, and move wearily along.
To my relief, the road veers away from the river onto
higher ground. Hardly anyone speaks and when they
do it's mainly to encourage an ox or horse to keep
going. My fingers ache and so do my toes. I take turns
putting a hand inside my cloak to warm, but I can't do
that with my toes, so I just keep wiggling them.

How much longer will this last and will I be able
to keep riding? Then I realize there's a warm spot by
my waist and I lay my fingers there next to my belt
pouch. There's a slight quivering. I dip my hands in
and touch the bracelet which is nearly as hot as bread
fresh from the oven. Fumbling a little, I pull the
bracelet over the sleeve of my left wrist. Almost right
away my whole body starts to warm. I sigh contentedly, then glance guiltily toward Thea and the wagon.
She and the twins are well wrapped and look comfortable enough.

By the time we finally stop in a grove of trees, the

moon gleams in the east and the first stars are beginning to twinkle. There's a large open-sided log building with a stone fireplace. I put the bracelet away and smile in anticipation of warming flames and hot food.

Thea is out of the wagon and I've dismounted from Izmeer when Thea nudges me and points. Against the dusky sky shapes rise, splashed with white – mountains.

"We'll see them more clearly in dayligh," Thea says.

All the way through the evening tasks – feeding and settling the animals and ourselves, getting ready for sleep – I think about Ali. I need to find a quiet, private spot to try and make a connection with her. In the end it's not hard.

Thea goes to sleep soon after the boys and everyone else rolls into their blankets or wagons.

Should I wear the bracelet or hold it in my hands? Do I even need it? I wrap a blanket around my shoulders and hunch into the shadow of Thea's wagon. Reach into my belt pouch, touch the sliver circlet, close my eyes. I sit like that for long enough to get stiff, but nothing comes. An owl hoots and Izmeer nudges me. I give up. Maybe Ali is disgusted that I haven't tried to talk to her before and she's not thinking of me.

Chapter XII
Eagle

In the morning I peel away blankets and crawl out to shiver in the cold air. I'm still wearing the clothes from the day before and the day before that. I've grown used to the smell of sweat and smoke, dust and horse or oxen. By the time we get to Shönspitze I'm going to have quite a reek! Someone has already started a fire so I pack the bedding away quickly and join others in the log building. Breakfast is gruel with dried fruit. I down two bowls full.

As I saddle Izmeer for the day's travel white flecks begin to drift down from the sky. A few land on my bare hands and on my face. They burn briefly on the skin of my face and then disappear. But on the ground the flakes gather.

"What is this strange white rain?"

"Snow," Thea says. "You've never seen snow? Haven't you realized that's what's on the mountains?"

I glance up at the distant triangular shapes striped with white, brown and green. "Maybe when I was small, but I don't remember. It's like bits of cloud have broken off and are falling. Why are they hot when they first touch skin?"

"Not hot, very cold. You're going to see more of it. I hope you brought plenty of warm clothes."

For the first part of the morning we move quickly to keep warm. Snow continues to drift down settling on wagons, animals and people alike. We shake ourselves periodically, but the white stuff continues to gather. As it melts it makes the road slippery. Travel becomes harder because the land turns hilly and rocky. The mountains ahead are growing larger, or rather, we're getting closer to them.

Toward mid-day when my stomach tells me it's time to eat again, there's a shout from the front of the caravan. A wagon tongue has broken. It's the driver who gave me brandy. Maybe he drank too much of his own tipple and got careless. Or he'll believe I really did give him the evil eye. The guards direct us to continue, passing the stopped wagon where Primarius is talking with the driver and another man. Once we are all past, the guards tell us to stop. We're going to take our break here while the tongue is fixed. It seems a difficult job to me, but apparently it's not an unknown mishap.

"All in a day's work," Distans says. "Primarius is a good leader. He knows to expect anything and is ready for it."

I dismount and take care of Izmeer, then get myself a bowl of the stew that is cooking over a quickly made fire. Take the food and wander off to look out over a valley. Beyond that steep mountains are draped in snow and low clouds. Nearby is a large flat rock where I perch to finish my meal. Afterwards I find a few nuts in my belt pouch to munch on.

A rustling in nearby bushes slightly down the hill turns my eyes. The bushes are covered with dry brown leaves and plenty of thorns. They're also dusted with snow. A faint clacking joins the rustling. Curious, I get up and walk closer, bending to peer between the branches. Is some animal hiding there?

I pick up a large stick and poke among the thorns. A shriek makes me jump back. The bush rattles, but nothing shows itself. Carefully I move nearer, edging some branches aside with the stick. A large bedraggled brown bird speckled with white hunches there, glaring at me – an eagle. A couple of years old by the colour and size of it. It puffs out its feathers.

We stare at each other – golden eyes meet mine. When I was small I thought Papa and I might be kin to eagles because we both have gold flecks in our eyes. Maybe that's why he can talk to eagles and be understood. Could I do that? I've never tried.

"Eagle! What are you doing there?" I say quietly.

The bird just glares. Does it see the similarity in our eyes? Can eagles even see colours? Why don't I know this by now, living with all those eagles in Aquila? Guess I haven't asked enough questions, though Papa sometimes said I asked too many. I stare at the curved beak under the eyes – deadly. Even in Aquila where eagles are accustomed to people you hear of an occasional attack. Usually it's something stupid – someone trying to pet an eagle or catch it or steal eggs. I'm not going to do anything foolish today.

The bird shifts slightly, maybe in response to a twitch or move of mine. One of its feet comes into view, talons, twice the size of one of my fingers, clenched on a twig. This creature could be my death or at least cause me serious injury. I should just back away and leave.

Then I see there are leather thongs wrapped around its talons and tied to a curved formation of branches. Has someone set this trap for an animal and the eagle got caught by accident?

This is strange, so similar to the story that I read in the Leather Book. The eagle tries to back away. I realize I'm still holding the stick. Maybe the bird is just as scared of me as I am of it. I put the stick on the ground. The eagle raises its head, opens its beak and screams defiance.

I take a step back. "I don't want to hurt you. If you're stuck, maybe I can help."

The eagle clatters its beak softly. Does it understand? Is it encouraging me? I move forward very slowly, watching to see if the eagle is shifting for an attack. It closes its beak and waits. I bend down cautiously and reach out. The eagle stays still. Now I see that one of its wings is partially spread and thorns are stuck among the feathers.

"This is going to take a little time," I say softly. "I don't want to scare you and I don't want to get torn by thorns myself. Or hurt by you."

The eagle ducks its head as if saying, "Get on with it. I'll ignore you."

So, very carefully I move aside branches until I can touch the young eagle. I begin gently to untangle its wing. The bird makes a soft chirping noise but doesn't raise its head. I continue working at getting it released. I gather up the leather thongs tied to the branched trap and pull it out.

Now the young eagle raises its head and takes a step toward me. I back up, holding branches aside. The bird brushes past my knees and hops out of the bush. I hunker in place, unmoving. The eagle spreads its wings, leans forward and launches into air. My breath catches in my throat and I have a sudden vision of leaping into the air myself and soaring off over the valley. The bird circles a few times, making a whistling sound, as if in thanks. I crawl out of the bush and wave. Did it come from Aquila and is heading back? Or is it a mountain eagle? I wish I could send a message to Rowan telling her what just happened. Wouldn't she be surprised! I'd love to see her face if that happened.

The eagle dives toward me. For a moment I think it's attacking so I back up and consider running. The bird lands in a flurry of wings right in front of me. It cocks its brown head and hops closer. It looks at me.

I squat. "You're welcome," I say. "I was glad to help."

But the eagle continues to sit there and I speculate on why. Could it be waiting to help me in some way, to thank me for what I've done? Rowan used to use her raven for sending messages. Now might be my chance to send a note to Papa at Aquila. No sense trying for my sister, because I'm not sure where Rowan is.

Continuing to keep an eye on the bird, I take a bit of parchment out of my belt pouch along with a stick of charcoal that Ali gave me. I write a few lines, fold the parchment, and reach out slowly. The eagle doesn't move, lets me tie the bit of parchment to its leg. I think clear thoughts of Aquila, where it is and what it looks like, and Papa. When I'm done, the eagle leaps at me, takes a nip out of my outstretched hand and is off into the sky again before I can complain. I hope this eagle will know how to get to Aquila. I watch until it's a speck in the east, and then gone.

I sigh, take time to smash the trap that held the eagle, then walk back to the caravan and find Thea. She bandages the slightly bleeding wound on my hand. I just say that I ran into a thorn bush. As the caravan with the repaired wagon gets moving again, I notice a young eagle flying some distance away. It follows us for a while before veering away.

Soon all my concentration has to be on the road, which is narrowing between steep outcroppings of rock. The rocks on one side gradually drop away and we're travelling along the edge of a hill with empty space on the left. Thankfully the snow has stopped and the sun is out, warming us a little. I keep my eyes firmly to the front, following Thea's wagon. We're all moving in single file. I know there are mountains all around, but don't dare move my head to look at them.

Unexpectedly, the scent of wet ashes hits my nose. The path has widened slightly, and we begin to pass an area of blackened spikes of trees, lumps of stuff I don't recognize. I decide not to think about that as I catch a whiff of scorched meat. The caravan slows even more, and a call goes out for people to help clear the trail ahead. There are charred branches and tree trunks scattered here and there.

"A fire must have gone through several days ago," Distans says.

By the time we've cleared the way my hands and clothes are black and grimy. Beyond the burn the trail grows wider as we travel into a valley. A narrow creek rushes through and we stop briefly to wash, replenish our water skins and containers. From what others in the caravan say, though, it seems now that we are in the mountains, we don't have to worry about conserving water the way we did in the desert.

The sun beats down and there's no snow here. How can the weather change so much in a short time? Then swarms of tiny biting creatures fly at us and there's not much we can do to avoid them. I try wrapping my face in an extra tunic, but that makes me too hot. The horses and oxen start to twitch, a few run and it's hard to control them, but soon we are out of the valley and moving up into cooler air. The biters are left behind.

In the distance a glistening green-white mass lies between two white-capped mountain peaks. A cold wind blows into our faces. I sigh and pull my cloak out of my saddle bags.

"It's a glacier," Thea says. "A huge sheet of ice. Rivers sometimes start from the base of them as they melt."

"Is this normal mountain travel?" I grumble.

"Poor Samel," Thea says. "Not really prepared for this excursion, are you, even though you wanted so badly to come?"

"And what was your first long trip like?" I retort.

"Look over there," Thea points. "See those scratches on that big tree? Made by a bear. And on the other side, that pile of rock? That was a slide where part of the mountain came down."

Without saying anything, I urge Izmeer forward and ride away from Thea and the boys. I'll stay near the front of the caravan for a while, maybe talk to Primarius. Let Thea get over her grumpiness, whatever it's about. As we get closer to the glacier, I see that it's swirled with grey and black, dirt maybe? Things aren't as clean as they seem from a distance.

"Hey, young Samel," Primarius says, "how are you? It's a hard trek, this mountain travel. You've done well rid- ing so far. We should reach Schönspitze late tomorrow afternoon."

"I'm glad to hear it!"

"It hasn't been bad so far you know. Why I re-member the first trek I ever took with a caravan out of Aquila. I was a green young wagon driver. We struck a sandstorm that delayed us for a whole day digging out after. Later a flood held us up two days, and finally a blizzard at the edge of the mountains stopped us entirely. We had to turn around and go back."

"That's awful! Why did you keep travelling after that?"

"The wide-open spaces, the companions I made, new places, adventures. I suppose it got into my blood and I haven't been able to shake it."

"I hope to travel more after this, but even if I can't, at least I have a few stories to tell when I get home."

That night we make camp on beds of green moss in a cleft between two mountains. I try for a while to get a vision of Rowan and then of Ali but am not successful. I hope they are both all right. I pull the blankets tightly around me and stare upwards. The sky is full of the stories of stars, and eventually an owl hoots me to sleep.

Chapter XIII
Schönspitze

Those of us who live in Aquila think of it as the greatest city in the land. I don't know if that's true, though it is the largest city I know, and very well protected. Surrounded by thick walls on three sides with the river on the third. At night you can see the lights of it twinkling from a long way in the desert.

I don't expect Schönspitze to be exactly like that. After all, it's in the mountains and could be hidden by trees or behind peaks. I spend the morning and early afternoon craning my neck and searching. But I see nothing that looks like any sign of a city. We're travelling along a high track that falls off into valleys on either side. It makes my head whirl to look down, but the road is wide enough for two wagons to pass each other, so we must be safe.

Then, suddenly there's fog obscuring the road completely and hiding everything ahead. I slow Izmeer, expecting the caravan to stop while our forward scout makes sure the way is safe, but instead the wagons speed up. Quickly I move right beside the wagon holding Thea and the twins.

"Don't worry," Thea says before I can speak. "There's always mist here. We're very close to Schönspitze now. We're fine."

The fog is so thick I can barely see her. I feel it brush against my skin as if it's a curtain of thin cloth. How will the wagons and animals find their way without falling off the road and tumbling down the mountain? I can barely make out Thea's wagon, but nothing else. There's no sound either, not even the clop of Thea's ox or the squeak of her cart wheels.

At my waist, my belt pouch is throbbing faintly, a sign that the bracelet is active. Does that mean I should take it out? Will it help keep me and Izmeer safe?

A faint glimmer lights the borders of the road; it's coming from an edging of white stones. My skin prickles and I push back a sleeve, noticing goose bumps up my arm. Izmeer snorts and his form shifts to camel. I grab for his neck to keep from falling off. He snorts and changes back, begins to trot. The ox pulling Thea's wagon is running. I don't think she noticed Izmeer change. Fog still surrounds us. How long will it last?

And then abruptly we're in the clear with a late afternoon sun sinking slowly behind jagged peaks in front. One huge peak dominates, craggy and snow-covered, its top hidden by clouds. The whole caravan has inexplicably stopped now that we're out of danger.

Thea points. "Schönspitze. Beautiful peak. That's what the city is named after."

Little by little it dawns on me that not all that I see ahead is mountains. Surely that's the point of a steeple, and there is a fragment of tiled roof. The town is built higgledy-piggledy on several levels, up and down the sides of two mountains. It's difficult to make out details, for the buildings seem to merge with the mountains and shadows lie over it all. The sun is too low in the sky, though. When we entered the mist it was early afternoon. Now it's nearly sunset.

Then I notice the archway hewn out of stone, filled with solid wooden gates. To the left and right of the arch are crenellated towers, and on top of each tower stands a guard holding a bow with an arrow in it.

"Hail the town!" our caravan leader calls. "You know me. I am Primarius, from the city of Aquila. We come to trade."

"Hold!" one of the guards shouts back. "The gate will be opened."

It's a long enough wait that more than one of the wagoners begins to fidget. A few are grumbling. I have time to speculate about what's just happened.

Both the magical mist protecting the city, which Thea never mentioned and the possibility that Izmeer might suddenly change back. What else hasn't she told me?

Is there always this sort of delay or is there a reason the guards are more cautious today? I don't ask Thea because she hasn't been to this city in a long time, and besides I don't trust her to tell me what's going on. I glance at her. She has an arm around each of the boys and is murmuring softly to them. Both of them are staring at the towers.

At last the gates begin to creak, but the caravan still doesn't budge, though horses stamp and oxen low. Perhaps the animals can smell food and water. I catch a glimpse of Distans leaning down from his horse to speak with someone in armour. Then, bit by bit the wagons start to roll forward. I could ride ahead but decide to stay beside Thea. The boys are sitting holding hands, looking at everything with big eyes.

By the time we reach the arch it's dusk, and two guards in armour holding torches stand one on each side to stare long at every face and briefly inspect the interior of each wagon. The guards' helms are raised, so they can't be too fearful of us. One of them holds the roll of parchment that Primarius handed over. As I stop for my own inspection, I notice that the guard on my right is pale skinned with flowing hair, a woman. Though her hair is white, she isn't old, rather close to Thea's age it seems to me. The one on the left, also a woman, has a face dark as a starless night, head topped by black curly hair. Long bows are slung over their shoulders and sharp tipped pikes in their hands.

Thea exclaims suddenly, "Nacht and Tag! You're soldiers now!"

The stern faces break into wide smiles. "Thea, is it you? So many years. Wie gehts? Are you back now for a while? And are these your children? Who is the young man with you?"

Thea nods and shrugs in the appropriate places. "My boys are Kosto and Pello. This is my sister's son, Samel. We shouldn't hold up the line. Come see me at the old house."

The two guards wave us through the gate into a wide enclosure. Wagons are already drawn to the side, lined up and more guards are doing a thorough inspection.

Primarius approaches. "Thea, you and young Samel won't need to go through the same inspection our wagons do. I've mentioned to one of the guards that you're from Schönspitze and that you have little baggage in your wagon, nothing to trade. Just wait over here."

"Thank you," Thea responds, and we move aside.

Distans nudges his horse toward us and leans down. "Perhaps we'll see each other in the town."

"Who knows," Thea shrugs.

"We're returning to Aquila in a week if you decide you want to come with us."

"I doubt we'll be finished our business that soon, but I'll keep it in mind," Thea says.

Distans hesitates as if about to add a few more words, but then moves away. Soon a city guard comes to poke around the wagon. It doesn't take much time, and then he gives each of us a pendant on a chain. It's a square wooden tile carved with a symbol of two mountain peaks and inlaid with copper. A pass, he tells us, so we can go in and out.

"You have to give them up if you leave for any reason, even just a walk on the mountain. The tiles are spelled, so they offer you a measure of protection, but they'll scream if you try to take them beyond the gates."

I open my mouth to say "Scream?" but Thea is vigorously shaking her head at me. She tells the guard "Thank you," then clucks to her ox and the wagon moves ahead. The rest of the caravan stays behind. On Izmeer I follow the wagon as it trundles along streets paved with cobblestones. They wind here and there, uphill and down. At times a street is so narrow that only one wagon could move through, so I keep behind Thea. The buildings of the town are stone or wood or a combination. A few windows have open shutters and show flickering lights – candles or lanterns. Few people walk in the streets and those who do, hurry on their way as we approach.

Thoughts and questions are roiling in my mind like the fish I once saw in a river whirlpool. Thea and my mother came from a city that uses spells and magical protections. No wonder Thea and her children can shift shape. I have a feeling Rowan had no knowledge of this either. Maybe it's not surprising at all that my sister and I have found and can use a pair of magical bracelets.

Finally, we reach a stone house with a tall central tower and two-storey wings on each side. Round windows above an arched double door make the tower look as if it has eyes, a nose and a mouth. Each wing has two square windows on the second floor and one large rectangular window on the main, so there appears to be a face with square eyes and a rectangular mouth – no nose. Will this house swallow us whole and will it ever let us go? I shiver and blame it on the cooling evening air. No sense letting my imagination run away with me. I focus on the details of the house. All the windows have glass in them, which is another sign that this house was built for wealthy people. A dim light shows through one of the lower windows.

Thea guides the ox and cart into a curved entry way and stops. I follow on Izmeer. She sits staring at the house. The boys, are quiet, too, not even babbling to each other.

"Is this your house? Are we going to knock?" I ask.

"There's a bell," Thea responds, but she keeps sitting.

I get off Izmeer and tie him to the wagon. I'm tired and hungry and I'm sure Izmeer and the ox feel the same. Maybe if I move Thea will take the hint.

"I lived here with two sets of grandparents," Thea says dreamily. "Your mother, too. All except me dead now. Maybe no one's here to look after the place."

"One way to find out," I say, and slowly walk up to the door. "I noticed a light from one of the windows. Maybe you're expected." I reach for the rope tied to a bell.

"Wait!" Thea scrambles out of the cart and lifts down the boys. They follow close at her knees.

The four of us cluster in front of the wooden door. While I wait for Thea to make up her mind to ring the bell, I study the carvings. Old, dark, and hard to make out, but here and there I think I recognize a cluster of leaves, a frog or toad, a sun, a moon, and a scattering of stars.

At last Thea pulls the bell rope, starting a pleasant chime that echoes along the street. Oddly, a deeper tolling reverberates from inside the house. The boys clutch at their mother's knees. We wait some more. Thea is reaching for the rope to pull again when one half of the double door creaks open slightly.

A bent, grey-haired figure in a long dark dress stands in the doorway. "Go away," a woman's voice rasps.

So much for being expected.

"I have a letter," Thea says. She rummages in her belt pouch and pulls out folded parchment. "A message that I was needed."

"You can't come in." The old woman turns slowly away and begins to close the door.

"It's my family home," Thea says.

"No orders," the woman croaks.

"The letter is from Anwalt. He looks after my family's affairs."

"The advocate," the woman says. "His house." She takes one step out and points down the street. "Blue windows." Then she steps back and shuts the door in our faces.

The twins begin to whimper. "Help me put them back in the wagon," Thea says.

"Do you know where to go?" ask.

"I think I remember."

Just down the street stands a smaller stone and wood house with blue window frames and shutters. We have to leave the cart and Izmeer on the street and walk to the narrow front door. I grab the knocker in the shape of a circle and rap it hard against the wood. I'm colder and hungrier, and very tired.

The door is opened by a wizened old man, wrinkled as a shrivelled grape, so bent that his chin nearly touches his chest. He holds tightly to the door, shaking slightly. I'm positive the man might fall over if he lets go of the door handle.

Thea must feel similarly because she speaks quickly, "Sorry to bother you. I'm looking for the advocate who's in charge of the Burgrave's house.

This is the first that I've heard the house we just visited called that. What does it mean? Who is or what is the Burgrave? I have lots to ask Thea later.

"Anwalt," the old man rasps and peers at us for several moments. Is he going to cast some sort of spell to decide whether he'll let us in? My teeth are chattering from cold, and I touch the pouch with the bracelet in it, gathering a little warmth. The old man nods quite normally and pulls the door wider, gesturing us in with his other arm.

We step forward, but before we can enter, the twins run across the threshold. Thea and I follow quickly into the warm house. There's a scent of recent cooking: onions and some kind of meat dish. My stomach grumbles longingly.

Down a short, dark hallway the old man leads us to a small room on the right. There are several upholstered wooden chairs and a low table. He gestures toward the chairs and Thea and I sit. The twins huddle at their mother's knees.

"I'll fetch him," the old man says and leaves.

Kosto toddles to the table and pats it. Pello stands and watches him. I wonder what this room was used for. It's not large enough for much of anything but waiting. What is an advocate? A tall, thin man with dark hair scattered with grey enters. Thea and I stand.

He bows. "You are Thea. I remember you as a child and young woman, but you may not recall me. My father used to take care of your family's legal affairs."

"Yes," Thea says, "Vaguely. You wrote me the letter?" She nods at me. "This is my cousin's son, Samel."

He nods at me. "Zarmine's son. I'm sorry she's dead." He turns back to Thea. "I have news that will surprise and perhaps shock you."

"Oh?" Thea grabs the twins who have started toward the advocate's legs.

"Do you remember your grandfather? On your father's side?"

"Of course. He disappeared. No one ever found out what happened to him."

The advocate clears his throat. "Well, he has resurfaced. Alive."

Thea opens her mouth, but no words come out. The twins begin to wail. I notice that Thea has pressed her nails hard into one of each of the children's arms. Just then she realizes it and lets go. "But," she says, "he was dead! Everyone I talked to said . . ."

The advocate nods. "So we all thought. I am sorry. I could not think how else to tell you except bluntly. And it didn't seem the sort of thing to write in a letter, in case the wrong person read it."

"He must be ancient. How can he still be alive? Are you sure it's him? Where is he?" Thea's words rush out, her voice grating.

"It's him all right. He's been living at the house and asked me to send for you."

"The housekeeper, at least a woman who could be a housekeeper, wouldn't let us in," I say. "Wouldn't she know he sent for Thea?"

The advocate glances at me, then back at Thea. "She is very cautious, and her eyesight isn't that good anymore. She may have seen you as a child but might not remember you. I'll give you a letter authorizing your entry to the house. That will satisfy her."

"But . . ." Thea starts.

"I'm sure you have many questions," the advocate says. "You must be tired, however, from your journey. Questions can wait. Sit, I will be back with the letter."

"I guess we could go find out where the caravan is staying if the housekeeper still won't let us in," I say after Anwalt has left.

Thea sighs. "I'm so tired of complications. Why can't life be simple for a change?"

"Hah! Wouldn't that be a surprise."

"Are you sorry you came?"

"No. I can hardly wait to see what happens next." I'm considering asking her about our arrival and magic and all the things she hasn't told me, but Anwalt returns just then.

As it turns out the housekeeper does let us in without saying a word when she sees the letter with Anwalt's signature and seal. She shuts the door behind us and shuffles off down the hall.

My first impression of the house is that it's rather dusty and neglected. A few creaking floorboards, a cracked door, a couple of damp stains, lots of spider webs. As we walk down the hall, I notice a room full of books on shelves to the left and a smaller room to the right. Candle lamps light the way here and there. The housekeeper gestures for us to go inside the small room.

The twins huddle at Thea's knees. Thea takes their hands and moves forward a little. "Where is my grandfather?"

The woman shrugs and keeps moving. "Please tell him I'm here."

The woman disappears into dimness and we enter the small room. I'm thinking we should just have followed the woman. It would have been quicker and besides, this is Thea's house, too.

Thea sits on a narrow settee and pulls the boys into her lap. "This room is a disaster!"

Besides the settee, the room holds a chair, a desk, and cupboards. And every surface is filled – a pillow on the chair, books on the desk and knickknacks on the shelves. Everything is furred with dust, too. I sneeze.

"If she is the housekeeper, she's not doing her job," Thea says.

I poke my head out the door to see if the woman is coming back. In the centre of the hall is a slightly sagging spiral staircase, going up, probably to the tower. No sign of the housekeeper.

"Come on," I say. "Who knows when she'll be back? This is a big house so she may have to hunt a long time to find your grandfather."

Thea and the boys follow me down the hall. Behind the library is a large room with couches and chairs; behind the small room is another with a long table, chairs and side cupboards filled with dishes. Besides the tower stairs, there are stairs between the living and dining room going up. When we reach the large kitchen with a fireplace and cupboards with closed doors, the housekeeper sitting at the scarred table with a couple of scorch marks on its surface, looks startled. Did she think we would just wait and wait? Did she even let Thea's grandfather know we were here? In one corner there are stairs going down.

"Where is my grandfather?" Thea asks. The woman shrugs.

"We need rooms," Thea says. "And what do we do with our ox and cart, Samel's horse?"

The housekeeper points out the window. "Stable." She points up. "Bedrooms." Then she pours herself a cup of tisane.

"I'll look after the wagon and the animals," I tell Thea. "You find us some bedrooms."

Not far from the house is a narrow street that leads to the back of the house. In the gathering dark I lead the ox and cart, follow the street along a wall to a gate. The gate, wide enough for a carriage with horses, leads to a large yard. In the moonlight I can see overgrown grassy areas, straggly bushes and plants, a few trees, and sitting areas with rickety looking benches and tables.

The stable is to the left of the gate. I take care of Izmeer first, finding a box stall, unsaddling and brushing him. I watch him carefully, but he remains a horse. I notice a well in the yard; go out and lower the bucket. The water appears clean and good. I rummage for a couple of handfuls of oats in Thea's wagon for Izmeer to eat. Another stall can hold the ox. The wagon I leave beside the stable, but I unpack it, hauling our belongings to the kitchen door.

When I bring the bags, baskets, blankets, and boxes into the house, I find the kitchen empty, though a large pot hangs over a banked fire in the fireplace. I set down the last of the bags and peer into the pot. It's filled with what looks like chicken soup and it smells all right. I rummage in the cupboards and unearth a couple of bowls and spoons. Fill each with soup. Finish one bowl. Carry the other with me.

Thea is upstairs in the largest of four bedrooms. It holds two beds, several chests, a small table and a dusty armchair. The windows look out onto the back yard of the house. The twins sit on the floor rolling a couple of wooden balls back and forth.

"You've picked this one?" She nods. I hand her the bowl. "Do I get to choose my own?"

The boys set up a clamour and come running as they smell the soup.

"Thank you," Thea says. "Yes, go and pick a room. The housekeeper wandered off after telling me she'd ring the bell for the evening meal."

"Oh, so I didn't need to bring you food."

She shrugs. "I'm hungry enough and the boys are, too."

"No sign of your grandfather?"

"Not yet. He could be in the tower."

"I'll go look."

The tower has a couple of small bedrooms on the second floor, and one large room on the third. No people in any of them. The round window in the top room looks out over the roofs of the town to the mountains, though I can see little of them by the light of a half moon. I'd be like an eagle in a nest up here. There's a narrow bed, a chest at the foot of the bed. The chest is filled with bedding that smells faintly piney. A small table and a chair, both covered in dust, sit by the window with another chest beside it. This holds scraps of parchment, reeds and quills for writing, and a pottery inkwell with dried residue in it. Along the wall by the door are several wooden pegs, empty, but useful for hanging clothes.

I return to the kitchen and bring up our luggage. Leave most of it with Thea.

A clanging bell catches me in the midst of putting my things around the tower room. Rushing down the spiral staircase, I nearly knock Thea down when I reach the hallway near her room.

"Hey!" she says. "Little ones here."

"Sorry."

Kosto and Pello grin at me and hold out their arms. I take one of them, Thea takes the other. They learned to go down the stairs at our place in Aquila quite easily, but they are still new to this place and the stairs are more complicated. We have to take care of them. Lots to think about with children. Did Papa or our mother ever get tired of looking after us? Maybe Papa is tired of looking after me, though I don't think I need much looking after these days. Well, he's getting a rest from me now.

How long will we stay here? Thea might decide to remain for a long time if her family business isn't easily solved. I guess I should think about whether to go back with the caravan in a week. I want to explore the city or town, whatever it is, before I leave.

The table in the kitchen holds bowls, spoons and knives, bread and butter. The housekeeper stands by the fireplace and the pot with a ladle in her hand. The twins stop in the doorway and stare at her. Thea nudges them forward.

"What do we call you?" Thea asks.

"Helfrith," the woman says squinting at the twins. "Bring the bowls." She fills them nearly to the brim and we sit. She doesn't say anything about me sneaking food earlier, although she must have found my dirty bowl.

"Where is my grandfather?" Thea asks as the twins start on bread and butter, for the soup is very hot.

"He comes in his own time," Helfrith says. She puts the ladle into the pot and moves it off the hearth. Then she walks out of the room.

"This is so annoying!" Thea exclaims. "He asks Anwalt to send a letter saying I'm urgently needed and then he isn't here."

"He could be hiding somewhere in the house."

"Where?"

"We haven't searched down those stairs." I point to the corner of the kitchen. "I could do that after we eat."

"Fine! I'll get the twins settled and you go looking."

"Any suggestions for favourite places he had in the house?"

"I don't remember any," Thea says. "Do the best you can."

The stairs down are wide with a good railing. At the bottom is a door on the left and a passage straight ahead. The door is locked. It occurs to me that it may lead to Helfith's rooms. Could Thea's grandfather be in there with her? I knock a few times, but there's no answer.

I follow the passage, which leads past two storage rooms, both unlocked and filled with boxes, trunks, broken chairs, odds and ends. Beyond these rooms I come upon a wine cellar, racks with dusty bottles. There's a distant sound of splashing water. I wander on past the racks, peering behind, and into corners. The wine cellar ends in another door which stands open.

The sound of splashing water is louder. I hope the house isn't about to wash away. I take a step through the door. A pair of large brown eyes above a wide grinning mouth stare at me. The head is as wrinkled as a dried grape and nearly as brown. If it wasn't for the stick-like arms resting on narrow bent legs, all clothed in green, I wouldn't have thought this was a man, but it is. One of the hands holds a bulbous flask that is tipped and dripping water into a small pool near the feet of the man. The feet are bare and also wrinkled. Perhaps he's been soaking them in the pool.

"Who are you?" The voice is low and croaky, as if he doesn't use it much.

"Samel. And you must be Thea's grandfather."

"Aha! A smart boy. So, she's here at last." He stands. "Call me Grandfather Frog."

Before I can question that or find out if I've heard correctly, he's off into the wine cellar, moving in a hop-skip way that adds to his looks matching his name. I follow, nearly tripping on the flask he's left behind. At the top of the stairway to the kitchen the old man stops. Over his shoulder I see Thea standing by the kitchen table with her mouth open.

"Shut it," the old man says, "unless you want to catch flies!" He guffaws loudly and takes a couple of steps into the room.

I close the door to the stairway.

"I thought you were dead," Thea says.

"And I knew you weren't. You had two babies. Learned to shift shape. Couldn't stop your cousin from drowning."

"You've had me watched, spied on? How dare you!" Thea takes a step towards her grandfather.

I move between them. "He's old," I say.

Thea ignores me. "You look different."

The old man chuckles again. "Died and came back to life, didn't I? Of course, I look different."

"Impossible," Thea says. "What are you going on about? How do I know it's really you?"

"Tisane. I want a tisane. Put a pot of water on the fire. And I'm hungry."

Thea glares, but does as he asks. The pot of soup is gone; maybe there were no leftovers. I decide that if Thea can search the cupboards for beakers, I can look for more food. And I find it – a half loaf of dark bread, a piece of dried fish, a pot of berry preserves and several small apples. Grandfather Frog pulls a chair up to the table and perches. He breaks a piece off the bread, dips it into the preserves, and begins munching.

"Is it really your name?" I ask. "Grandfather Frog?"

"What?" Thea turns from the hearth. "No, that's not his name." She wrinkles her forehead, rubs it. "Wintan is what he's called."

"Was called." The old man mumbles around bits of bread. "Reborn, remember."

"Stop mumbling on. What really happened when you disappeared?"

"Tisane first! It's a long story."

By the time Thea has poured the water and steeped the dried leaves, the old man has eaten more bread with preserves and is keeping an eye on the dried fish simmering on the stove. I nibble on an apple to keep him company. Thea watches us without speaking, but she glares at us. When I ask if the twins are asleep, she just nods.

"The twins!" Grandfather Frog says (I prefer that name to Wintan; he doesn't look like a Wintan at all). "I want to see them."

Thea pours the tisane and thumps a beaker in front of the old man. "In the morning. Now, tell your preposterous tale."

"Some of that fish first. It should be soft enough to eat now."

Chapter XIV
Grandfather's Tale

It began when my wife died, my dear Warda. I was grief stricken and that fool of a cleric didn't help. He said she'd killed herself, couldn't be buried in temple grounds. Half-mad the man was, everyone knew it, and no one paid him any attention. She was buried as she ought. The cleric was furious.

"I know people thought he took his crazed revenge and killed me; I heard the rumours after I returned. They locked him up when I disappeared. Hah! I set it up to look that way. Had a last argument with him where lots of people could see and hear. He even threatened me with retribution. Probably meant the gods would punish me, but people took it as if he intended it personally. I'd stolen one of his gloves. Planned to drown myself and leave the glove, mess up the ground as if there'd been a struggle, leave a little of my blood and my cloak."

He stops to take a breath and I look at Thea with my eyebrows raised. Is this old man telling truth or just making up a tale to entertain us? Thea shakes her head slightly. I eat a bit more apple. Did he really set things up so that a cleric was unjustly imprisoned?

"What happened to him?" I ask.

"Who?" the old man asks.

"The cleric."

"He wasn't right in the head, hadn't been for a long time. Eventually he was sent to an isolated monastery in the mountains.

"Anyway, I made all my final preparations at the lake north of Schönspitze, but then I just sat there for a while, thinking. My great love was gone, and the younger people had little time for me. I could no longer do some of the physical things I used to do in youth – climb mountains, dig in the mines or cut down trees. What if people decided to shut me up with a caretaker in a couple of rooms? I had to get away. So, I jumped in the water."

"I don't remember anyone talking about shutting you away," Thea interrupts.

"You were barely past childhood, involved in your own affairs. You didn't hear all the talk. Anyway, I didn't drown. Was sucked down by the currents into a deep tunnel and spilled out in a damp cave. Wandered in my wits for a while, danced in a dream, tangled in a trance. That cave held enchantments. I lay for a long time, felt no hunger or thirst, no cold, no discomfort of any kind. I thought I'd shrunk, become an egg, hatched into a tadpole, turned into a frog. Did all that really happen? I don't know."

"At least you're willing to admit it might have been visions."

"Did I say that?" He shakes his head. "How long I remained there I have no idea. I dreamt of power and spell craft, shapeshifting, speaking to animals, unimag- inable things that I no longer recall. Though I was reborn, I'm still old and my memory isn't as good as it was. Still, I get hints now and then, a brief memory or a fragment of dream. Things to do with water and time, with hidden powers of the earth, how metals form and rock, the importance of fire and wa- ter, air and earth. Secrets that I no longer remember, only bits and pieces."

"Dreams," Thea snorts. "None of it was real. You went off and lived in a cave."

The old man shakes his head. "Believe me or not, it doesn't matter. There was a pool or a pit, a kind of cauldron of renewal, I think. Somehow there was food and water and at times I was awake. Then again, I think I got lost in my mind. I heard whispers on the air, saw light in darkness. Now and then mist ob- scured everything. Occasionally I heard the sound of wings.

"I dreamt of scrolls secreted in ceramic jars and in niches in the rock. Words were written on parchment and leather, carved into stone, etched on wood. Ob- scure languages, but I could read them."

I gasp, for this part of his story reminds me of another old man, the sorcerer, Hrashak. Could it have been the same cave? Grandfather Frog stares at me waiting for me to explain the gasp. I just shake my head, and he continues with his story.

"Mist came again that lasted for a long time, and then water covered me. Eventually I found myself outside on a wet slope of grass with animal skins nearby. Had I hunted and skinned animals or had someone left these for me? I never found out. I wrapped myself in the skins and gradually I remembered who I was and where I came from. In searching for berries and roots to eat I found familiar landmarks, so I walked home. None of my family remained here. I spoke to the advocate and he helped me find the housekeeper; she's his sister who came back to the city after her husband died. I swore them to secrecy, let no one else know that I had returned, though eventually the news trickled into the town.

"Thoughts of the cave haunted me. I had found answers there, but I lost them. Don't even know what questions to ask now. I've been searching all the books in the house, trying to find stories about caves, water, magic, anything that might help." The old man shakes his head. "That's all."

Thea stares at him. "It's not all. How did you know where I was and what had happened to me? You had someone spy on me! And you didn't let me know you were alive. What kind of person does that?"

"I didn't know who I could trust."

"More stories! I'm supposed to believe you died and were reborn? Found a magic cave? Ridiculous!"

"But Thea," I say, "there is magic, especially here. What about that mist and these pendants they gave us? Even you can …"

"Stop it! We're not talking about this anymore." Thea gets up from the table and leaves the kitchen.

"She's tired," I say to the old man. "Has been travelling a long way with her twins. They're hard work."

"Children always are."

"Speaking of children, you knew my mother. What was she like then?"

"Ah, Zarmine. Loved the outdoors. Always in the garden – we had one then, it's gone to weeds – learned the names of plants at an early age. Knew which were good to eat and which dangerous. Asked lots of questions. Could drive you crazy with her questions." He chuckles.

"What else? Did she argue? Get along with people?"

"She had a temper. Learned to walk away if she was angry, but it took time to teach her that. Learned to be persuasive instead. If she didn't get her way, she'd try to wheedle you into it." He sighs. "I wish she hadn't left."

"But if she hadn't met my father I wouldn't be here."

"True." He yawns. "I'm off to bed. You?"

"Not yet. I think I may go out for a walk. Is it safe here at night?"

"This neighbourhood should be fine. And the city pendant will give warning if there's danger. I'll see you in the morning."

He doesn't even give me time to ask what kind of warning the pendant might give. Maybe screaming. I shake my head and put on my cloak before leaving the house.

It's full dark now, but the moon adds brightness and there are myriads of stars. Thea's family home is the largest on this street. They must have been rich and important at one time; maybe they still are. I'll have to ask Grandfather to tell me more. Most of the houses are one-storey, stone with thatched roofs. A few have roof tiles or wooden shingles. The street curves uphill to the left of the big house toward the advocate's house; to the right and down is the way back to the town gates.

I turn right. There are no trees of any kind along this street, though I can see the tops of evergreens here and there. Glowing moss grows in the cracks of stones and there are patches of grass. Did my mother walk these streets? Play skipping games, toss balls? Did she have friends?

Light spills from a window, a door opens and two figures step out. I stop, not sure whether I should worry. I catch a glint of leather armor and weapons. Am about to turn back and hurry away, when a woman's voice stops me.

"Hail, young one. You came with Thea."

"Guten Abend," the other says.

I take a step toward them, and light from the window shines on the pale skin of one of the guards that Thea recognized at the gate.

"Oh," I say, "greetings. I don't speak your language."

"We're Nacht and Tag," the darker of the pair says. "We speak more than one language."

"Sisters," the other adds, "same mother, different fathers."

"Can we buy you a drink?" the first asks gesturing toward the door behind them. "Ale, wine?"

"No thank you. I'm just out for a walk before bed."

"Down to the gate? We'll walk with you. Safer that way."

"Gr . . . that is, I've been told it's quite safe here."

"Oh yes," the pale one says, "but you never know."

"A caravan just in, there's always a little rough and tumble," the dark one adds.

Their words don't quite ring true. It seems to me that if there's danger I should be told about it and so should Thea. But I can't quite bring myself to ask what they're not telling me. The three of us walk quietly along the street, the two women tall on either side of me. I notice lights flickering here and there in windows. An owl hoots, a dark shape glides over the roof of a house.

"Um, have you lived here long?" I ask.

The one on my right answers, "All our lives. Born here."

"Friends with Thea all that time until she went away," the other says. "Her cousin, too."

"That was my mother."

"What happened to her?"

"She died. Drowned."

"I am so sorry," they say in unison.

"What was she like when she lived here?"

"Like?" asks the dark one. "A child."

"Always riding off to the woods. Her grandparents set a guard to watch her most of the time," says the other.

"It was dangerous even then?"

"Woods have wild animals and hunters," says the pale-haired one.

Despite what I've heard so far, I still can't picture my mother as a child. When we reach the gates, I see that they are shut, barred across with two wooden poles, and chained. Up on the wall a figure turns and bends down.

"No worries, Korat," Tag calls softly. "We're just taking a walk with Thea's young cousin."

The shape of an arm waves and then a quiet voice, "Take heed."

I make to turn back and am about to say good-bye when I notice that both my companions have turned with me.

"What is it?" I ask. "You're not acting as if it's safe."

Nacht takes my arm and leads me a few steps further. "We'll walk you home."

Tag, on my other side, touches my shoulder. "Come. There may be other ears listening."

We go in silence for a while. At Grandfather's house the two guards follow me to the front door.

"You'd better tell me," I say. "If there's danger, Thea should know about it."

"It's nothing clear or obvious," Nacht says. "There have been incidents."

"Occasional damage to the walls," Tag adds. "Sabotage, perhaps or attempts to scale them."

"We've increased the night guards," Nacht says.

"What else?" I ask.

Both of them shrug. "Oddly behaving animals," Tag says. "A bear circling near the gate one morning. A pack of wolves howling several nights in a row."

"Wolves!" I exclaim. "What about foxes?"

Nacht shakes her head. "Nothing really to worry about, just unusual."

"Best you go in now," Tag adds.

The door is locked and though I ring the bell no one comes. I have to knock hard and long before Helfrith hears and lets me in. While we wait I'm thinking about the bodies of wolves that were found near Aquila last year, not like normal wolves at all. Those were due to Hrashak's sorcery, but he's dead so the odd behaviour of animals around Schönspitze must be something else. Maybe the protection of the mist doesn't work on animals.

"Tell Thea we'd like to see her some time," the dark guard says.

Nacht and Tag wave good-bye as the door opens and Helfrith peers out. She doesn't say a word, but she looks daggers. I will have to find out about getting a key.

Before I head to bed I go out the back door and check on Izmeer and the ox. I refresh their water from the well and give them new hay, as well as a little more grain. They nuzzle my hands in thanks. I stand in the court-yard listening and looking; all is peaceful and ordinary.

Up in my room I lie on the bed but can't sleep. I get up and light a couple of candles, wander about the room, rearrange my belongings. At the bottom of my saddle bags I discover the Leather Book, having put it away there after reading it the last time. I open it at random. The pages flip to a story called 'The Frog King.' I light more candles, place them on the table and settle down to read.

The Frog King ruled over a land deep in a marsh filled with sink holes and small islands. No people had ever reached that place, but a few adventurous frogs had gone out and seen the land of people. These daring ones told of the wonders of that other world.

The Frog King didn't believe the stories. How could anyone be larger or more powerful than he was, who ruled over such a large territory? How could people have animals bigger than themselves that they rode on? And houses built of stone and wood rather than mud and sticks to live in?

Some of the King's advisors agreed with him, others supported those who had been away and returned. The arguments spread throughout the kingdom and the croaking and cheeping went on and on, day and night. No one was getting any sleep or getting any work done.

Finally, the Frog King decided to send his eldest son to go take a look. Everyone waited and waited, but this son did not return. At last, the King sent his second son along with two other frogs who'd been to the human world before. They were to act as guides, helpers and guards. None of them returned either.

A frog who'd been to the human world told horror stories of what might have happened, said he had just got away with his life when he travelled there. It was easy to get stepped on or caught in nets, run over by great rolling boxes. The rest of the frogs, he said, should forget all about that dangerous land, leave well enough alone.

But the Frog King couldn't do that – it was two of his children missing after all. He considered sending more of his people because he had no more sons to send, but no one else wanted to go. He considered going himself, but his guards and other people set up a great clamour of arguments.

"What will we do if you don't return? You guide us, settle our quarrels, tell us what to do. We can't lose you."

Then the Frog King's youngest child, a daughter nearly grown said, "I will go. I'm small, I can slip in and out of places, I'll hide and no one will see me."

The King didn't want to let her go, but eventually she wore out his resistance. Again, they waited, but this time the expedition did return, though many had given up that they would.

The daughter came back with a young man who had fallen in love with the Frog Princess when she was turned into a human by a spell that went astray. She had found no signs or news of her brothers. Now the young man wanted to stay and live with the frogs. Perhaps he could learn to shape shift. He and the princess began to learn how to rule from the Frog King so they could take over in the future.

I tuck the book away while thinking about the story and the old man who said he spent time as a frog. Is it a coincidence that I found this story, or should I take it as a sign? But a sign of what? My sister and I are no strangers to odd events that may or may not be connected. Thea's grandfather thought he'd found answers in the cave, though he can't remember them now. My sister and I searched for and found each other. But that wasn't enough. She's been off looking for and finding two missing children. What am I searching for? Is it just for knowledge about my family? I'm nearly a man, soon old enough to make my own way, but uncertain of what I want to do. I don't know if this journey will help me with all that.

I get out my bracelet and think of Ali, then Rowan. Either of them would be good to talk to, to ask advice of. Should I worry about the strange events at Schönspitze? How much of Grandfather's story can I believe? No matter how hard I concentrate on them nothing comes, so I finally go to bed.

Chapter XV
Burgrave House

The next morning I'm wakened early by sun streaming through the round glass window of my room. The faint sound of music just ended haunts my ears. I listen for a while but hear nothing. Perhaps it was the tail end of a dream. I get up and push open the window, breathe in chill mountain air. Beyond the roofs of Schönspitze and its eastern wall lies the road leading away from the gates toward Aquila, my home. What is Papa doing now? If he's awake he'll be getting breakfast and then heading off for the school. So predictable. I don't want a life that's as dull as that. Though I didn't always think of life in Aquila as dull.

I get out the bracelet, sit in the middle of my bed, finger the silver ivy leaves. Silver is a metal that belongs to the moon. Ivy is a climbing and trailing plant. Do those two things connect in some important way? I've never thought about that before. My sister, who has knowledge of plants, herbs and healing, might know. I picture her long black hair, grey eyes, and her smile that flashes quickly and is gone.

"Rowan," I whisper.

The whisper echoes in my head, rolls around the room, floats out through the window. I think of it buzzing through the air like a bee. How far can bees fly?

"Samel."

Am I imagining her voice? "Rowan, are you there?" Then I see her face floating in front of me. I close my eyes to concentrate. She's sitting cross-legged on a low bed. Can she actually be in the room Papa had built for her? "Are you home, in Aquila?"

"Yes. Your message by the eagle came and we sent one back. You probably haven't gotten it yet. I don't know how fast eagles fly. Where are you?"

"In Schönspitze with Thea and the twins. In the house where Thea and our mother lived. And Grandfather Frog is here. Thea thought he was dead, but he's alive after all this time!"

"Grandfather Frog? What are you talking about?"

"Long story. He's Thea's grandfather. Our mother's, too. Our great-grandfather, I guess. When did you get to Aquila?"

"A few days after you left. Too bad I missed you and Thea. Thea's grandfather is not really a frog, is he? A shape shifter?"

"Not a frog. I don't know if he's a shape shifter. We just got here yesterday. Will you be staying in Aquila a while?"

"Yes. I'm going to work at the arts school when it's finished. Teach about herbs and healing."

"Really! Big changes."

"Yes." There is a pause and I'm about to speak when Rowan says, "You came past Hrashak's castle with no problem?"

"We didn't go close to it. Why?"

"Julina and Varonne are there now. I'm a little uneasy about them. A flock of ravens is keeping an eye on things there."

"Ravens? That's odd. You had a raven once didn't you?"

Rowan's face flickers like the flames of a fire about to go out. "Can't hold … glad … talk …care." She's fading fast.

"Greetings to Papa and my love."

I don't know if she heard my last words. I put the bracelet away. A sigh escapes me. It's harder being away from home than I thought. My stomach feels odd, queasy. What does it mean about Julina, Varonne and the ravens? Varonne was Hrashak's daughter, and Julina is her mother, though she had left Hrashak long ago. A growl from my belly drives everything else but food out of my head for a while.

No one is in the kitchen and I can't see any food laid out. I hear voices from down the hall. Thea and the twins are in the small room at the front. The boys roll a wooden ball on the floor; Thea is dusting.

"Where's Helfrith?" I ask. "I'd like something to eat. Should I help myself?"

"Who knows? The house is a disgrace. I thought I'd do a bit of cleaning."

"She's old and she's only one person," a deep voice croaks.

Thea and I turn in unison. The twins begin to wail and immediately there's a smell of goat. I'm not surprised. If I hadn't seen him before I might feel rather like moaning myself. His bald head gleams as rays of light from the window strike it. Like yesterday, he's dressed in a green jerkin. As he moves forward, dust motes rise from the floor and his clothes. Thea starts sneezing.

"Frog!" one of the boys sobs.

"Eat us," the other adds.

"Hush!" Thea admonishes. "This is your great-grandfather. Stay calm! He won't hurt you."

The twins fall silent; fingers find mouths; eyes are round.

"Welcome boys. It's true I won't eat you. I like to eat cake."

One of the boys whispers, "Cake."

"Thea, tell me their names." The old man bends down to peer at them. The boys, surprisingly, hold their ground, but there's still a strong scent of goat.

"This is Kosto and this, Pello. I have to get them some potion."

"What sort of potion?" Grandfather asks.

"If they get upset they . . . change."

"What do you mean?" the old man frowns, then nods. "They can shape shift?"

"Yes, didn't your spies tell you that? They can't control it yet, change to goats when they get upset."

"No need to worry," Grandfather responds. "In this house," he says to the boys, "you can be goats or boys or anything else you want to be. No one will hurt you."

The boys stare at Grandfather. One reaches out a hand and the other takes it. "No hurt," one whispers, I think it's Pello. "Cake," whispers the other.

"I think they might be hungry," I add as my stomach grumbles loudly again.

"Helfrith is setting out food in the next room," Grandfather says. "And I went out earlier and fed your camel and ox."

He points to a door directly opposite from the windows and moves towards it. It's the room with the long table and many chairs. Plates, bowls, cutlery and drinking vessels are set on the table. A side table holds several covered pots and dishes. Helfrith isn't to be seen. The boys run forward and grab hold of the table edge.

"Help yourselves," Grandfather says. "We can talk as we eat."

Warm bread and cold meats, cheese, gruel, honey, butter and fruit preserves; Helfrith hasn't stinted. I load a plate and set it down, then help Thea to get the boys settled. Grandfather is already seated and spooning gruel.

"Why did you send for me?" Thea asks. "Just to tell me your story?"

Grandfather swallows. "Can't a man want to see his granddaughter?"

"You've been back a while, haven't you? Why wait so long to let me know?" Thea picks up a piece of cheese that Kosto has dropped and sets it aside. She wipes gruel from Pello's face and hands, cleans his spoon and gets him eating again.

"I had other things to do."

"What things?

I frown, remembering what the old man said yesterday he'd been doing. "Books," I say. "He's been searching for something."

Grandfather sighs. "I'd forgotten what the young are like. Precipitous, nosy, without discretion." Then he grins at me, that wide, frog-like grin that makes me feel a bit like a fat fly.

"Was it a secret?" I ask. "If so, I'm sorry."

"Never mind," the old man says. "Books, yes. Whatever happened to that old leather-bound book your cousin had, Thea?"

"The Leather Book? Why I gave it to Samel. What do you want with that?"

"To refresh my memory about a story or two. You have it, Samel?"

"In my room. Do you want me to get it now?"

"Later." Grandfather pushes his plate away and settles back in his chair. "While you all finish eating, let me tell you about our family, Samel. It's important to know where you came from."

We settle ourselves and pass food. Grandfather eats a few spoonfuls of gruel, then pushes his bowl aside. He wipes his mouth and hands.

"We were traders at first, left a place somewhere in the east, the family tales aren't clear about where or why. I've found no records about that, but family tradition maintains it was an ancient city. We travelled much and found this place, became merchants and eventually amassed enough wealth to have influence and build this house. My grandfather became the Burgrave or ruler of Schönspitze. He ruled wisely and well, and when he died the townspeople conferred the same title and power on my father, and later to me. It was assumed that our family would continue in this way. When I went away, I left a letter appointing Thea to this function."

"I didn't want it." Thea shakes her head emphatically. "Told the townspeople to chose someone else."

"But this house," Grandfather continues, "belonged to the family, not to the city. You ran away, Thea, and left the house to fall into disrepair."

"I left to go and help my cousin when she needed me!" Thea slams a spoon against the table.

The twins and I jump.

Grandfather frowns. "And you let her drown."

"Wait a minute," I say. "That wasn't Thea's fault! An old sorcerer was responsible."

"I need to hear the details of that story some time," Grandfather says, "but not now."

"Didn't your spies explain it to you? You know so much else about my life. You could have written to me, let me and Zarmine know you were alive," Thea mutters. The twins start to sniffle. "Finished eating? Let's get you cleaned up. Then we'll get to work on the house. I don't see why you couldn't have hired people to help you keep up the house," she flings at Grandfather. "You must have money. Or did you spend it all?"

Thea doesn't wait to hear the old man's response. She takes a boy by each hand and stomps out of the dining room. The twins are babbling, but among the nonsense, I hear, "no cake" in a disappointed little voice. I look anxiously at Grandfather to see what he will do or say.

The old man grins. "I like that girl's spirit."

"She's a grown woman."

"I stand corrected." He taps a long finger on the table top. "I know a lot about Thea and what she has been doing, but you I didn't expect."

"Is that good or bad?"

"We'll see." He stands up and I expect him to walk away or to tell me to leave him, but he surprises me by saying, "Want to come along?"

"Yes. But what do I call you?"

His eyes flash, his lips twitch. "Grandfather is fine."

He leads me to the small room near the front of the house, that he calls the salon. It's much tidier and not as dusty as before. Someone, probably Thea, has washed the window because it gleams in the sunlight.

"I'll have to hunt up my key," Grandfather says, closing the connecting door to the dining room behind us and throwing a bolt. Then he goes over to close the hall door. "I don't mind that Thea cleaned in here, but I use this room to think and read, and I'd rather it not be disturbed." He rummages in the centre desk drawer, manipulates something and a narrow drawer pops out. It holds a key, which he takes out. "Lots of secrets in this house if you have the patience to hunt for them," he says.

That sounds as if he wouldn't mind if I did find some of the secrets. I grin and he nods at me. He sits in one of the chairs and gestures me to another. I settle myself and wait. He doesn't speak for a while, so I look around the room. There could be more secret cupboards in here, but if he's going to lock the doors, I'll have to search other parts of the house instead.

I'm distracted from my thoughts by Grandfather crossing his legs and leaning forward. "That Leather Book, have you read much in it?"

"A story here and there. An odd book, though. At times I've looked for a story I read before and can't find it. I have a really clear memory of the story, but it's as if I must have read or heard it somewhere else."

"Aha! But it's a magic book, you see."

"My Papa doesn't like me to have anything to do with magic."

"And you? What do you think?"

"I've seen magic. I'm not afraid of it."

"But you should be. Oh, not the folk magic that a hedge wizard or wandering witch might practise, although even they can cause problems if they don't cast their spells properly or use the right herbs."

"My sister knows all about herbs."

"Her mother taught her, I imagine. She was your mother, too of course. At any rate, my wife also knew the secrets of plants and she passed that on to Zarmine."

"I don't know much about this family. Papa didn't talk about it."

"Perhaps he didn't know. It doesn't matter though. I can tell you anything else you wish to know or you can look in the library. There's quite a collection of books, scrolls, and so on in there. Different languages, too. Family histories, stories of other lands, poetry, philosophy, herbals and so on. I've become even more familiar with the library since I returned." He opens his hand and contemplates the key lying there. "Haven't found what I'm looking for yet."

"And you think the Leather Book might have what you need? I can go and get it right now."

The old man shakes his head. "It's not that easy with magic. You can't confront it too directly. Have to sneak up on it. We'll wait until the time seems right.

Now, I want to think alone for a while. Why don't you go and explore the house?"

He unlocks the door and lets me out. I hear the key turn as I leave. Instead of exploring right away, I sneak up to my room. If Thea is going to clean, I don't want her to find me.

Chapter XVI
Explorations

E ach day I remember to take time to play the flute because a musician must practise. I guess I'm not giving up on that, at least not yet. It's too much fun, though it can be hard work, too. I wish I'd brought a drum, but there just wasn't space. I fool around with some composing. I'd like to write a piece about our journey here, but nothing I come up with satisfies me. Now and then when I'm playing, there's echoes, as if another musician somewhere else in the house has joined in. But I never find this person, or any musical instruments. It must be just the echoes of a large house.

Most of the next three days I spend wandering the house starting with the cellars. I guess I'm looking for signs that my mother lived here. In the cellar I find

nearly empty wine racks, storage rooms filled with
old furniture and other bits and pieces. Then there's
the strange pool where Grandfather often sits playing
with water – dripping, stirring, pouring it from one
container to another. He never explains what he is
doing or why the pool is there. Was it accidental or on
purpose? I haven't felt comfortable asking.

There's also a niche at the far end with a cot,
a chest and a chair. Grandfather's bedroom? Why
would he choose to sleep here rather than in one of
the upper bedrooms? Maybe it reminds him of the
cave, or it could be that he doesn't like climbing a
lot of stairs, though in that case it would make more
sense for him to sleep on the main floor. Who knows
how an old man thinks. Or an old woman, for that
matter. Helfrith's rooms are also in the cellar near the
stairs, but she keeps them locked. She's often in the
kitchen and doesn't seem to like me around much
so I'm not able to do as thorough a search there as I
would like. I suppose I could ask questions, but I'm a
guest in the house and I don't want to be rude. Papa
brought me up better than that.

I meet Thea and her boys here and there on my
explorations. Once in a while the boys are in goat
bodies and Thea lets them be. I guess she's taking
Grandfather's words literally – they can be what they
like here. But I've seen the boys change back on their
own, too. So maybe Thea is teaching them control.
Often Thea cleans; the boys stay nearby.

Grandfather unearths ancient wooden toys – a small wagon, a horse on wheels, and a set of blocks. The boys play noisily with these in whichever room their mother occupies. I wonder whether there are other interesting things to find. Now and then Thea tries to involve me in her cleaning and I do help, but always manage to escape to keep on with my exploring or to go out and visit with Izmeer and the ox.

The library holds me for more than a day because there is so much to peruse. At first, I go row by row looking for my mother's name, but I don't find it. Thea comes by and shows me how to properly dust books. I end up sneezing a lot. It's easy to get lost in the great assortment of scrolls, tablets of clay or wood or stone, parchments stitched to leather or wooden covers, books of vellum. Many are old and fragile, others written in languages I don't even recognize much less can read. A few scrolls that I can make out deal with the history of the Burgraves, how they governed the city, expenses, political issues; these don't interest me. But I do come across others – for instance, a children's story book with drawings of a retelling of the Frog King story that I found in the leather book. Grandfather may have read this and it influenced his belief that he turned into a frog.

When I'm about to re-shelve the children's book, I notice at the back of the dark space something pale. I reach in and pull out a crumpled sheet of parchment. Smooth it out carefully. The writing is faded and the parchment cracked. I take the sheet to a table and light a candle to help me read. The writing looks familiar.

Dearest Zarmine,

I can hardly wait for tomorrow! I've bought an extra horse and told the other musicians that you'll be joining us when we leave in the morning. They were a little doubtful, but I convinced them that a healer would be a useful person to have along.

Are you still planning to sneak away, leaving only a note to let your family know where you've gone? It seems hard, but you know them and I don't, so if that's what's required for you to come with me, so be it.

I'll be seeing you in only a few hours so I won't say much more. Just that I love you and I hope you sleep well. I'm not sure I'll be able to sleep at all!

In great anticipation and joy,

Yarvan

Quickly I look around, but there's no one else in the room. I roll the letter up carefully and tuck it into my belt pouch next to the bracelet. Did my mother hide this here suddenly when someone entered? My eyes itch and when I rub them there's wetness. My mother and Papa were young once like me and so much in love. It makes my face hot to think about it. A tear rolls down my cheek; they should have had a long life together. Rowan and I should have had two parents for a lot longer. But there's nothing to be done about it, life is what it is.

I rub my eyes dry and go back to searching the shelves for things to distract me; find some of the stories that grandfather mentioned about the family as traders describing caravans travelling across grass-lands, encountering stampedes of wild cattle, wild-fires, and blizzards. I spend quite a time with these, imagining what it must have been like to be the first to explore parts of this land.

Our first close view of mountains, craggy, green, brown and white. We've seen them in the distance for several days, vague shapes on the horizon. Have heard so many stories. Great bears and huge wolves are said to roam the forests, gemstones supposedly scattered about in the valleys. I hope the truth lies somewhere in between. The women are nervous, keeping the children close to them at all times. Even the men, though they pretend to be joking, jump at the slightest noise.

If luck is with us we'll find a good location for our settle-ment. A fertile valley would be ideal but might be difficult to defend. That's of prime importance. All of us remember what it's like to run from fire and swords.

A plateau on a mountain side with plenty of trees to cut for houses is what I'll search for. We have tents and the wagons to live in until we can build. We've arrived in early summer, are travelling through a meadow, wild flowers in profusion — yellow, blue and pink.

To travel and not know exactly where you're going or where you are going to end up, what dangers you may face must have been both frightening and excit-ing. Were there truly great bears and wolves in this area? I shiver and turn back to the shelves.

There are also journals with lists of goods and prices in crabbed handwriting, difficult to decipher. One scroll has a drawing of a long and complicated family tree, but I don't see any names I recognize. A person could spend many days looking at all this, but I choose to move on for now. I can always come back here later.

The room next to the library holds upholstered chairs, window seats, small tables, low couches that could be used as beds, several chests. I examine everything carefully but find no secret cupboards, just a few faded ribbons, perhaps belonging to my mother or Thea; there's no way to tell. I imagine what this place might have been like when two sets of grandparents and two girl cousins lived here. Noisy and busy, maybe similar to now with me, Thea and the twins added. Helfrith seems to find it more difficult than Grandfather. He likes to talk to us, while the housekeeper mostly disappears when she's not getting a meal ready.

On the second floor I examine three bedrooms thoroughly, leaving Thea's and the twins until last. Beds, tables or desks, chairs, cupboards and chests. It's not as dusty in these rooms as it is downstairs. Obviously, Thea has been here before me. I'm surprised that she hasn't thrown out all the old clothes yet – men's tunics and breeches, a few faded dresses and robes, several shawls, and a heap of down-at-heel boots and sandals. Nothing that makes me think of my mother as a young woman. But at least I have the letter.

"Samel?" Thea stands in the doorway of the last bedroom. "What are you looking for?"

I've been expecting her to ask and have already decided to tell her the truth. "Signs of my mother. Also, secret cupboards or passages. Do you know of any?"

"Grandfather put you up to this."

"He suggested I might like to explore."

"Of course. He wants to keep you busy while he goes about his own business."

"Which is what?"

"I haven't figured that out yet. I'm thinking of going to see the advocate again and asking what he knows. In regards to your mother, I think she took some of her things with her when she left and had others sent on later. I took more along when I left to visit her in the north." Thea frowns. "I remember how puzzled we all were that she could sneak away without us knowing. She wasn't a shape shifter." She shrugs. "Ah well, it was long ago."

I peer around Thea into the bedroom. "Where are the boys?"

"With Helfrith. She's taken them into the back yard to run around."

"You're starting to get along with her?"

"She's taken a shine to the boys. I think it's because they like to eat. Old as she is, she has done her best here. I told her I know that, but I also said that it's not fair she hasn't had any help. We're thinking of hiring a stable and yard boy, and maybe a girl to help with the housework. If there's any money. That's another reason for me to talk to the advocate."

"You didn't answer my other question."

"Which is?"

"Do you know of any secret hiding places in your room?"

"No. And when we were children here I didn't know of any secret passages."

"I'll go on to my room then."

Clothes and bits of this and that are strewn over the bed, chair and floor. Thankfully Thea hasn't been up here. Papa wouldn't be pleased at the mess, so I tidy while searching. The walls are stone except for a section by the bed which has wood panel skirting. It's there I find the secret. When I press against an edging carved with flowers, a square of wood slides aside, revealing a small cube-shaped recess. Inside is a wooden box.

I take the box out. It's plain and shallow with a hinged lid. I open it to find a grid of small sections holding a collection of rough gemstones. Some compartments are empty, others hold scraps of parchment with the names of the stones. There is amethyst, beryl, citrine, emerald, hematite, jasper, lapis lazuli, moonstone, opal, ruby, sapphire, tourmaline, and zircon. Who could this collection have belonged to? Were they found long ago in some part of the mountains? I could ask Grandfather, but whoever hid it wanted it kept secret for some reason. Do these stones have significance? Or are they just a child's collection kept private? I could ask who used this room.

Ali would like looking at these stones, would probably know much more about them than I do. I'm sorry that I was so grumpy with her for a while before I left. It wasn't her fault that I was angry at Papa and Rowan, that I wanted a journey of my own. Ali has been my friend for most of my life, always on my side. I said good-bye to her so abruptly. Will she still be my friend when I return? When will I go back? I'm not done with this place or this journey.

I put the box of gems back into the recess, accidentally banging it against the side wall. With a creak, a much bigger section of panel moves aside, and I'm faced with a dark space where I can see a couple of steps leading down. Quickly I shut the door of my room, then light a lantern and enter what I suspect is the hidden way that my mother found to leave the house.

The stairs are dusty and there's a smell of damp, along with plenty of spider webs. The narrow passage leads steeply down, twisting and turning to eventually end in a narrow wooden door. I push against it, but it doesn't open at first. It takes a few good thumps of my shoulders to dislodge it a crack. I peer through. It's the stable, and there's some obstruction that stops the door from opening all the way. I'll see if I can find the door from the stable end some other day.

Chapter XVII
Inside and Outside

Black as obsidian – where does that idea come from? Along with the thought comes a faint sound of humming like someone singing a familiar tune. I look all around, stare hard into darkness. Gradually I make out a dim light; the longer I look at it the brighter it becomes. I feel grass under my bare feet, move slowly forward through warm night air. The glimmer can't be the moon because it's too low.

"Samel?"

"Who's that?" I ask.

"Ali."

And then I see her sitting tailor fashion under the fig tree in the back yard of the artists' house with a lantern beside her. How did I get here? I went to bed in the tower room of Grandfather Frog's house.

"It's the stone," Ali says. "The piece of obsidian you gave me. I'm using it to see you."

"But how can I be here?"

"A dream. A vision. We saw each other once before, briefly, right? I didn't think I imagined that. I've been thinking about you, wondering how you are, where you are. I put the stone under my pillow last night."

"And you're not really in your garden either?"

"No. Remember how I dreamt about you and your sister before you found her? I hoped I could dream about you."

"We're in Schönspitze. It's strange here, but interesting. Thea's grandfather, who disappeared a long time ago, and everyone thought was dead, is actually alive. And he has this huge house. I haven't had time yet to explore the town very much. The trip was good. Thea changed my camel into a horse. I met an eagle."

"Sounds like you've had an adventurous time. I know about the eagle. It came at the celebrations for the opening of the school."

"Ali, I'm sorry I was so grumpy to you."

Ali sighs. "It happens. I miss you."

"I miss you, too. Oh, what do you know about gemstones?"

"What kind?"

"Um amethyst, lapis, ruby."

"Oh, lapis lazuli is lovely, you can make blue paint from it. Did you find some?"

"A rock collection."

And then the garden is fading, blowing away like mist on a windy morning. Ali's figure recedes, is gone. I'm lying in my bed in the tower room at Schönspitze and it's morning. The room is too empty with just me in it. I wish Ali could be here so that I could show her the rocks I found, the secret passage. She'd enjoy seeing the house and we could explore the town together. Why are these visions and dreams so short? Can I learn ways to make them last and to be more reliable when I want them? I'll have to think more about that.

Grandfather isn't at breakfast. After serving us, Helfrith goes off with a tray of food and knocks on the door of the salon. When the door opens, she hands over the tray and leaves us. I guess Grandfather is in there and doesn't want to be disturbed.

"I'm going to the advocate's house after we finish eating," Thea says, wiping gruel from Kosto's hands. "Do you want to come or are you still searching for secret hiding places?"

"I've stopped searching for now. I'll come along."

Seeing the advocate's house again, I realize that it's definitely small compared to Thea's family home. Much narrower, made of wood, and only two stories high. The same old man who opened the door before is there to let us in.

"I'm sorry to come without an appointment again," Thea says, while I hold onto the twins to keep them from running down the hall. "I'm hoping that Anwalt will have time to see me, if not this morning, then later today."

"Let me ask." He shows us into the same small waiting room.

A short time later he returns. "The advocate is having breakfast, please come with me."

"Oh, but we don't want to disturb …"

"He asked me to show you up."

It becomes clear to me that the ground floor contains the offices of the advocate, while the second floor holds a four-room apartment. The clerk shows us into a sitting room. Anwalt rises and gestures us to chairs.

"Would you like tisane, some food?"

"Thank you, no we've eaten. I'm sorry to bother you."

Anwalt reseats himself. "How can I help?"

The boys toddle over and stand by Anwalt's table. I go to them and take their hands to lead them away. The advocate smiles and offers a plate of fingers of toasted bread spread with jam.

"Thank you," I say, gathering up boys and plate. We sit on the floor in a corner. The boys munch happily.

"I've been wondering," Thea says, "about the reasons why my grandfather sent for me. Are there taxes to pay, documents to sign? What do I need to do?"

"Hasn't he told you?"

"He's told us a story about how he came to be missing and how he returned. Other than that, he hasn't said much."

"It's awkward." Anwalt takes a sip from a ceramic beaker, puts it down and studies Thea. "Before your grandfather returned you were the heir to the burgrave house and all their business."

"I know. I didn't really want it, but I was advised not to give it up too soon. Good thing."

"Well." Anwalt brushes crumbs from his front. "It should really be your grandfather who explains it all to you."

Thea doesn't respond to this, just waits. I can see that it's a battle of wills. Who will give in first? The advocate might just send us back to Grandfather Frog's house. Maybe I can get Grandfather to explain what he wants. I could tell him I won't let him see the Leather Book unless he does.

But Anwalt surprises me. He sighs and sets his breakfast things to one side. "You do have a right to know. When your grandfather asked me to send for you, he said that he wanted to get you involved in the businesses, prepare you to take over. He thought that since you now had children to take care of and think about, you might want to ensure a good future for them."

"Maybe he's planning to disappear again."

Anwalt shrugs. "Perhaps. Who knows the mind of that old man? On the other hand, he is very old and may be thinking about his death, which could come at any time."

"Tell me about the businesses. Our family governed the town at one time, but I know that's no longer the case, there is another burgrave. But our family also had mines and a timber business as well as an apothecary shop. What's left and what shape are the affairs in?"

"There's the house, of course. It needs work." Thea nods. "The apothecary shop was sold. After your grandmother died and your cousin left there was no one in the family who had the skills to keep it. All except one of the mines was sold. Most of the forest lands remain, though not much cutting of trees has been done for quite some time. I don't know any details of your grandfather's plans for you. You will have to ask him."

"I have a feeling it's not going to be easy to get him to explain," Thea says. "He's gotten into habits of concealment."

"Try," Anwalt says. "If you don't have any luck with him, let me know and I will come and talk to him, but I prefer that you do it."

"I appreciate that." She hesitates, then continues. "What about money? We really need a man or boy to work in the yard. Is it possible to hire someone?"

"I'll see to that," Anwalt says. "There's a great deal of money from the various sales. Your grandfather has some in the house. I've got the rest in a strong room."

"Thank you. We'll go now and leave you in peace."

"Wait," I say. "Sir, can I ask you a question?"

"Of course. What do you want to know, young Samel?"

"I'm using the top bedroom in the tower. It's an interesting room; you can see over nearly the whole town. I just wondered who might have used that room before."

The advocate frowns. "No one recently. When the whole family lived there, they used mostly the second floor as bedrooms. Perhaps servants lived in the tower? Thea do you remember?"

"Yes, we had a couple of maids who lived in the tower at one time, and a cook and her husband lived in the cellar as Helfrith does now. Why do you want to know, Samel?"

"Just curious. There were a few odds and ends in the chests – scraps of parchment, old goose feather quills."

"Hmm, Zarmine might have used the room once. I'm not sure."

I nod.

"Anything else I can help you with?" Anwalt asks.

"Nothing else today," Thea says.

The old servant shows us out.

Even though I should probably help Thea find and talk to Grandfather Frog, the thought of being indoors doesn't appeal to me. Other than my brief evening walk I haven't explored the town yet and there are the mountains and forests all around.

"Do you mind if I go and wander a bit?" I ask Thea as we leave the advocate's house.

She sighs. "Go ahead. Just don't go too far. I could use your help later cleaning or looking after the boys."

I stroll through narrow cobblestone streets past mostly one-storey houses with tile or thatched roofs. Here and there a housewife scrubs a front step. Now and then a man leads an ox pulling a wagon. A group of children chase each other, giggling. I recognize no one, shiver in the breeze, wish I'd brought a warmer cloak or worn more layers. Two children, each carrying a long loaf of bread, pass me leaving behind the scent that pulls at my nose and turns my head toward more of the same. A bakery. I scrabble in my belt pouch for coins, find a few. Enough to buy a small warm and crusty loaf. Tear and chew as I walk.

On a small square of grass two girls twirl a long rope while others run in and skip. I watch them for a while. It reminds me of children in Aquila and makes me homesick. Then it comes clear what the girls are chanting.

"Bear, bear, turn around,

Do not touch this magic ground.

Run, run, run away.

We don't want you to stay."

I shiver and move on. Do even the children cast spells here or was that just an ordinary skipping rhyme? Two men walk past me.

"Was there another bear sighting last night?" says one.

"No, false alarm," says the other. "But people are on edge, see shadows where there are none."

They turn down a street where a small tree grows. A rough wooden sign swings from a branch. Curious

to hear more about bear sightings, I veer in that direction, after the men. The sign has a crudely drawn mug
on it.

"Ale," says one of the men. "That's what I'm in
the mood for."

The other nods and they enter at the door next
to the tree. I don't recognize the men, so they're not
from our caravan. Locals probably. Maybe bear sightings is why Tag and Nacht didn't want me wandering alone at night, though it seems far-fetched that
a bear would actually come inside the city walls. It's
still overcast and cool out and I'm feeling chilled so
I enter the house. The men are sitting on benches at
a square table. I find another table and bench, plump
down rather heavily. The men pay me no attention.

The clatter of dishes and the chatter of voices
drifts from a door in the back wall as I enter the dim
room. We three are the only customers. Besides the
benches and tables there is a fireplace against one
wall, but the fire isn't lit. One of the men rattles his
fingers against the table top. I'm thinking about calling out for service when the other man pushes back
his bench and rises. Just then a woman enters through
the back door. The woman is in shadow so I can't tell
whether she's young or old.

"Ale if it's fresh," one of the men says immediately. "Have you any pastries?"

The woman nods, then crosses the room toward
my table.

"No ale for me," I hasten to say. "But a tisane would go down well if you have it."

The woman continues on without a word and I think she's about to leave by the front door, which seems strange. Instead she opens a pair of wooden shutters.

The brighter light blinds me for a moment, and I blink my eyes a few times. The woman is a dark shape against the window.

"Ale's fresh and I can give you bread with jam, or honey. Also red leaf tea." She's speaking to all of us, her voice low and musical. I see her clearly now. About the age of Thea perhaps, with black hair and dark eyes.

"Two ales and bread with jam," the two men say in chorus.

"Just tea," I add.

The woman nods and returns to the back room. The men ignore me and engage in conversation. They don't look like soldiers, no weapons or armour. Can't be storekeepers or they'd be busy at their work. Itinerant labourers, maybe, picking up work here and there when they can.

"Any more news?" one of the men asks.

The other mumbles words I can't quite make out.

The woman returns with their ale and bread, then leaves again.

For my order, I hope. I'm still chilled. I wish there were a fire in the fireplace. There is a stack of wood, though. I wonder if it's allowed for customers to light a fire. I don't have a tinder box nor flint with me. The men are hunched forward talking quietly. I catch the occasional word.

"Getting dangerous … traders from Aquila … the Burgrave … negotiating … defend."

I start as the men thump down their empty beakers, throw a few coins on their table and leave. I mull over what I've heard. Does it connect with what Tag and Nacht told me about strange happenings? With what I know about the caravan and Lord Davus' support of it? Who might be responsible for all this upset? If Papa were here, I could ask him and perhaps we'd talk the way we used to when he'd tell me about protocol and politics in Aquila.

I shiver and wonder when my tea is coming. Has the woman forgotten me? Just then she arrives with a plate and a beaker.

"Sorry to be slow. Fresh bread out of the oven. Thought you might like some even if you didn't order it. Boys your age are generally often hungry. I had to wait a bit for it to cool enough to cut." She sets the food and drink in front of me. "You're new here, a stranger to Schönspitze."

"How do you know?"

She smiles. "It's not that large a place. Strangers are noticed. And besides, we've all heard of the return of the former burgrave's granddaughter."

"Did you know her when she lived here before?"

"Not really. I knew who she was, of course." She taps me quickly on the shoulder. "Enjoy. And don't worry too much."

She's gone before I can ask what she means, or what else she might know. The scent of warm bread and honey pulls me out of needless thought. There's something about this mountain air that makes me eat more than usual. After I've drunk the tea, though, I'm anxious to get moving again, find Grandfather, ask him some questions. I pull a few coins from my belt pouch and leave them on the table.

Just outside the alehouse, a solitary man approaches. I pay him little attention until he stops next to me.

"Samel?"

"Oh, Distans. You're not with the caravan today?"

"I have business to take care of. And I was hoping to see Thea. Will you all return with us? We're leaving in two days."

"Nothing's decided yet. Why don't you come and see Thea now?"

"No time, but will you tell her I asked about her? She can let us know what she decides about returning to Aquila."

"Yes, I will."

Chapter XVIII
Speculations

I've forgotten to get a key to the house, so I expect Helfrith's frown to greet me when she answers to my ring. Instead it's Grandfather who opens the door.

"Come in my boy! I wondered where you'd got to."

"I did a little exploring of the town."

"Ah. And what did you see?"

"A lot of houses, cobblestone streets. I found an alehouse."

"Not drinking this early in the day, surely?"

"I don't drink ale at all."

"Good, good. Come in. There's something I want to talk to you about."

"And I have questions for you."

"My turn first."

He leads the way into the small room on the right, the salon, as he calls it. It's not as dusty as before, but messy with papers and books scattered everywhere, on the desk, on chairs, on shelves and on the floor.

"There's a story I want to tell you," Grandfather says. He clears papers off a chair and gestures me to it. "Perhaps you've read something similar in your Leather Book. I heard the tale long ago as a boy and remember only fragments." He takes another chair. "Let me tell you what I remember, and you can see if it sounds familiar." He leans back in his chair and closes his eyes.

"Once there were two boys who lived in the mountains. They were friends, close as brothers. And like brothers, sometimes they disagreed, sometimes they quarrelled, but mostly they got along and they looked out for each other, defended each other, stood up for each other. Their favourite activities included exploring, hiking, climbing, camping. As they grew older they wandered farther afield and one day they discovered a cave. At first they were wary – dangerous animals could live in caves – so they watched for a few days, but the cave seemed uninhabited. They didn't realize that there was another entrance.

"Finally, one day the boys took courage and entered the cave. They found a fire pit, wood, furs, cooking pots and implements. These weren't dusty and didn't look abandoned but had been taken care of. All signs that a person lived or had lived there.

"One of the boys wanted to leave immediately. 'This is someone's home,' he said. 'We're intruding.'

"The other shook his head. 'No one's here now. We haven't seen anyone for days. Maybe whoever lived here has left or they could be hurt. We should try to find them. Look, there's another opening, more chambers maybe.'

"They explored further. One of the boys noticed several niches carved in the side of the second chamber. Most were empty, but one held pendant with a carved wooden 'R.' In another, they found a small scroll.

"The boldest boy picked it up and partially unrolled it. A glitter of silver dust rose into the air.

"The other boy said, 'What if it's magic? Best put it back.'

"His friend refused and peered at the writing. "I can't read this." Neither could the other boy.

"A voice stopped them. 'What are you doing here?'

"They turned and found a most beautiful girl – raven hair shading in places to silver, midnight blue eyes, alabaster skin. Both boys fell in love instantly."

Grandfather opens his eyes and shakes his head. "And that is all I remember of the story except I think one of the boys died or was killed not long after. I have the feeling that cave was very important. When I was away and I found myself in a cave by a pool of water I remembered the story.

"Like I said earlier, I'd gotten pulled or pushed there by underground currents. I thought I was in a frog body and seemed to be in a dream or trance. I was there a long time until a great rainstorm came and flooded the cave and washed me out through an underground river and down to Schönspitze again where I came out in a pool by a waterfall. I found myself back in my own body.

"What I didn't say to you and Thea was that at times I could hear one or more voices. Sometimes they were merely murmurs, then a word would pop out at me like cinders flung from a fire: 'time' or 'try' or 'test'. Once I heard someone say, 'It's the silver.' I still puzzle over those words."

I start and drop the silver bracelet I've been fiddling with from my pouch. It clangs on the floor and rolls under a chair.

Grandfather hears the noise and bends forward to look at me. He says, "Those words mean anything to you?"

His brown eyes shine like embers in a dying fire. They could flare at any moment. I can't look away. There's pressure behind my eyes as if a headache is about to start.

My throat feels a little tight; I clear it and words tumble out of me. "Do you know about the bracelets?" I manage not to look at the chair where mine rolled.

"What bracelets?"

"You don't know." I take a deep breath. "My parents had a coucouple of silver bracelets made."

"Aha!" Grandfather leans further forward in his

chair. "And you have them now?"

"Not exactly. Our mother had one and Papa had the other."

"Had?"

"Hmm. They didn't really like them."

"So they gave them away."

"Not really."

"I don't understand. What did happen and why didn't they like them?"

"It wasn't the look of them. The bracelets were . . . sort of . . . magic."

"Yes!" Grandfather bends even farther forward.

"Careful," I say. "You don't want to fall out of your chair."

He sits back. "Tell me more. Who has them?" His eyes fasten on my face and he frowns slightly. "Surely you have one of them?" He rubs his forehead. "And your sister has the other!" He peers around the room. "That noise was one falling."

I groan. "Yes, you're right." Quickly I dive under the chair and grab my bracelet before Grandfather can, if he can. I slip it onto my arm.

"Tell me more about these objects," Grandfather says, his eyes on my wrist.

"I think my sister and I might have found each of ours around the same time, though we were far apart. At first mine just helped me to make breezes when I played one of Papa's flutes. Rowan started having visions and the bracelet made them clearer. Once mine started a piece of parchment on fire. Then

Rowan and I began to be able to see and talk to each other."

I pause. Should I tell Grandfather the last bit? I'm not actually sure if it's to do with the bracelet or the obsidian stone or both. It could be something entirely new, too. Still, Grandfather is interested in this and he has all those books. Maybe he's read about stuff like this.

"The other night I dreamt of a friend of mine. We saw each other as clearly as I see you now and we talked."

"Very good!" Grandfather says. "Thank you for telling me all this."

I frown and study him. I've told him more than I ever told anyone else at one sitting other than Ali. She wondered if Hrashak had ensorcelled me. Why would I suddenly tell Grandfather all this?

"Have you been doing something to get me to talk of this now?" I ask.

"Like a spell?" Grandfather's eyes twinkle. "If I could do that kind of thing, I might have that bracelet on my wrist right now."

"I don't think so. You'd have to be a lot more powerful than . . ." I stop.

I have gotten to like Grandfather. Enjoy spending time with him, listening to his stories. But I don't entirely trust him. He hid from his friends and family, though perhaps he hadn't had any control over that at first. Still, once he returned home, why didn't he let Thea know?

"Why did I keep watch on Thea and her boys without letting her know that I was alive?" Grandfather takes the thought out of my head. "It's not hard," he continues. "I watch people's faces. I'm old; I've had a lot of experience. I can often tell what people are thinking."

"So why did you not let her know you were alive?"

Grandfather sighs. "I may know a lot, but I wasn't sure who to trust. Had they wanted to shut me away? Did I feel a push before I landed in the water?"

"Wait a minute. Once before you said you jumped in the water."

"Did I?" I think the old man looks a little shifty. "I don't always remember exactly."

"Hmm. And did you really think it might be someone you knew who pushed you? Like Thea? She was a young girl then wasn't she? Why would she do that?"

"It's hard to remember what I thought then. I'm a different person now. Anyway, by the time I came back, so many were dead and gone. I needed to trust someone and I chose our advocate's son. But as for the rest, if I let too many know that I was back and alive, they might on purpose or by accident tell someone who could harm me."

"Your housekeeper didn't know who you were?"

"Yes, she was the only other one. She's the advocate's sister, a widow. But that's all."

"What did people think? Who did they imagine was living here?"

"At first Anwalt just let it be known that a distant

relative had surfaced and he was dealing with it. I didn't go out much except well wrapped up."

"And no one guessed who you really were?"

"You saw how unbelieving Thea was. I'm ancient. How could I still be alive after all this time? Perhaps there was speculation, but so what? No one knew for sure."

"And now? Are you preparing to reveal yourself? Or maybe more people have figured out who you are."

"Hmm. Perhaps. A few." He smiles at me. "I'd like to get back to something else though. You said that I'd have to be a lot more powerful than . . . who? If I wanted to take the bracelet from you."

"Umm."

"So be it. You don't quite trust me or don't know whether you can." Grandfather reaches over and picks up a bell from a nearby table. He rings it loudly until the housekeeper comes to the door.

"You want something?"

"Bring us a tisane, will you, Helfrith? And biscuits or cake, something sweet to go along with it."

The woman nods and leaves.

"Food and drink help the thinking and talking," Grandfather says.

And he says no more until the housekeeper returns with a tray. She sets it on a low table in front of the old man and leaves again. Grandfather sits for a few moments without speaking.

The whole time we're waiting I'm thinking hard.

How much more should I tell him? He knows about a cave. Hrashak had found knowledge or power in a cavern. I have no idea where that place was, though it seems to me someone had suggested that it wasn't too far from the castle where Hrashak lived. That castle was Papa's home many years ago. It belonged to Papa's grandfather. Papa's father would have been living there if he hadn't died. Papa thought that his uncle, Hrashak was involved in that death, though he never admitted it. If I tell Grandfather about the cave, he would likely want to go there. I have no wish to go back to the castle, even if Varonne and her mother now live there. What I saw of Varonne while we were her father's prisoners hadn't made me want to trust her or spend any more time with her. Perhaps she's changed, though, and Rowan seemed to think that Julina, Varonne's mother, had helped find Papa and me. But even Rowan didn't completely trust Julina.

Grandfather pours steaming amber liquid into cups for himself and me. "It's hot." He picks up a square biscuit. "She makes good gingerbread. I like to dip it into the tisane before drinking it." He suits deed to words.

I pick up a piece of the gingerbread and nibble. Very tasty. Eating that piece gives me a good excuse not to speak, at least not about Hrashak and the cave. There are other things to discuss. I swallow the last bit of gingerbread.

"Thea was going to talk to you," I say. "She needs to know why you sent for her, what you want of her."

"Yes, she told me. I gave her the deeds to the house, the silver mine and the forest lands we still own. Other documents, too. She's in her room studying them."

"So, you do want her to take over here?"

"This is her home. I think she stayed in the north looking after the land and cottage just to please Rowan. It's not Thea's favourite place."

"You think you know her that well after not seeing her for so many years?"

"I know her."

"I guess if Thea is going it stay here it means I have to decide when and how to go. I could take the caravan back to Aquila. That's soon."

"I hope you won't leave for a while yet. You've seen only a little of the town and of the surroundings. There's the forest and the silver mine. And lakes and rivers. A waterfall."

"Hmm." Casually I say, "And the Leather Book?"

"Oh, of course! You were going to show it to me."

The old pretender! He was the one who said he was anxious to see the book. Still, I'm not satisfied with his story. I want to know more of what he's really after. "What will you do after Thea takes over? Will you stay here or go searching for the cave?"

"That is difficult to say at the moment. I need more information." He hunches forward, his movement casting a shadow that briefly makes him look as if he's got long hair and a beard.

"Hrashak," I mumble, then press my lips together. I didn't mean to say that out loud.

"What's that?" Grandfather Frog says. At times his hearing seems unnaturally good.

"Nothing."

"You said a word. A name perhaps?"

"Not important."

"Why say it then?"

"I was thinking aloud. I guess you remind me sometimes of another old man I knew once."

"Oh, yes?"

I set down my cup and stand. My body is tingling as if my arms and legs have gone to sleep; I need to move. "I think I should get the Leather Book now and show it to you. Maybe it will have what you've been looking for in all these other books." I lurch around the room and then make for the door before Grandfather can stop me.

On my way up to my tower room I catch a glimpse of Thea in her room, hunched over reading. The twins are lying asleep in the middle of her bed. She has separate cots for them, but during the day they often nap on her bed. She doesn't notice me, so I go quickly and quietly up.

Chapter XIX
Second Eagle

I stop in the doorway of my room, mouth agape. An eagle perches on the sill of the open window, talons denting wood, golden eyes fixed on me. By the white mottling on its chest and its brown head I make it about two years old, but even a young eagle can be dangerous. The bird chirps softly, however, and extends a leg, rocking precariously on the other. Quickly it grabs hold of the sill again. There's something fastened to the eagle's leg. Ah! This could be the message from Papa and Rowan. It's not that easy to tell eagles apart, but I think this might be the same eagle I sent with a message to them.

Slowly I walk forward, not wanting to startle the bird. It hops down to the floor and I stop. It cocks its head, then extends the leg with the message. I crouch and fumble at the ties, trying to be quick, aware all the time of the curved beak above my head and the talons close to my awkward fingers. At last I get the message untied, back up slowly, and open it.

It's much as Rowan described in my vision. She's in Aquila with Papa. They are both fine, and happy to get my message. I wish they'd written more, but of course you can't expect an eagle to carry too much, and they probably didn't have time to write a lot and keep the eagle waiting.

"I wish I had food to give you," I say to the eagle. "I could go down to the kitchen and see what there is. Would you wait?"

The bird's golden eyes stare into mine. It chitters softly. Yes, I think it's going to stay.

"I'll be quick," I say and rush down the spiral staircase.

Thea looks up as I thunder past. "What's going on?"

"Tell you later," I call.

No one is in the kitchen or the pantry and I'm lucky enough to find three raw fishes in a covered pan. No time to find someone to give me permission. I grab the smallest fish by the tail and flip it onto a wooden trencher. Then I run upstairs again.

The eagle is crouched by the open window peering about the room. Its head jerks to me as I enter. Its eyes go to the fish and it hops forward with a squawk. I put the trencher on the floor and back away. The eagle grabs the fish and leaps out of the window. I run forward and catch only a glimpse of the bird rising.

Laughing, I sink to the floor and read the note from Papa again. He's written love from Papa and Rowan. I wish he'd mentioned Ali.

Then I remember. I came up here to get the Leather Book to show Grandfather so I'm surprised he hasn't been yelling for me. I find the book in the trunk at the foot of my bed, under my cloak. Once again, I run down the stairs.

"You owe me several explanations!" Thea calls after me. The twins howl in chorus.

"Sorry if I woke them," I call back. They'll keep her busy for a while.

Grandfather is taking a drink from a flask and he chokes slightly as I enter. There's an old looking scroll on the desk in front of him. Seems like he's forgotten all about me.

"What is it?" he asks, corking the flask and tucking it behind a wooden box.

"The Leather Book?" I hold it up. "You wanted to see it."

"Ah, yes. Bring it here."

He clears an area of his desk and lays the book down, strokes the cover as if to clean it. The book isn't dusty. Though it looks old and worn it's never held dirt. Interesting. I didn't realize that until just now.

"Aren't you going to open it?" I ask.

"All in good time. I have to think about the story I want to see."

"Don't you just look in the list of contents and then turn to the page of the story you'd like from the list?"

"Oh no, this book isn't as simple as that."

"Are you trying to tell me it's magical, too?"

"Didn't I say that already? Perhaps even as magical as your bracelet. I think you said that at times you had trouble finding a story you'd read before." He grins at me. "Did you think I would have forgotten about that?" He shakes his head. "We'll discuss the silver circlets later. Now, should it be the cave or something else?"

"So where did this book come from?"

"Don't know. It's been in the family for a long time."

"There's lots of good stories. I've read about the Kingdom of Eagles and about the Frog King."

"Interesting, but I want anything about caves."

He runs a thumb along the edges of the pages and ruffles them. The book flips open. I lean forward.

"The Arrogant Burgrave," Grandfather reads aloud. "No!"

I can't stop my giggles. "The book has never done anything like that to me. But then I usually just look for a good story."

Grandfather slams the book shut. "You try."

Gently I open the book. I'm not thinking of anything in particular. The pages open to The Frog King. "Here," I say, "read this one. I think you'll like it."

The old man takes the book and settles back in his chair to read. While he's doing that, I wander about the room looking at the shelves. There are lots of books and scrolls, of course, even some clay tablets and incised stones. What I'm more interested in are the objects. There's a rusty curved knife, several grey stones with sparkly bits in, a carved wooden horse, a set of wooden blocks with letters and numbers painted on. I fiddle with these to try and spell my name. I can't find the 'e' though, so all I can get is 'Saml.' Instead, I build a tower, which wobbles as I get past eleven blocks. Then it tumbles with a crash.

"Can't a man read quietly in his own room?" Grandfather glares at me.

"Sorry."

There's a knock on the door to the dining room. "Enter!" Grandfather yells.

Helfrith stands there. "A thief," she says. "Stole one fish meant for the evening meal."

Oh no, should I offer to pay for the fish? But before I can admit to my crime, and receive my punishment, Grandfather speaks.

"I gave it to a beggar who came to the door," the old man says. "I thought two fish would do us, with vegetables and bread."

Helfirth ducks her head and leaves the room. I glance quickly at Grandfather, but he has turned back to the Leather Book. Why did he lie to Helfrith? Does he know what I've done with the fish? I sniff at my hands. Yes, the scent is here, and this old man is just as secretive and scary as Hrashak. He turns a page, sighs, and closes the book.

"I enjoyed this story. Before I experienced the cave and all that went with it I wouldn't have believed it either, just like the Frog King didn't believe in the world of people. But I think he was wrong to send his children off one by one into danger."

"Isn't it usually the younger people who go off on quests and things?"

"In some of the stories. But older people can have adventures, too." He shakes his head. "I really wish I could find that story of the cave. I'm sure I read it in this book many years ago, though I suppose it could have been in a different book. Still, I haven't been able to find it anywhere else."

The old man closes his eyes and holds the book against his chest. I go back to studying the shelves, but I don't actually notice many details. There's pressure at the back of my throat, a sort of ache as if something has to come out. At my wrist there's a circle of warmth. The bracelet is making itself felt. What will happen if I tell the old man about the cave and that other old man?

"Hrashak," the word falls into the quiet of the room and for a moment I think that I've spoken it aloud. Then I realize it's Grandfather Frog who spoke.

I don't turn to look at him but pick up a flat stone that has a spiral carved on it and pretend to study it. My shoulders feel tight. There was a spiral passage into the Sand Shrine at Aquila. Papa and I walked there just before we were about to go looking for my sister. The spiral took us to a room where a wind came and carried us away.

"I heard another story," Grandfather says. "Not so long ago. I think it happened to you. You were taken prisoner by a sorcerer in the southern mountains. What was his name again?"

"Hrashak," I mumble, and put the stone back on the shelf.

"Ah. And why did you think of him a while ago when we were talking? What brought him to mind?"

I turn around to face Grandfather. "He was old like you. Maybe that was it."

"Yes, perhaps. But was there nothing else? Earlier I'd been talking about the cave I found myself in. Hrashak lived in a castle in the mountains, did he not? Might there have been a cave nearby?"

"He was a dangerous old man!" I burst out. "He kept us prisoner and threatened us. He had illusions of conquering Aquila. Talk, talk, talk. That's what he did. He wouldn't leave us alone! Maybe you make me think of him because you won't stop talking."

I should leave this room before I say something that I'll regret, but I can't seem to take the first step toward the door. Does Grandfather Frog have powers like the old sorcerer? Is that what's keeping me here?

"Are you using spell craft on me?" I burst out.

Grandfather pushes his hands, palms out, away from him. "I don't use spells on friends."

"Coercion of some sort then. I really want to leave, but I can't."

Suddenly the bracelet flares brightly and heats uncomfortably. I shake it off and let it clang to the floor. Quickly I put a foot on it. What if it chooses to leave me?

"Now that is interesting," Grandfather says. "How does the bracelet connect to Hrashak and do they both have something to do with a cave?"

I frown and sink into the nearest chair. "He wanted them, the bracelets, but he couldn't take them. They have that much power." I hope this will be a warning to Grandfather. Then I add, "Our parents had them made, that's what Rowan told me, but no one could find the silversmith afterwards."

"Samel," says Grandfather, leaning forward, "I know that you don't entirely trust me, which is fine. One should be cautious with anything magical, and even with trusting people. I have my own motives for wanting to know more about the bracelets and about Hrashak. You have your reasons. Still, I think that we could gain a great deal if we collaborated. I know things that you don't and vice versa. What do you say? Shall we pool our knowledge?"

I study that odd old face that looks so much like a frog, and yet it's not ugly. As far as I can tell he is being honest with me right now, though I'm not sure that he always is. I had guessed early on that he would be interested in the bracelets and in my adventures with Rowan and Papa. Just as I'm interested in what has happened to Grandfather.

Rowan and I talked about the bracelets, speculated about what they might help us to do. Papa didn't like them, and after she killed the old sorcerer, Rowan didn't want to have anything to do with hers for a while. Still, she didn't get rid of it and she took it on her recent journey. Which I'm glad of because otherwise we wouldn't have been able to speak to each other at all for a long time. Did she use it for any other purpose? I haven't tried to do much with mine lately. Maybe I should test it in new ways. Grandfather has been waiting patiently for me to answer his question. He hasn't tried to hurry me, and I've felt no compulsion.

"Yes," I say, "I'm ready to collaborate."

A knock on the door leading to the dining room interrupts Grandfather before he can do more than smile. The door opens on Thea.

"How long are the two of you going to stay shut up in this room? Helfrith has supper ready, and the boys are clamouring to see you both."

"And you," Grandfather says as he bends slowly out of his chair. "What do you want of us, Thea? Questions for me, I'm sure, about the house, the mine, our forest lands. Well, food and conversation go well together."

As usual, Helfrith leaves us to eat by ourselves. Did she do that too when Grandfather was on his own here? It seems odd that she wouldn't keep him company, but then Papa and I never had any servants so I don't know how they usually act.

After setting plates in front of Kosto and Pello, Thea starts in on the state of the house and how it needs not only time but also money spent on it. She doesn't give Grandfather any opening to protest or discuss this and moves on to talk about the silver mine.

"I want to see it," she says. "When can we go? Could Helfrith look after the boys or is it safe to take them?" She turns to me. "Or Samel, maybe you could look after the boys unless you want to see the mine, too."

"I can look after the boys," Grandfather says, "whether Samel goes or not."

"What do you mean?" Thea protests. "You have to show me the mine."

"I haven't been there in years," Grandfather says. "Have no desire to see it. Anwalt can take you, and there's a caretaker who can show you whatever you want and answer any questions."

"The businesses belong to you. You don't want to see them?"

"I'm an old man. Time to pass things on. This house and the rest will belong to you and your sons. If you want it? You can decide when you come back from the forest and the mine."

Thea smiles. "I don't have to wait until then. I've decided to stay. This is my home. I've missed the mountains."

"Wonderful!" Grandfather ruffles the twins' hair. They giggle. "Now let's eat!"

"What about Samel, though?" Thea asks. "I think the caravan leaves in a day or two. If you don't go with them, Samel, we'll have to work out how to get you back to Aquila."

"No rush for that," I say. "I want to stay a little longer. But that reminds me. I saw Distans. He wanted to see you, Thea."

Thea sighs. "We'd better send a message that we're not going back with them."

Chapter XX
Visions

Grandfather and I don't get a chance to continue our discussion that evening because Thea has more questions for him, but I don't mind because I want to get up to my room and work with the bracelet. I light a single candle and place it in a lantern on one of the wooden chests; it casts a warm glow over the walls, makes me feel safe, but thinking about evenings in Aquila when Papa and I would play the flutes together. I get out the silver circlet and polish it a little with a soft cloth. It never seems to get really dirty, but at times its brightness is dimmed. Tonight I want all the power I can get. I glance out of the window to see that there's a half moon low in the sky; that may help. I slip the bracelet onto my left hand.

First, I try to find Rowan, to see her face, to hear her voice. I think of her in her new room in Aquila, at the market, and at the school, but nothing happens in that regard.

Papa's wooden flute that he gave me for my own at the beginning of this journey lies close at hand. I play softly so as not to disturb anyone else in the house. Almost immediately a tiny breeze springs up, fluttering my tunic sleeves and rattling a bit of parchment that lies on the table. I stop playing and the breeze dies. Put down the flute, close my eyes and wait again. Nothing.

Next, I think of Ali, but I can't see or hear her either. I try holding the bracelet in my cupped hands, search everything that's happened, every thought I've ever had to figure out why I've I been having so much trouble with it lately. Where does its strength lie and are there ways to bind its magic? Perhaps the silver or the way the ivy leaves are shaped and joined is important, but I don't know how to use that knowledge. Could there be a connection with Grandfather's cave or his silver mine? Hrashak's castle and what may be occurring there might have an effect on my attempts to use the bracelet. Or maybe the mist that protects Schönspitze is making it difficult for the bracelet to connect with Rowan. The ramparts of the mountains around me may act as a barrier as well. I just don't know enough. I want so much to see my sister and Papa, and Ali, talk to them.

On impulse I get out the gemstones and lay them in a circle, seat myself in the centre. I touch a single leaf of the bracelet with a finger, follow the curves and lines of it, the facets that catch and hold light. A glow of many colours springs up around me, light from the stones. The leaves of the bracelet shimmer and seem to shiver, as if about to move. I've seen ivy vines growing in the palace gardens at Aquila. I close my eyes and think of one of those green plants, clinging to a wall or tree, climbing to the sky. Silver moonlight touches the leaves. The plant rustles, grows before my eyes and reaches for me. I am entangled in green and silver. But I'm not afraid and don't try to get away. I'm held gently. And then the visions start.

At twilight someone with long hair dances on the top of a green hill, a woman whose face is vaguely familiar. Have I seen her recently? The face blurs as she moves, and her long hair blows back, the face more prominent, with high cheekbones and a square chin. Perhaps I was mistaken and it's a man. I can't tell for sure, but the dance is like song made motion. Arms and legs wave and stamp, fingers and hands undulate, head and body sway and dip, turn and turn, weaving coloured light and shadow into a tapestry I can't detail. The figure flickers in and out of sight until darkness closes in.

Mist rises over a river, spills into rolling grasslands. Through the vapour I catch glimpses of people on horseback leaning low over their horses' heads. They move as one with purpose and power, but I can't see where they are going.

A lantern illuminates carved rock walls. Small hollows here and there gape emptily or hold objects: the stump of a candle, a pottery jar with a wooden stopper, a fur coverlet, a tattered parchment scroll. I'm not sure who holds the lantern; I don't think that's my hand, but it's like I'm sitting on the shoulders of the person walking through curved passages. The sound of hammering begins and grows louder. Ahead, there's more light.

Grey stones lie in a heap; a great fire blazes nearby. A man hunches over a forge, picks up a crucible of melted silver and sets it aside. He grasps a metal rod, raises a hammer and beats on the metal. Light blazes into my eyes. I shake my head, open and close my eyes to try and get rid of the spots.

In my hands the silver bracelet lies warm and barely glinting. The gemstones' glow is fading. The visions have stopped, and I feel as tired as if I've run up and down the stairs several times tonight. All I can think of is sleep and my bed looks inviting, but I don't move to it yet.

Wind sighs around the tower room, whispers words I can't decipher. Did Grandfather really hear a voice in a cave talking about testing and silver? Rain taps against the window, drips into puddles as large as the pool in the cellar. A frog dives with a splash, deep deep into darkness. What waits in that lightlessness? Who was Hrashak really and what are his former wife and daughter doing now?

The sound of wind deepens, two notes, E flat and D vibrate in the air. The gemstones flare brightly once more, and I see Ali sitting in her room on her pallet bed holding the black stone I gave her. She stares into its shadows, finds sparks from fire mountains to light the darkness where we stand, while above us a mountain belches smoke. The earth shudders under our feet.

"Samel," Ali whispers, "be careful."

A shadow rises behind her. I try to call out to warn her, but my throat closes and I fall off a cliff. On and on, down and down. Strangely, I'm not frightened. Will I be carried by the wind as Papa and I were once before? Will I land again in the courtyard of Hraschak's castle?

"The cave," says Grandfather's voice. "I want to find that place again. It's not just any old cave, but a special one. A source of power. Don't you want that power, too Samel?" Darkness descends.

I wake to morning and the scent of rain through my half open window. Vaguely I'm aware of odd dreams as fragments linger in my mind – mist and silver, dancing and horses, stone, fire. The rain ends as I pull on wrinkled clothes.

Thea is up already and in the kitchen with Helfrith. A boy leaves as I enter. Thea tells me he's been hired by Anwalt to look after the stable and the yard. He brought a message that the advocate will pick Thea up after breakfast to take her to the mine and the forest. They'll be away all day so the housekeeper and cook is making a lunch for them and packing it in a wicker basket.

"Do you want to come, Samel?" Thea asks.

My first impulse is to say no because I want to talk more to Grandfather about his cave and how it might be connected to Hrashak and maybe to the bracelets. But then it occurs to me that the mine that Thea is going to see is a silver mine. What if the ore that became the bracelets was dug out of that mine? It would make sense that Mother took the metal from a place her family owned. Perhaps there will be remnants of power that I can sense there to help me figure things out.

Grandfather arrives in the kitchen holding a little boy at each hand. All three of them totter slightly off balance. My hands go out at the same time as Thea's, to stop an imminent fall.

"We're fine!" Grandfather says irritably. "None of us is going to tumble, right boys?"

"No," chorus the twins.

I'm glad to see the twins happy with the old man, but if I stay I'll probably be drawn into taking care of the boys. Grandfather and I likely won't have time to talk. My mind is made up on the spot.

"I'm going with Thea and Anwalt today."

I eat a hurried slice of bread with preserves, run back up to my room to fetch a warm cloak. Grab my belt pouch with the bracelet in it, and at the last moment tuck in the wooden flute as well. By the time I get back downstairs Anwalt has arrived.

"You're coming, too?" he says. "I didn't arrange for a horse for you."

"I'll take Izmeer. He needs the exercise."

The new yard boy helps me get Izmeer saddled. He tosses his head, lots of high stepping, so I know he's excited to be getting out. When I reach the front of the house three husky mountain ponies wait under the care of a bearded man.

"This is Altman," Anwalt says. "He'll guide us today."

Before we can start off, there's a shout and a tramp of footsteps.

It's Distans. "Thea. Samel," he says, a little breathlessly, "I see you're off somewhere. I wanted to let you know that the caravan is leaving the day after tomorrow. We extended our stay a little. If you want to come back to Aquila with us you should let us know by tomorrow at the latest."

"Thank you," Thea says. "We're off on a trip for the day. We'll let you know later what we decide."

I glance back as we start off. Distans still stands in the street, a rather forlorn figure. I thought Thea liked him, but she's treating him rather carelessly. She could have told him right now that we're not planning on going back with the caravan. Unlucky fellow.

We leave from a smaller gate at the northwest edge of the town, giving up our safe passage pendants, which we'll pick up when we return. A chill wind and a scattering of snow make me glad for my cloak. For a while the horses' hooves clatter on cobblestones until we reach a dirt track that winds into dense forest.

"It's not far to your family's lands, Mistress Thea," Anwalt says. "I sent a message there yesterday, so the caretaker is expecting us."

He seems about to say more when a shriek from the sky stops him. We all look up. Dark wings and a curved beak slip across blue sky.

"Eagle," Altman says curtly.

"A few live in these mountains," Anwalt adds. "We don't bother them, they don't bother us."

"Except for a few poachers," Altman says.

Is it my eagle up there? Was it poachers that had tried to trap it? The eagle follows until the deepening forest hides it from sight. We move along a winding trail, the scent of pine following us. Snow thickens both in the air and on the ground. I'm thinking that this might not have been the best day to take an excursion. Izmeer tosses his head and huffs, blowing a gust of snow from his nose. My fingers are aching, and I didn't bring any gloves. I pull my sleeves as far down over my hands as I can.

To keep Izmeer's and my spirits up, I start to whistle, a simple tune I learned for the flute when I first started to play. It's a song about warm spring breezes, short, but I repeat it a couple of times. As I'm starting the third repetition, I realize snow is melting off my arms and off Izmeer, and a warm wind is blowing. I'm last in line, so I don't think the others have noticed. Up ahead, snow still swirls. It's the first time I've called wind without the flute. I try whistling another tune, just making it up as I go along, though I keep thinking of warm wind. The magic holds. I ride happily until we reach a dilapidated hut nearly hidden in the trees, but we don't stop.

"Who lives here?" I ask.

"No one," Anwalt says curtly, "not anymore."

I notice that our guide, Altman, is making strange movements with his hands.

"Who did live here?" I ask.

"An old woman," Anwalt answers. "People said she was a witch and she kidnapped children and ate them."

"Really?" I say.

"There was no proof," Anwalt adds hastily.

"Ah," Thea nods. "Probably a wise woman who knew herbs and healing. Some of the people in the village where my cousin and her daughter used to live called them witches, too."

Mother and Rowan? I never knew that.

"The old woman who lived here was more than that," Altman says. "She could tell things about you that no one else knew. People said she could curse or bless you."

"What happened to her?" I ask.

"She disappeared," Anwalt says and both he and the other man ride quickly ahead.

"Do you believe them?" I whisper to Thea who is riding beside me.

"I remember when your mother and I were girls there were always stories about an old woman in the woods. We were warned to stay away from her. At the time I believed the stories that she ate children or changed them into animals. Now I don't. People say all kinds of things that aren't true because someone doesn't live the way everyone else does."

"Hmm." One of the reasons I don't talk about the bracelets to just anyone is because of what other people might say or do. Still, a city that uses magic for protection should be more tolerant of an old woman in the woods.

I turn for another look at the hut, but it's hidden now. I hope the old woman who lived there wasn't harmed. After a while we reach a clearing with a log house. A man steps out of the doorway as we reach it.

"Waldron," Altman says. "The Burgrave sent us."

"Yes, I got your message. I'd heard rumours that he'd returned, but thought he'd forgotten all about me and his forests."

"I'm his granddaughter," Thea says. "I hope you'll show me what you've been doing. The forest is thick."

"Too thick," Waldron says. "The undergrowth needs thinning or we'll be in danger of a bad fire. Come, then, dismount. There's a shed to keep your horses out of the snow, though it seems to have stopped snowing now."

Waldron's cabin is just one room. It's rather crowded with all of us, only two chairs by the table and a narrow cot to sit on. Altman comes in to get a beaker of hot tisane and then heads back out to stay with the horses. I take my tisane and walk over to the single window, staring out into trees and more trees. Doesn't Waldron feel shut in by all this woodland? Behind me, he's launched into a tirade about the need to thin the forest.

"Dead wood and fallen trees, fine, I gather and cut or I invite selected trappers or small holders in to do the work for a portion of the wood. But that's not good enough. We need to start clearing out under-brush and cutting other trees so that there's room for better growth. I could take you around today and show you."

"Are there maps of the property?" Thea asks. Waldron must have nodded or made some other gesture of assent because Thea continues. "Fine, then make me a copy with your notes and indications of where cutting should proceed, what should be done first. Also, include costs of extra people to do the work, and so on. Can you bring all that to me in Schönspitze in a few days?"

"Of course, but don't you want to see the land, the trees?"

"Yes, after I've seen your plans and recommendations. I'll come out with you a day or two after that, and we'll get started."

"What about the old man? Will he agree?"

"He's turned everything over to me."

"Good. More tisane?"

"Thank you, no. We have a silver mine to look at today, too, so we should get moving."

I'm feeling a bit sore and stiff when I get back on Izmeer. Not enough riding the last few days, I guess. The sun shines brightly through the trees, and the snow on the ground starts to melt. Izmeer frisks along, head high and tail arched. He probably had water and food in the shelter. Which reminds me that it's been a while since my meagre breakfast and the tea didn't do much to fill me. Luckily, there's still a few nuts and dried figs in my belt pouch, though they are a bit dusty. I munch and eye the saddlebags on Thea's and Anwalt's horses. That's where our lunch is packed.

We pass through another clearing. A bird shrieks and I glance up. A dark shape against the bright sky, recognizably an eagle. Maybe it's my friend following along. Suddenly the bird dives and disappears behind the trees. Hunting.

We leave the clearing and gradually I realize that we're going higher. Trees fall away behind and low shrubs cover the mountainsides. The rocky, narrow trail makes me want to stop, find something solid to grab onto. I stroke Izmeer's neck, but he seems calm. Perhaps he's thinking of the trails we travelled to reach Schönspitze. Some of those were more difficult. Just ahead the trail reaches a place where the side of the mountain on our left falls away into a steep valley.

Altman turns his head. "Everyone all right? Just trust your horses, they'll be fine. The mine is on the other side of this curve."

It seems to take forever to get to the curve. Altman rounds it and disappears first, then Thea. Anwalt is next. Soon I'll be alone on this side, with the steep cliff next to me. I keep looking straight ahead. A shiver strikes my neck and I want to pull my cloak up, but I don't dare make any moves. It occurs to me that my horse isn't really a horse and has little experience with mountains. I hope Izmeer isn't frightened.

Anwalt turns his head. "Just a few more steps, Samel, and it's wide and flat again."

Then he's gone. There's a rattle of stones and I glance quickly to my left. Dust and stones are rolling down the cliff, but I don't see any people or horses.

Izmeer has stopped and I wonder why. Then he shivers and changes, only this time he stays a camel a bit longer than he's done before. I have to remember to ask Thea about this! Then he's a horse again and trudges slowly on. I'm tempted to squeeze my legs to make him speed up, but the trail is so constricted that I don't want to make any extra moves. Finally, we're around the curve and in a wide open rocky flat with a mountain at one end.

I let out a long breath and take in deep one. There's a very small dilapidated wooden hut that won't hold more than one or two people. Everyone clusters around the opening to a cave into the mountain.

"Come on, Samel!" Thea calls. "We're waiting."

I slide off Izmeer and my legs nearly fold up. I grab my horse's mane and he nickers. I pat his neck.

"You and me both," I say. "I'm not looking forward to the ride back."

"We're going to have our picnic first, just inside the mine."

Altman unpacks hay and grain for the horses and brings water in a bucket from a nearby spring. Inside the mine we sit on rocks and spread our food on a flat slab. At first, I'm too shaky to eat or to notice much about the mine, but gradually I calm. I reach into my belt pouch and touch the bracelet. It warms against my fingers. Everyone but me chatters and eats. With everyone around it's not a good time to talk to Thea about Izmeer. I nibble on bread and cheese and look around.

Heaps of grey stones lie about on the floor. The walls are curved and there's a tunnel leading away from us, deeper into the mountain. It looks very dark down there. Is Altman planning to take us farther in?

"Well, Mistress Thea," Altman says, "how far do you want to go? There are torches here. He points at a niche I haven't noticed before."

"Just a little way," Thea says. "Who is in charge of this mine?"

I don't hear Altman's answer. He lights a torch, then leads Thea and Anwalt on. I stay sitting by the entrance. Why did I come on this outing? So far I haven't seen or learned anything useful to me. Things never turn out the way I expect. Maybe that's the way my sister felt when she came to find us and we ended up prisoners in Hrashak's castle.

The bracelet is out of my pouch and on my wrist before I really realize what I've done. Rowan once said she thought the circlets had minds of their own. It's scary to think that, but I have no time to explore that thought. The silver bracelet gleams warmly against my skin. I sense silver on the ground, in the piles of chipped stones, in the walls around me, deep down the tunnel. It's not the same silver that the bracelet was made of though. For some reason I think of Ali, see her face clearly in front of me. Her lips open to speak; I think she's going to say my name.

"Samel?" Ali's face is gone, and Thea stands in front of me. Anwalt and Altman are behind her. Thea stares at the bracelet. "What have you been doing?"

"Finding out that there's a lot of silver in this mine," I say and pull my sleeve over the bracelet. "Are we ready to go back to Schönspitze?"

Chapter XXI
Hrashak

That evening after our meal when Thea has settled the boys, she and Grandfather go into the small front room and shut the door. They're going to talk about the forest lands and the mine, Thea's plans for all that. She's definitely going to stay in Schönspitze. What am I going to do?

I can barely remember how angry I was with Papa before I left home. I've had my journey, seen the mountains, found out more about Mother's family. Helping Thea with her boys has made me realize children aren't easy. It's probably even harder as they get older, not always clear what is right to do. Papa's mostly been good to me, probably he's done the best he can. Maybe it's time for me to return, to join Rowan and Papa, try to be a family again. I could let the caravan know that I want to go with them the day after tomorrow. But I'm not quite satisfied with that.

I wander into the kitchen looking for company, but Helfrith isn't there. She hasn't talked much to me, though she seems to like the twins. Maybe she's better with younger ones. Still, I take a lantern down to the cellar, not sure exactly why except that I don't feel like being on my own right now. The housekeeper's door is closed as usual. She likes her privacy, I guess. She and Grandfather make a good pair.

For something to do I walk on past the store-rooms and through the wine cellar to Grandfather's pool. The flame of the candle dances on the dark water, but I've never seen the pool itself so completely still. The old man often drips water here or stirs the pool with his hand or a stick. I just feel like standing and thinking for a while, letting my mind drift like a leaf on water. I stare into light dancing on darkness.

Gradually I realize that the pool is showing me pictures and scenes. Something is definitely happening with visions. There is so much I don't know about the bracelets, about any abilities for magic that I might have. In the pool I see trees, a moon shining on water. A raven flies across the moon. Mist rises, clears again and there's a fire with a man hunched in front of it; he raises an arm holding a hammer, brings it down onto an anvil, and sparks fly into the sky. Stars glint over rolling land and a small animal runs up a hill. There's a sudden blaze of sunlight and a figure dances on top of a hill. I've seen some of this before.

"Samel? What are you doing here all alone?"

I turn to see Grandfather hunched behind me. In the half light of the torch and the flickering water he looks more like a frog than ever. I'm surprised that he used words rather than croaking.

"Just thinking."

"Come away. It's not good to gaze into this pool for too long. You can lose yourself."

He leads me back through the wine cellar.

"Is it late?" I ask. "I thought you and Thea would be talking for a while yet."

"She's gone to bed long ago. I assumed you had, too."

"I guess I lo…lost track of t…time." My teeth chatter over the words.

"You're cold and damp." He ushers me into the kitchen. "Sit. I'll make red leaf tea."

He hobbles around filling a kettle with water, stirring up the wood stove, hunting for something in the cupboards. Soon he brings cups for each of us, then sits down to wait for the water to boil.

"Hungry?" he asks.

"No." The heat from the stove feels good. I pull my chair closer to it.

Soon the kettle steams and Grandfather fills an earthenware pot. He pours for each of us. I wrap my hands around the cup, waiting for it to cool enough to drink.

"Why did you go down to the pool?" Grandfather asks.

"You and Thea were busy. I was trying to decide what to do, I guess. Whether to go home with the caravan or stay here for a while."

The old man clears his throat. "If you're going, there's something I'd like you to tell me before you go."

"What's that?"

He coughs, then clears his throat again. "Tell me more about Hrashak."

I lean back. "Why?"

Grandfather taps the table. "You know why. He found a cave. I want to know everything you know about that old man and what he found."

Of course he does. I've known that for quite a while and have managed to avoid talking any more about those things. Why though? What would it hurt? He's a grown man, even if he is old and maybe not totally in his right mind. But that's not up to me to judge or to worry about. I'm only fourteen. What happens to the old man is not my responsibility. So why not tell him everything I know?

"Please," Grandfather says. "It's important to me."

"Hrashak." I sigh. "He was a watcher, too. He'd watched my parents, my sister and me. Wanted the bracelets but knew he couldn't just take them; they resisted that. He caused my mother's death. Maybe he tried to get her bracelet and she fought him, but who knows. Anyway, he decided he had to capture us, and that's what he did – got Papa, Rowan and me in his castle. Tried to persuade us to help him use the bracelets to gain power to take over Aquila because he thought he had a birthright there. I don't know if he could have done it. He might have had an army hidden away, but if so, I never heard anything of it later. Rowan killed the old sorcerer and we got away."

I take a few sips of tisane. My eyelids droop. I just want to go to sleep, but Grandfather isn't ready to let me do that.

"There was a cave, too, wasn't there. A place where Hrashak first found his power."

I frown. "How do you know about that? Papa found out about that afterwards from things some of the soldiers in the castle told him."

Grandfather shrugs. "I don't remember exactly. I pick up gossip, chatter here and there. Helfrith and Anwalt tell me what they hear about the town. What more do you know about it?"

"Hrashak was Papa's uncle, and probably involved in Papa's father's death. Anyway, when he was a young boy Hrashak started going riding in the mountains. He found a cave with scrolls or fragments of scrolls. There was magic, spells, things like that written on the scrolls, but difficult to decipher maybe because the writing was faded or because it was written in some obscure language. Anyway, he never could get as much power as he wanted. That's all I know. Can I go to bed now?"

"Hmm?" Grandfather stares at my face as if he's not really seeing it, his eyes seeming to look into distance. He shakes himself briefly. "Power," he murmurs, then smiles at me. "One more thing. Do you have any idea the location of Hrashak's cave?"

He's going there, of course, why else would he ask me so much about it? What have I done? This is an old man, ancient. He's planning an excursion through the mountains to a cave he may or may not find. What will Thea say when she finds out?

"It had to be near the castle, right?"

I shrug. "Who knows?" I yawn.

"All right, bed. In the morning you can get ready to return to Aquila. Thank you for telling me about Hrashak and the cave."

I stumble from the kitchen and make my way slowly up the spiral staircase, barely managing to keep my eyes open long enough to find my bed and flop onto it. Undress? Not now. Grandfather. He's going to do something . . . but I'm too tired.

Chapter XXII
Plans

Eagles scream and soar, black shadows against pale blue; sun blazes into my eyes. Am I in Aquila? I pull my eyes from the eagles, stare all around and discover I'm not at home, but in a valley in the middle of mountains, no buildings to be seen anywhere, no river. I'm feeling very hot, which is odd because I remember the mountains as cold. Snow lies on the peaks. Then I notice that the snow is melting, water beginning to trickle down in streams.

"Samel!" the call echoes through the valley. "Samel."

I wake to sunlight pouring in the round window of my tower room in the Burgrave's house. The door of the room bursts open. Thea stands there, hands on hips.

"Didn't you hear me calling? And why are you lying in bed dressed? You were going to sneak out, leave with him before I could stop you, right? Really, Samel, I expected better of you. He's an old man and no matter what fantasies he spins, you shouldn't encourage him."

I keep opening my mouth and trying to talk, but Thea's spate of words pours right over me. It doesn't help that my head's still a little foggy from the dream and it's warm in my room. My clothes make me itch and my skin is sticky.

"I need a bath." As Thea has finally run down I can say what I've been thinking.

"Hurry up about it then," she throws at me. Just before she leaves and slams the door, she adds, "I'll stall him with breakfast."

There's a wonderful room at the back of the second floor. It holds a huge bath tub that can be filled with cold rain water from a tank on the roof, and heated water from a metal cylinder that just has to have a fire lit under it. Luckily the cylinder still feels hot from someone having an earlier bath. I sink in, noticing that my legs are more muscular than when I left Aquila. All that horseback riding has made a difference.

My mind sorts through all that's happened as I lie and soak. Now and then I think that I hear a rumble of voices or a shout. Grandfather and Thea arguing. Grandfather Frog has obviously been talking this morning about going to search for the cave, Hrashak's or the one he found himself in. They could be the same, but who knows? Short of tying the old man up or locking him in a room, I don't see how we can stop him.

By the time I get downstairs both Thea and Grandfather seem to have run out of words. They are sitting at either end of the table in the kitchen glowering at each other. I wonder where the twins are. Helfrith puts a plate of fried eggs and a pot of gruel on the table as I enter, and then she scoots out the door to the basement. She probably has heard enough of the argument. Maybe she's afraid of what might happen if it continues. Does Grandfather have power as Hrashak did? I've never seen him use it other than thinking he compelled me to tell him what he wanted to know. What magic could a frog do? Cause a flood maybe and drown us. Bring a plague of flies?

"Samel," Thea says, "you're finally here. Tell my grandfather he's too old to go travelling through the mountains."

I'm trying to think what to say when Grandfather slaps the table. "This is still my house and I can send all of you away. You want to live here, Thea? Take charge of the businesses? Then you'll have to let me do what I need to do." He doesn't say, "Or else," but he doesn't need to.

Thea's head droops. "I've just found you again and don't want to lose you once more. What if you drown in some mountain lake or rocks fall on you in the cave? Will you ride or walk? It might be a long journey. I just don't think you can do it."

"This time I'm not going alone," Grandfather says. "Early this morning I sent a message to the guard post at the gates. I asked if Nacht and Tag would be willing to go with me on a journey."

Thea growls. "You annoying old man! Why didn't you say that earlier?"

Grandfather grins. "I was having fun making you angry, and I wanted to find out why you really objected. Now I know." He reaches across the table and touches Thea's hand. "I'm glad we've found each other again, too." He turns his head and nods at me. "And I'm pleased to have met, you, Samel, my other granddaughter's son."

I smile. "I'm glad I met you, too."

"Good. So will you come with me on this little journey or are you in a rush to return home?"

I barely have time to think about my answer to this question when there comes a ring of the doorbell followed by loud knocking.

"I'll get it," Thea says.

"Well?" Grandfather continues after Thea leaves the room. "What will you do?"

"When are you leaving?" I ask, to give me more time to think.

"The sooner the better, but it depends on Nacht and Tag. Ah, here they are."

Boots strike against the floor. A whiff of sweat and leather, a tang of horse and metal enter the kitchen with the two women guards. Although the kitchen is large, it suddenly seems to have shrunk.

"Burgrave!" Two voices chime. "What can we do for you?"

"I'm not the Burgrave anymore," Grandfather says.

"Sit," Thea says. "Tisane? Food?"

"We've eaten, thanks," pale-skinned Tag says.

"I have a proposition for you," Grandfather says. "A journey I want to take and I need guards. Are the two of you willing? Can you get time off?"

"Wait," Thea says. "I'm not sure my grandfather should be doing this."

"Let's hear the details," the dark-skinned guard says.

Grandfather rushes in, describing a journey south through the mountains. Neither of the two guards asks why he wants to take this trip. Dark-haired Nacht merely nods and says that there are trails. Tag adds that they can surely get time off guard duty at the gate.

I'm thinking furiously as all this goes on around me. Shall I go or not? Papa, Rowan and Ali wait for me in Aquila. I've had my journey, I should be able to go home. But once I get home, then what? Do I just fall back into my old ways? I want something different, but I don't know yet what that is. There is more to see and do here.

It's dangerous, though, travelling through mountains; I've already found that out. And Hraschak's castle? I'm not anxious to return there. On the other hand, Grandfather has never said that he wants to go to the castle. He wants to find a cave, a very special cave that might be near the castle. How foolish is that? One certain cave in a wilderness of mountains. How could you possibly find such a thing? Grandfather says that he will pay for food and tents. Will the two guards bring their own horses?

"Surely," Nacht says. "Is it just you going?" She glances at Thea.

"I can't go," Thea says, "and I'm not certain Grandfather should either."

Tag shrugs. "Not up to you, is it? He can decide what he wants to do."

Thea slides back in her chair, opens her mouth, shuts it again. Grandfather grins and nods.

"We can be ready day after tomorrow, I think," Nacht says. "As long as we can get the time off. We'll head back now and send you a message." She turns to Thea. "We've done treks before, we know what's needed, what to do. We'll keep him safe."

"What about the young one?" Tag asks. "Samel, you coming? It'll be an adventure."

"Yes, I'm coming," answers my mouth ahead of my thoughts. And I know suddenly that my mouth was right. The bracelet warms at my wrist. Certainly I have to go. I may not understand why, but it is the next thing for me to do.

The two guards leave shortly after and Thea, shaking her head and muttering to herself goes upstairs to get the boys for breakfast. I realize that there has been thumping and other noise from upstairs for a little while now. Grandfather grins at me and slaps his hand on the table.

"I'm glad you're coming," the old man says. "I have a feeling about it. We're supposed to travel together."

"A magical feeling?"

"What do you mean?"

"My bracelet is warming. That makes me think it wants me to go with you."

"So that's good."

"I'm not sure. The bracelets have been helpful to my sister and me, but at times, Rowan thinks, they have minds of their own and those may not be in our interests."

Grandfather waves a hand. "But you really want to go, don't you? See more of the mountains, find the cave and discover what secrets it holds."

I feel a chill. "I don't know."

"The way to deal with fear is to acknowledge it and then to open the door and walk into it. I'll be with you and so will two guards of the city of Schönspitze. We won't take foolish risks. After all, you'll be with an old man who was reborn. What could be more powerful than that?"

I can't think of an answer to that question because nothing is simple here. But before I can say any more about my mixed feelings, Thea enters with the boys.

"Sam," the one I think is Pello says.

"Eat!" yells the other.

Grandfather leaves to get ready, and I help Thea with breakfast for the young ones.

"Samel," Thea says when the boys are well into their food, "I guess can't prevent my grandfather going, much as I may wish to. He is an adult and though I don't think he's in his right mind about this, he isn't actually incapable of making decisions. So, I have to let him go. Anyway, I don't see how I could stop him short of locking him up and I don't want to do that. But you are not of age to make your own decisions. And in the absence of your father . . ."

"Wait, you're going to try and keep me here? You can't." And I run from the room and all the way up the spiral staircase.

I still have confused feelings about going on this journey, but Thea trying to stop me makes me more determined to go than to stay. I shut the door to my bedroom and push a chest against it so that no one can get in. I'm going to pack and then I'm going to try and talk to Rowan.

It doesn't take long to arrange my clothes in my saddle bags and a few odds and ends in my belt pouch. Not so many days ago I was living out of these bags. I look around the room one more time to make sure I'm not leaving anything behind that I might need.

Then I realize that I'm just putting off using the bracelet. In the past it's been my sister who was reluctant to use the silver circlet. She feared its power, but I always told her it was like learning to play a musical instrument. The more you practised the better you got. What's holding me back now? Rowan might say I shouldn't go on this excursion, but she can't stop me either. And besides, she went off on her own twice. I've had my journey to Schönspitze, but there's more to do, more I want to see. Rowan said she was worried about Julina and Varonne at Hrashak's castle, but Grandfather has no intention of going there. It's the cave he's after, and that's probably not very close to the castle. So, do I even want to tell Rowan what I'm doing? No. I'll tell her once it's all over and we're back here safe and sound.

Chapter XXIII
Distractions

I'm floating on the wind among white clouds that make me think of giant balls of cotton. Cotton grows near Aquila, but I'm not there now. Below I see mountains, a river and valleys, trees, rocks and snow. This reminds me of the time Papa and I were lifted magically and carried away, but there's no sign of Hrashak's castle, and the old sorcerer is dead so there's nothing to fear from him. A shriek tears the air and then a massive eagle, wings spread, is floating alongside. My arms are out, though I have no feathers. It's amazing that I'm flying. How long will this last? I hope I don't crash. Could I grab hold of the eagle and ride on his back? He might not like that. It would be great if I could change shape and become an eagle. Or any other bird. Fly wherever and whenever I wanted, see more of the world, go back to Aquila easily and then off to wherever I like. The eagle banks and turns. I follow. Where is he leading me? On my left wrist, the silver bracelet glints in the sunlight. I stare at it and wish for wings, wish to be . . .

Morning and what a dream I've had! I'd like to just lie here and savour it, but there's lots to do, and no time to dwell in dreams. I need to find Grandfather to see if he's heard from the guards. I want to groom Izmeer and pack oats for him, give him a little exercise. Avoid Thea as much as I can.

I sneak downstairs very quietly. No one to be seen as the smell of fresh bread entices me to the kitchen. A couple of round loaves lie on the table. There's a dish of butter and a bowl of honey. I break off two wedges of bread, butter one and honey the other. I could go searching for Grandfather, but don't want to spend time wandering the house in case Thea comes down and starts haranguing me again. So I leave by the back door making sure to shut it gently. Alternate bites of bread from each hand as I hurry across the yard to the stable. The stable boy, Bubel, is filling the water pails at the well.

"Help you?" he asks.

"I've come to take a look at my horse, brush it, feed it, maybe go for a ride."

"I take good care of horse and ox."

"Yes, I know. I didn't mean to say that you don't take good care of them. But my horse is like a friend. I want to visit with him."

"Ah," the boy nods.

Izmeer nickers quietly and nudges at the hand that still holds a bit of bread and honey. I feed it to him, notice that his water pail is full and so is his oat bin. Bubel has been up early. I snag a brush and start to untangle Izmeer's mane, remembering how I used to rake him with a wooden rake when he was a camel. If Thea stays here in Schönspitze when I leave for Aquila, how will I get Izmeer changed back? I could ask Thea to change him if she isn't too angry with me once I return safe and sound from my journey with Grandfather.

I glance around; see that Bubel has left the stable. Quickly I head to the dark corner where there is an empty stall. There behind the manger I find the spot where I'm sure the secret passage from my room ends. In fact, the manger is easily removed and I find I'm right. So this is probably how my mother sneaked out of the house. I put everything back as it was and return to Izmeer's stall.

"You want a ride?" Bubel stands outside the stall with Izmeer's saddle. "I can help."

The two of us make short work of getting Izmeer saddled and bridled. I mount and Bubel gives Izmeer a pat and me a grin.

"If anyone asks, I've just gone for a short while."

Bubel nods and runs to open the back gate for me. It occurs to me that I can ride to the town gates, find Tag and Nacht and ask them if they are able to get the time to guide Grandfather and me.

Izmeer's hooves clatter on the cobblestones. It's still early and I hope that I'm not disturbing or waking anyone who might become annoyed. Particularly Thea. Quickly I head away from the house and down the hill along the winding street to the guard post at the town entrance. Only a few people are out going who knows where. I pass a couple of cross streets, and then an inn. The gates are just ahead.

"Samel!" The voice startles and nearly sends me sliding off Izmeer.

I glance behind. Distans stands at the side of the inn waving at me. I turn Izmeer back.

Distans is smiling. "Were you coming to find us? We're returning to Aquila today. You've left it late, but I think Primarius will make a place for you."

"Oh no, Distans. I'm sorry, I should have let you know that I'm not coming. I have things to do here. I'll have to find a later caravan."

Distans' smile fades. "And Thea? She's returning later, too?"

"Umm, no. I think she's planning on staying here in Schönspitze. It was her home before, after all."

"Yes," he says slowly. Then he claps his hands. "Could you give her a message from me? It will take me only a moment to write. Can you wait?"

"I'm just riding down to the town gates. I won't be long. I'll stop on my way back."

"Good, see you then."

Neither Tag nor Nacht is doing duty at the gate, but the guard who is there opens the door to their post and yells in, "Tag, Nacht, you're wanted!"

After a few moments the pale guard emerges, yawning. "Samel, you're up early. We were going to send a message later. Everything's set for a start to-morrow morning just after sunup."

"Good. I'll tell Grandfather. We'll be ready."

Thea is in the kitchen when I return. The twins are there, too and they grin at me, waving spoons dripping with gruel. Before Thea can say a word, I hand her Distans message. The note is sealed with wax and a ring impression.

"What's this?" she asks, holding the note in one hand and removing a ceramic beaker from near Pello with the other.

"I met Distans and he asked me to give it to you. He seemed disappointed that you weren't returning to Aquila with the caravan."

Thea frowns and takes a spoon from Kosto, who has been beating on the table with it. "Can you watch the twins? They're almost finished eating. Wipe their faces when they're done and then let them play in the back yard. Stay with them!"

She leaves the room, opening the note as she walks. I'm glad I had Distans' message to pass on because it occupies Thea for a while. I don't even mind taking care of the boys while Thea isn't there to nag me about this or that or threaten to find a way to keep me from travelling with Grandfather.

The boys gurgle at me in between bites of bread and preserves. Then Pello slaps the table, showing me he's done. "Down!" he says. "Sam, put Pello down."

I stare at him. "A whole sentence!"

"Sam," Pello says. "Down!"

I get them both down and clean them up as best I can while they struggle against the damp cloth. Both get away from me and run to the back door.

Kello slaps the door. "Out!"

In the yard, they wander about poking at dried grass and picking up pebbles. Then they notice Izmeer and the ox, who have both stuck their heads out of their stalls in the stable. Bubel isn't around. I hope for his sake that he's having a nap somewhere.

Kosto bounces up and down. "Hor, hor!" he yells.

Pello starts to run toward the stable. I manage to grab him and then Kosto is off. I get him with my other hand.

"You want to ride, boys?"

"Ride!" Pello yells.

Kosto shouts, "Yes!"

I don't bother with a saddle, but I do put a halter and rope on Izmeer. Should I just put both boys up and hope they can hold on, or should I sit up there with them? Either way they could fall off. I glance back at the house. Thea is not in sight, not at any of the windows. I'll take a chance. The boys are standing very quietly beside me, each clutching one of my legs and staring up at Izmeer. They are very small compared to him.

Suddenly Izmeer bends his legs, front and back, and kneels. That's what he used to do when he was a camel. His warm brown eyes look into mine. I'm sure he knows what I'm thinking. I get the boys mounted, one behind the other. Kosto clutches Izmeer's mane; Pello grabs hold of Kosto's shirt. Slowly Izmeer rises and I steady the boys. Both of them look a little scared and stay very quiet.

Slowly I get Izmeer moving. He starts without a jolt and glides forward. We make a half circuit of the back yard. By now both boys are grinning, though they still hang on tightly. We complete the circuit without any mishaps.

"Enough?" I ask. "Do you want to get down now?"

"Down," Pello says. Kosto echoes him.

Again, Izmeer kneels and the boys scramble off all on their own. They each pat Izmeer's neck.

"Good horse," I say.

"Good!" Kosto says.

"Horse!" Pellos adds.

"Run to the door of the house," I say.

The boys toddle off and I quickly get Izmeer settled back in his stall. "Thank you," I say. "You're a good creature, Izmeer, camel or horse." Izmeer neighs loudly. With one last pat, I leave him and catch up with the boys who are standing by the kitchen door.

"Let's find some cake," I say.

"Cake, cake!" they both yell.

It's amazing how they've suddenly started saying much more than they ever have before. Maybe they've just needed time to get used to words, the way I've tried to get used to using the bracelet. I guess learning to talk is a little like learning to play an instrument.

Helfrith is in the kitchen. Though most of the time she has a rather dour look, she does turn up her lips in an almost smile whenever she sees the boys. The two younglings stop just inside the doorway and stare with big eyes at Helfrith.

"Cake?" Kosto whispers.

"Raisin cake," Helfrith says and opens the oven door. "Just baked. Needs to cool. Wash hands, then sit and wait."

Without any help, the boys scramble onto the chairs she places for them with a bowl of warm water for each. I take my turn washing also. Helfrith was probably watching us through the window and knows that we've been touching horse. I hope that if I'm quiet and biddable she'll allow me to have a piece of raisin cake, too. Grandfather enters from the basement just as Helfrith begins to cut the cake.

"A piece for me, too?" Grandfather asks.

"Me," Pello says.

"Cake for all," Helfrith agrees. "But Grandfather must wash hands, too."

"Wash, Granfa," Kosto says.

The old man ruffles both the boys' hair and they grin at him. Surprisingly Helfrith joins us at the table, pouring milk for each of the twins and cups of tisane for the rest of us. She usually leaves us to eat on our own. Quickly we find out why today is different.

"Going again," she turns to Grandfather. "Taking the young one." She nods at me. "There's danger."

"I know," Grandfather says impatiently. "It's not simple travelling in the mountains, but we're taking two of the guards to look after us."

"Guards can't guard from all things."

"Have you been talking to Thea?" Grandfather asks. "I'm going and that's final. Samel wants to come, too."

Helfrith stands and slaps the table. "Foolish." Then she leaves the room.

"Cake?" Pello says, eyes sad.

"No more cake right now," Grandfather says. "We'd better get everyone cleaned up."

"Do you need any help packing?" I ask as we wipe the boy's hands and faces.

"No," Grandfather says. "And Tag and Nacht will bring tents and supplies."

We lift the boys down. I put away the left-over food and clean the table. Grandfather gathers up the dishes and puts them on the sideboard. He reaches down to tickle the twins and they run giggling under the table.

Grandfather turns to me. "Are you ready?"

"Ready for what?" Thea stands in the kitchen doorway.

The twins run and grab her knees. "Mama!"

Instead of answering Thea's question, I ask my own. "What did Distans say in his note?"

Thea reddens. "None of your concern." She crouches down to kiss the twins. "What have you and the boys been doing?"

"Cake," says Pello.

"Horse," adds Kosto.

Grandfather laughs. "Adventures," he says. "Even at their age." He reaches over to pat Thea on the shoulder. "I remember you and Zarmine hiding in the stable, letting us hunt for you. When you got a bit older and could climb you asked to build a house in one of the trees in the back yard."

"You didn't answer my question," Thea says. "What are you up to?"

"Is that tree house still there?" I ask.

"I don't know," Grandfather says. "Why don't you take the boys and see?"

"Wait a minute!" Thea says.

"Out?" I say to the boys and they run to the kitchen door. I leave Grandfather to deal with Thea.

Chapter XXIV
Parents

Have you ever thought about what a frog's eye view is like?" Grandfather asks me later that day. "Looking at the rest of the world from low down or seeing all the tiny things among the grasses – flies and ants and hidden flowers. Or the way light flashes on ripples of water? What is important varies depending on where you're standing."

We're sitting by the pond in the basement, hiding from Thea. She doesn't like it down here Grandfather has told me. Is afraid of salamanders and spiders. Or she used to be. That may have changed. Still, it's peaceful here and I haven't seen any salamanders or spiders. There's no one asking questions about why we're going on our journey. I have my own doubts, which refuse to go away, but I won't let those stop me. It's not so long ago that I let myself get stuck in Aquila, grumpy and unhappy. I'm going on the journey because I'm curious about the cave, but also because I don't want to look back some day and regret that I didn't go.

"I never imagined being a frog," I say, "but I know what you mean about deciding what is important. When I found out that I had a sister, all I wanted was to find her.

"Of course," Grandfather says. "And she would want to find you. I don't know what Zarmine and youe father were thinking when they separated the two of you."

I stir the water with my bare foot. "They'd had some worrying experiences with the bracelets. And they thought someone might try to use the two of us. And in a way they were right, except that it was because of the bracelets that we were safe. Rowan thinks it wasn't right to separate us either, but I guess we weren't old enough to have an opinion at the time. I keep thinking that if my parents hadn't given up on the bracelets, tried to use them, things might have been different. Mistakes were made. And sometimes Papa has made me so angry! Still, I know he loves us."

Grandfather clears his throat. I glance over at him. "Are you crying?"

He wipes the back of a hand across his eyes. "I miss those of my family who are gone. I wasn't always the best father or grandfather."

"I think you're a pretty good great-grandfather."

A quick smile flits across the old man's face. "Thank you. That means a lot. You have to think that your parents did the best they could. No one knows what might have happened if they'd tried to use the bracelets. Things could have been even worse."

We sit in silence for a time. "I haven't told Papa lately that I love him. We weren't getting along."

"So tell him! No time like the present. Didn't you say you can talk to your family with that bracelet?"

"Um. I can't do it here. I mean I usually need a quiet and private place."

Grandfather waves an arm. "Use one of the storage rooms. Take a candle if you need light."

I put my socks and boots back on and do as he says even though I haven't much hope of connecting with Rowan or Papa. My bracelet hasn't been working so well lately except for those strange dreams and visions. It could be because of being in the mountains and so far away from Rowan. Shutting myself in a storage room in a basement doesn't seem like the best way to try.

Still, I set down the candle on a free space of the floor near a carved wooden box. Find a dusty cushion and lay that down to sit on. Hold the silver circlet in my hands and lean against the wall. Close my eyes. Candlelight seeps through my eyelids. I smell dust and damp. Picture my sister and father, think of the bracelet. It grows larger in my mind, shines brightly. Once Rowan and I created a doorway with our bracelets to help us escape a dungeon. All I want to do now is have a conversation.

For some reason I start thinking of my mother living here as a child, she and Thea with Grandfather and his wife. Maybe it's all the junk around me or the smell of old dust. I do my best to push those thoughts away. It's my sister I want to think of. Where might Rowan be? In her room in Aquila, on the streets, at the market, at the school? Images flicker quickly through my head like paintings.

"Samel?" She's sitting under a tree. I catch a glint of water beyond – the river?

"Rowan! At last. Can you give a message to Papa?"

"He's right here, tell him yourself." Then I see him, across from my sister. There's food between them – bread, cheese and fruit – they must be having a picnic.

"Samel, are you all right?"

"I'm fine. I just wanted to tell you … I … I'm sorry we haven't been getting along."

"I'm sorry, too."

There's a flickering around the edges. Not again! Why can't we ever speak for a longer time?

"Papa, I love you," I say quickly.

He opens his mouth, but before he can say a word, they're both gone. I open my eyes. The candle has almost burned out, but my bracelet is shining brightly. A sigh whooshes out of me. It blows out the candle. Guess I should open the door and go back to Grandfather. At least I got to say what I wanted. I hope Papa heard me. In the light of the bracelet the inlaid coloured stones representing petals of flowers glint on the carved wooden box near my right foot. As I reach for it my bracelet flares. Inside the box lies a thin shabby book. Maybe this is what Grandfather has been looking for and it got mislaid. Put away at some point when Helfrith was clearing up. The book has no title, but inside is written Thea's name and further on bits and pieces of writing under various dates. It's a diary. I shouldn't read it, should give it back to her. The pages flutter in a slight breeze and a piece of paper falls out.

I see words in faded ink, read a phrase here and there. "Sorry I haven't written … bought a couple of horses … knowledge of plants … wonder what we will see." Then at the bottom of a page: love Zarmine. My mother's signature.

My bracelet is dimming. I need to get out of this room into bright light. Quickly I stuff the papers and book into my belt pouch along with the bracelet. Head back out to tell Grandfather I'm going up to my room. He isn't by the pond. I guess I was away longer than I realized and he got tired of sitting or thought I wasn't coming back.

Surprisingly, I meet no one in the house as I make my way to my room at the top. Briefly I wonder if they've all gone out or are asleep. I don't spend long on thinking about that, though. I close the door and shove a chest against it. Sit on my bed and carefully open the letter, sorting and smoothing the pages. Finally, I think I have it in the correct order. It takes time to decipher some of the words partly because they are faded and partly because the letter writer, my mother, it seems, had scrawly handwriting. But eventually I get it all.

Dear Thea,

I'm sorry that I haven't written more often. I know you thought I was making a mistake, didn't want me to leave with someone you said I barely knew. I hope that someday you'll find out that you can get to know a person in an instant, with just one look. Because that's what it was like for us, Yarvan and me.

We've been travelling with the musicians most of the time, but just a few days ago we decided to set off on our own. We have a couple of horses. Don't worry, I'm not heading off into the wilderness alone!

Yarvan says we should find a caravan to join. I guess that will be all right, though I like having him to myself. I'm content, Thea, from my head to my toes.

We left the mountains and have moved into the grasslands. Now and then we find a village or a group of wanderers and stop so that Yarvan can play his flutes. I've tried singing to accompany him, but I don't have a very good voice, kind of hoarse and scratchy. We make hardly any money with our music because the people have so little. But they share their food and drink with us and offer what shelter they can.

I have had occasion to use my knowledge of plants. There was a child suffering from diarrhea, and an old man with a fever. I've started keeping notes about these incidents as well as about any new plant remedies I learn of.

Tell grandmother how useful her knowledge has been to me.

We plan to come back to Schönspitze eventually, but this land is so vast! I want to see as much of it as I can. We've heard of a large lake in the east at the edge of the grasslands and of a town on the edge of a forest to the north.

And there's such a variety of people! Hunters and trappers on the plains and in the forests, miners in the mountains. Crafts people of all sorts everywhere. Wanderers in tents in the grasslands. Every day I wake and wonder what we will see next!

Of course, I was happy in Schönspitze a lot of the time, but I always missed my mother and father. We were lucky to have each other, you and I, and lucky to have our grandparents. Still, I missed something and didn't know what it was until I met Yarvan. It's being extra special to someone. I like to think that was the way my parents felt about me, though I don't know for sure. Yarvan is my best friend. He knows me better than anyone. He takes care of me and I take care of him. We argue sometimes, but we sort things out together.

Oh, Thea, I can almost hear your voice: 'If something seems too good to be true it probably is.'

Well, maybe you're right. I could be living in a dream world and it's all going to end some day in hurt and disappointment. Even if I knew for certain that was going to happen, I wouldn't want to miss out on a moment of this. Why shut yourself away from the joy of the moment just because you are afraid of sadness sometime in the future? I hope that my parents had that kind of joy at least some of the time they were alive.

I wish joy to you, Thea.

Greet everyone I know for me and tell them I'm very hap-

*py. But if you can't bring yourself to do that, it's all right. I
still love you, my cousin.*

*I don't know when I'll write again or when I'll be able to
find someone to take another letter. I don't know where to tell
you to send a letter back, though I wish I could hear from you.*

*We met a group of traders travelling to the mountains.
They've promised to carry this letter for me. I've paid them and
I think they're honourable.*

Much love, Zarmine

I lay the pages carefully on my bed and wrap my
arms around myself. It's amazing how vivid my image
of my mother has become. I don't have any memories of her, but Papa and Rowan told me that she had
long hair, red like mine, and grey eyes like Rowan.
From the letter I get that she liked seeing new places
and meeting new people. She loved her family, but
that didn't stop her from travelling. And it's clear how
much she loved Papa.

Best friends. Taking care of each other. That's like
Ali and me. At this moment I miss Ali more than ever
before. Is she still angry with me? Usually she doesn't
stay angry, but I wasn't very nice to her for a while
before I left Aquila. Maybe she was waiting for me to
ask her to come on this journey? I've known Ali nearly all my life and we've been best friends, lived next
door to each other. Can you suddenly see someone
you've known for a long time in a different way?

I'm not old enough to partner for life and neither is Ali. I'm sure that's what our parents would
say. But why couldn't we travel together, in a caravan,

of course. I know now how dangerous it can be out in the world and I prefer to have the help of others around me.

There's such a strong feeling in me to see and talk to Ali that my fingers have moved before I even really think about it. I pull out the silver circlet and think of her. Try to see her in the garden at their house, under the olive tree. Imagine her sitting in her room and painting or walking down the street to the market. All the places we have been together.

Nothing comes. I don't see her, have no visions of her, don't hear her voice. Why? There are no answers. Too few answers in my life. Maybe Grandfather is right about searching for the cave. Maybe there'll be answers there.

I fold up my mother's letter and put it in my belt pouch. Stick the bracelet in there too. Curl up on my bed and pull a blanket over my head.

Chapter XXV
Oddities

The road we take out of Schönspitze is not the one the caravan used, which is good news to me because I've been dreading the narrow and steep areas I remember. Maybe we'll come to similar places, but for now the way is easy. We left so early that Thea wasn't up yet, but we wrote her a note, and I put her diary with it. Thankfully she didn't try very hard to stop me going on this journey. I suppose she could have locked me in my room, but maybe she thought that too harsh. Anyway, I'd have run away if she did try to lock me up, because there is the secret passage, which Thea doesn't seem to know about.

We left our safe conduct pendants at the gate and had to pass through the fog again, but this time it didn't worry me. A yawn sends cold air down my throat and I close my mouth quickly. Shake my head to knock some of the sleepiness out. It's cool enough to be wearing my heavy cloak; a bite in the air nips at my cheeks, so I should be wider awake. Only Tag and Nacht are truly alert, cantering their horses, leading the two pack horses, riding ahead and back, chatting, even laughing. What is it like to be a soldier or a guard? It's not something I've ever considered being. I suppose, it's good that some people want to do it.

Izmeer plods along slowly. Grandfather is strapped into a basket-like saddle on a grey horse that the two guards provided, and he's definitely dozing. If I'd known they had a contraption like that I might have asked for it, too. The sun hasn't shown itself, but the dawn flush gives enough light so that we can see each other and the road very clearly.

A scream pierces the air, bringing my head up quick. An eagle wings just ahead, following the same path as we are. Is it my friend? I can't tell for certain, though I hope it is. Having an eagle along makes me feel safer somehow, and more at home. Not that I should be worried or scared with two guards. Although the stunted trees that line the road could hide anything, I find no one there no matter how hard I look, while Tag and Nacht seem very relaxed.

Nacht canters back to me. "How you feeling, Samel? Awake yet?" She grins. "Sorry, I shouldn't tease. Not everyone's used to early mornings."

I try to stifle another yawn, but don't succeed. "Carvn startd ely."

Nacht laughs out loud this time, sending a nearby bird rattling out of the tree where it was perched. Grandfather jerks awake, looks around.

"What? What's going on?" he says.

"Nothing at all," Nacht says. "Go back to sleep." She rides forward again and leans to say something to Tag. They both chuckle.

"Hate perky morning people," Grandfather grumbles.

I yawn wide enough to nearly split my jaw. "Me too."

The old man peers at me out of half-closed eyes. "What was that scream a while ago?"

"An eagle." I study the sky. The bird has disappeared.

"Eagles are good luck," Grandfather says. "Of course, you know that being from the City of Eagles."

"Hmm. We like our eagles. They keep watch for us."

"Schönspitze could use birds like that. Odd things have been happening."

I pull Izmeer closer to the old man. "You know about that? Wolves howling near the walls, a bear wandering around by the gate? Attempts to climb the walls?"

"More than that. A couple of guards disappeared during a ride a month or so ago. Never found them. And …"

"Wait a minute! Guards disappeared?" I glance ahead to make sure that Tag and Nacht are still there.

They are. "Why didn't you mention this before?"

"They knew." He nods at the two guards. "Everyone knows."

The two guards have swords strapped at their hips and bows at their backs. There are also spears tucked into leather holders at the side of each horse. Are we well enough protected?

"Except me! I didn't know."

"Would it have made any difference? I thought you wanted to go on this journey. Since that disappearance the guards are more careful. Tag and Nacht are experienced. The two that disappeared were young, new."

I shake my head and don't answer him. Soon the old man nods off again. And. He said 'and' and didn't finish the sentence. What else has happened around Schönspitze? I consider riding closer to the guards and asking them, but I'm not sure I really want to know. It's worrying, nonetheless. Hrashak is dead, but is someone else trying to take his place? Trying to find or has found the secrets of the cave that gave the old man some of his power? There's another old man riding beside me. Maybe I should be more careful around him.

By now it has grown lighter, but not any warmer. I huddle in my cloak and pull up the hood. A flake of snow floats past my eyes and lands on my nose, melts. What on earth was I thinking? Was I living in a dream? Imagining that summer had suddenly returned to the mountains and we'd go on a pleasant ride? Izmeer snorts. I glance down at him.

"Yes, you're right," I say and pat his neck. "I'm stupid and foolish." I sigh. "But I'm not turning back." If Grandfather is up to something bad maybe I can stop him. But if someone else is trying to use the power of Hrashak's cave I don't know what I can do.

Tag calls, "Everything all right, Samel?"

"Fine," I call.

Tag's horse strolls back. "It's frigid," she says. "Are you warm enough? We have extra blankets and robes. It will warm up once the sun is further into the sky."

"Good to know. I'm warm enough, thanks."

She canters off and I attempt to distract myself by looking at the scenery. We've left the steep peaks of Schönspitze behind and are riding through a shallow dip. There are still mountains, but they're further away, all of them streaked with snow, some wreathed in clouds. Does any of that snow near the top ever melt? How much water would it make? I imagine rivers rushing down the slopes and filling this valley, washing the road away and us. No, that's not going to happen. I have to stop this silly imagining. Tag and Nacht know how to survive here and they don't seem at all worried.

Maybe the guards who disappeared were not paying attention, being careless. I feel like waking Grandfather up and asking him what else he knows and hasn't told me. I look at him. He's wide awake and grinning at me.

"What?" I say.

"You're looking worried."

I frown. "Did you make up that tale about the guards going missing?"

He shakes his head vigorously. "Not at all. It happened a few weeks before your caravan arrived."

"What else?"

"What else what?"

"You were going to tell me something more before you fell asleep."

"More?"

"You said 'Never found them. And …' What were you going to tell me? Something more about the missing guards or about other strange things?"

Grandfather clears his throat. "There was a lightning strike on the guard tower at the gate. But that could happen."

"Has it ever, before?"

"No."

I sigh. "Did you really not know about me coming with Thea? You'd been watching her."

"I knew she'd arrived in Aquila. I thought she'd want to bring Rowan because they lived together before. I was busy with other things and I didn't have Thea watched all the time. Why do you ask?"

"Because I don't trust you!" I realize that I've shouted when the echoes come rolling back. And Tag and Nacht stop their horses and look back at us.

"Problems?" Tag asks.

"Just a little nervous," Grandfather says. "I think

it would be better if one of you rode at the back and one at the front."

Neither Grandfather nor Tag are looking at me. I want to protest that I'm not scared, but I keep my mouth closed. After all, what Grandfather is suggesting makes sense.

The day winds onward like the road, peacefully. Rows of mountains march into distant haze, a stream gurgles now and then beside the road or in a valley. An occasional small house or two surrounded by a stone wall nestles among trees. I can't imagine living way out here, but smoke rises from the chimneys. I shiver, though not from cold. My mother and sister lived alone in a cottage in the northern woods. I think they had neighbours and a village not too far away, but I prefer a city, with lots of people, markets, things to do. How would you spend your days out here? Rowan talked about taking care of a garden and animals. Helping to heal with herbs. At this moment Aquila seems terribly far away.

My back and legs are sore by the time Nacht calls a halt. There's an abandoned hut by a small spring. We dismount and I nearly fall off Izmeer. Grandfather gets lifted down by the two guards. They set him on a dilapidated bench by the side of the hut.

"We won't bother with a fire," Nacht says. "There's plenty of other food to munch on – travel bread, cheese, apples, dried meat."

After taking care of my horse, I stretch and stomp. There are kinks and aches, but gradually I feel better.

I guess I'm out of practice riding.

Grandfather watches and laughs. "Wish I was young enough to move like that," he says.

I settle beside him and take a bit of bread and cheese. The two guards are still seeing to the horses. Grandfather hands me a water skin.

"Thank you."

I lean against the back of the bench and stare at the sheer sheets of grey rock across the valley. The top is lightly sprinkled with white and at the base there is actually green growth. Tag and Nacht come and sit down on a couple of tree stumps.

"What's it like here in the winter?" I ask.

"Cold," Grandfather says, "deep drifts of snow. We wouldn't be doing this trek on horseback if it were much later in the year. In winter people strap curved boards on their feet and glide over the snow."

I stare at him. Now he's really telling lies.

"It's not so bad," Tag says after a swallow of water. "There's hot springs not far from Schönspitze. Skiing out there and soaking in the winter is great."

"What are hot springs?" I ask. "And skiing."

"Places where hot water bubbles or sprays out of the ground and forms pools," Nacht says. "Wonderful any time. Soaks aches and pains right out of you. Warms you to the tips of your toes and fingers."

"Why hasn't anyone taken me there?" I ask.

"No time," Grandfather mumbles, as he swallows a morsel of bread. "If you stay long enough you might get there. And skiing is what you do on those curved boards I mentioned earlier."

"Talking about long," Nacht says, "when do you think we'll reach your cave? We prepared for overnights."

"It's not my cave," Grandfather says.

"Never mind who it belongs to," Tag says. "How long?"

Grandfather glares at each of them in turn. Then he tilts his head up and appears to study the ridge. He hunches his shoulders.

"It's not up there is it?" Tag asks.

"He doesn't know where it is," I say. "I think he has a general idea."

"A general idea!" Both guards speak at once.

"We brought food for four days," Nacht says.

"But we can hunt if we need to," Tag adds.

"Four days," Grandfather says, "might be enough."

He won't answer any more questions and soon after that we set off again. Mountains and valleys, ridges and peaks, lots of trees and rocks, a waterfall. The sun warms us enough that I can remove my cloak. How does Grandfather expect to find the cave? He and I talked about Hrashak's castle so I imagine that we are riding in that direction. Though not too near the castle, I hope.

A chuckle escapes me and I quickly look around but no one is paying me any attention. I've just remembered the two guards' faces when I said that Grandfather had a general idea where we were going. Still, it is worrying though I'm sure the old man has some kind of plan.

It would be nice if he'd share it. Maybe I can get him to explain a little more tonight. I brought the Leather Book. It might start him talking.

After several hours more riding sunset spills over the mountains. We stop by a stream in the shelter of a rocky overhang. I discover how well the two guards have prepared. The pack horses carry one large tanned leather tent that will hold the four of us. Other bundles hold pots and pans, bowls, eating utensils, an axe and a saw, bedding rolls, food. The horses are unpacked and unsaddled first, led to the stream and left to feed and water themselves. Tag asks me to watch that they don't wander too far away.

"We'll tie them to pegs by the overhang later," he says.

The tent goes up quickly, a dead tree is chopped and a fire kindled. Once the horses are secured, I'm sent to gather more firewood. I don't mind this chore as I can find plenty of wood and still stay close to the light of the fire. Animals probably roam not too far away – bears maybe, wolves, foxes. After I've dropped four armfuls, Tag tells me I can stop. Grandfather beckons me. He's propped up against a couple of saddles and wrapped in a blanket near the fire.

"Didn't I tell you they'd take care of us?" he asks.

"Yes." Tag is busy with a pot over the flames. Nacht has gone to fill another pot with water. I lower my voice. "But how are you planning on finding the cave?"

"Several ways," he says equally quietly. "Water for one. After we eat I'm going to ask for help so I can go and soak my feet in the stream."

"And that will help how?"

"I know the sound and feel of water. I've been watching it, listening to it, feeling it for a long time now from before you arrived. Did you think all that work at the pool in the cellar of my house was just an old man's foolishness?"

"I didn't know what it was." I stretch my hands toward the warmth of the fire. "What else?"

"Did you see me looking at maps?" I nod. "So I know the direction of Hrashak's castle."

"South of Schönspitze, right?"

"Yes. And I'm also hoping that you will help me."

"How?"

"Your bracelet. Let me know if you get any sensations from it."

"Sensations?"

"Feelings, like whatever happens when you use it. You haven't told me details, but I have a hunch that you know when it's working."

"Hmm."

"Food's ready," Tag says. "Stew made from dried meat and vegetables."

All the times in the last weeks that I'd eaten stew with the caravan, it almost always tasted so good at the end of a day when we'd travelled far and ridden hard. This night is no different. There's something about eating in the open air that really gives you an appetite. Afterwards I offer to wash the dishes at the stream and Grandfather says he'll keep me company. Tag and Nacht are happy to let us; they have a few things left to do to get the camp ready for the night.

"Shouldn't you tell them the whole story so that they can be prepared for whatever might come?" I say as I plunge my hands into cold water.

"No." Grandfather leans into the boughs of a fallen tree that make a comfortable looking armchair. "I have no intention of telling my life story to everyone or anyone who might come along."

I sigh and begin to scrub the dishes with sand.

"You don't agree and that's fine. Now let's both be quiet so I can listen to the water."

Water chills my hands, runs down a metal bowl, drips back into the stream. Sand from the bottom of the stream on my fingers, rubbed over the next bowl. The rush of the stream over rocks sounds almost like wind. Voices in the wind, voices in the water. Sometimes I think the wind is trying to speak or sing to me, whispering among the leaves of a tree, rattling at my window in Aquila. Wind has different voices depending on how hard it blows and what it moves.

Water in the cellar of Grandfather's house dripped slowly off my fingers or swished across my feet. It spoke of damp stone and an old man's obsession. This stream speaks of snow on mountains melting in the sun. But now it's night and dark except for the flicker of firelight and the rays of a lantern. Water finds hollows and cracks in rock, carves a way through and down, drips and drips until it reaches a larger space.

"Yes!"

"What?" I drop a bowl and open my eyes.

"Well done," Grandfather says. "You made a link. We're on the right path."

"Are you two done washing the dishes yet?" Nacht calls. "We've got the tent all ready for sleeping."

The fire is banked, the dishes and other things are packed away. Nacht will stand the first watch, Tag the next. Grandfather and I are not expected to do anything but sleep. I lie awake for a while listening to the old man try to get comfortable, moan and groan a little. Eventually he starts snoring. The only thing I can hear from Tag's side is long slow breathing. I'm warm and there is enough padding under me. I listen to the wind sighing through the trees, hear a faint gurgle of water. Did I really help Grandfather find a direction for the cave? How far will we ride tomorrow?

Chapter XXVI
Mountains

The next day I'm wishing I could see something other than mountains for a change, though I have to admit they aren't all the same. High, low, with snow and without, bare rock or partially green, wreathed in clouds or stark against a pale blue sky. Ali would probably find much to paint here and could name a variety of colours. I remember umber, sap green, cerulean.

Those words are like music, tunes in my head. What notes would represent mountains? I fumble with my saddle bags, find the soprano flute and pull it out. Take off the gloves I've been wearing, touch polished wood. When did I last play? On that ride to the forest and the silver mine? I blew away the snowflakes with the breeze I made.

I start with high notes, trills like wisps of cloud dancing over snowy peaks, then try lower ones for heavy rock and deep caves. Mountains really demand very low tones I think, but this is the only flute I have. A big drum would be even better. I imagine a sonorous beat keeping time with my flute. Soon I notice that Izmeer's mane is fluttering and so are the edges of my cloak. Grandfather rides a horse length ahead of me; he turns his head and gives me a wave. The ends of the leather strips tying him to his basket saddle are dancing in the warming breeze. I blow the beginning of a tune I learned from Papa, The Road Circles On and On. I catch up to Grandfather.

"My wife used to play a wooden flute," he says. "Warda, that I mentioned when you first came."

I move the flute from my lips. "Did she?" I recall hearing echoes of music in the house and wonder if there is such a thing as ghost playing.

"Keep going, sounds good!" Tag calls from behind me. "I didn't know you could play music."

"You don't mind? I can stop if it bothers anyone."

Nacht turns from the front, "Not at all! Keep it up."

Neither of them realizes, of course, that I've also created this gentle wind. What would they say if they knew? Maybe they'd be impressed or maybe they'd look at me askance. Since they don't know, I can put the flute to my lips and blow a long low note that echoes like faint thunder along the edges of the ridge to our right. I stop playing immediately. Grandfather has slowed to ride beside me and he gives me a know-ing look. Both guards swivel their heads, looking all around, up and down. The sky is clear, no sign of a storm.

"That was strange," Tag says. "I've never heard echoes like that."

"Maybe you should hold off playing," Nacht says. "There's always danger of a snow or rock slide in the mountains. Not something we want to encounter."

I put the flute away and keep a close watch on the mountains nearby. I've never heard of rock slides or seen one, but I can imagine what it might be like. Great sheets of stone sliding down the side of a mountain, boulders bouncing. I duck my head just thinking about it. What would it sound like? Clat-tering and roaring, booming like thunder? But the mountains around us stay quiet and unmoving. Ex-cept … there on that distant rock face where the sun gleams strongly, a reflection off something shiny … a shiver or quiver?

"What animals live out here?" I ask. "Bears and such?"

A shifting shape is definitely there, dark, almost the same shade as the mountain with bits that are pal-er and glisten. I glance at Grandfather and point. He turns his head, stares for a while, shakes his head.

"You see something up there?" he asks. "My old eyes can't."

"Where?" Nacht says.

She and Tag both slow their horses and gaze intently. I point again. The movement is still there, slightly lower on the slope now.

"Rockfolk," Tag nods. "Too far away to be a bother to us."

"What are rockfolk?" I ask.

Grandfather is the one who answers. "Legends and stories. Creatures made of stone. Mostly they are said to sleep in caves, but if something warms them enough, like a nearby fire or the sun, they may wake."

I stare at the slope of the mountain again but can see no motion now. "In the stories are they very big?"

"Different sizes I'd think," Grandfather says. "Though I heard tell of one that was twice the size of an ordinary man. They're slow."

"And they're not real?"

"Did I say that?" Grandfather answers. "I heard of one fellow who saw a huge one and ran as fast as he could to get away. Of course, he may have been lying."

"Do they attack people? What do they eat?"

"Not sure what they eat if anything," Nacht says. "I've heard of sightings, too but never an actual attack."

"Still if they fell on you it might just look as if you'd been hit by a rock slide or fallen down a mountain," Tag adds.

I nudge Izmeer with my heels so that he outpaces even Nacht at the head of our line. If there are creatures as described around here I want to get away as fast as possible. The others speed up, too; maybe they feel the same. But the horses get tired and we don't enjoy the jolting so eventually we slow again.

Near midday there's a good stopping place by a tall narrow waterfall. We fill folding buckets with water for the horses. Grandfather seats himself on a rock just out of range of the spray.

I sit on the ground near him. "What is this water telling you?"

"It's familiar," he says. "I've encountered some of it before. Water can make its way great distances underground, find passages in many places."

"Do you think you'll know when we're close to the cave?"

"I hope so. The cave held a scent, a flavour of power. I haven't sensed that yet, but I have a feeling I will soon."

As we eat our cold meal I think more about the cave and the power that may be there. Is it in the rocks or the metals? Silver perhaps that sleeps in the earth until woken by fire. Fire wakens rockfolk, too. Are they part of the magic and power? Maybe they are guardians and the one we saw could have been watching to see what we intended.

Rocks and fire and water. Do these act together to create power? In the market at Aquila I once saw a trader with pebbles that could attract metal. He couldn't explain why or how this happened, except that it was a special kind of stone and not very common. He also had a fragment of rock that he kept in a small sack. He opened the sack to show me the brightness. At the time I hadn't found the silver bracelet. It shines, too, but differently.

The movement of water, the stillness and weight of rock, the heat of fire. All these can be for good or ill depending on the circumstances. Wind has force, too, blowing lightly and warmly or storming destructively across the land. I can call wind with the wooden flute, and my silver bracelet helps me do other things. What does that make me? I'm just a fourteen-year-old boy and yet, at times I can do unusual things. There are still secrets around the circlet that I haven't penetrated, though. Questions I don't even know to ask.

Grandfather wants the power he sensed in the cave. Could I find such help in the cave for myself? Papa and Mother didn't like the capabilities they touched in the bracelets. They thought them dangerous. Rowan wasn't happy with the forces that helped her kill Hrashak. That old sorcerer found his own cave of power and it seemed to have driven him mad. He believed that he could conquer Aquila, City of Eagles, a city that has a large and skilled militia. Grandfather could be mad, too.

"Ready to go, Samel?" It's Tag smiling down at me. I stand, shivering slightly.

"We've been climbing higher into the chill of the mountains," Tag says. "You should put on extra clothes."

As we ride I doze a little. The thump of the horses' feet becomes the drums of the Lord's Militia.

Where are they marching? An eagle flies above them or it could be some other bird, a black one. Black birds are not good omens for some people. A raven sits in the mouth of a cave, water splashes from a tiny rivulet into a deep, dark pool. My sister Rowan had a raven once that followed her. Birds don't live in caves, though, at least not any that I know.

The raven flaps great wings, darkness whirls about me. A faint spark flickers in the darkness, grows larger. It is a silver bracelet. Mine? As it enlarges I see that it frames a hunched figure unrolling a scroll. But the bracelet is falling, striking a rock, sparks fly and ignite the scroll. Fire in a forge, a blacksmith, his hammer raised to strike metal on an anvil. More sparks fly and silver fire surrounds a dancer on a hill. The dancer stumbles.

"Samel! Samel, are you all right? You nearly fell off your horse. Keep awake!" Nacht is by my side, holding on to my arm.

"What? Oh sorry, I must have dozed off." I take a deep breath of cold mountain air.

"We have some distance to go yet before we camp for the night. Do you think you can stay awake? Have a drink of water."

"Yes, I'm all right."

The cold air and cold water both help to make me more alert. What I'd really like to do is walk for a while, but that would only slow us down. Once again, I wish that I had a basket like Grandfather instead of a regular saddle. I yawn and quickly cover my mouth with my hand. More deep breaths, another gulp of water. This one sets me to shivering. Somehow, I manage not to doze off again, though I have to slap my own cheeks and shake out my hands and arms. Poor Izmeer, he's trying his best to carry me well and I keep wriggling.

The sky darkens, and at last we reach our stopping place, a grove of trees on the edge of a valley. This time there's no waterfall or stream but a spring of bubbling icy water. The two guards begin the process of setting up camp. Grandfather and I share the trunk of a large tree to lean against, both of us quiet and dozy. Izmeer crops grass nearby and now and then he raises his head and looks at me in a way that seems sad. What do horses and camels think about? Food and water, running, rutting, sleeping? Is Izmeer missing Aquila and the other camels there? He seems more like a friend than just a horse or camel. My sister talked often in the same way about the horse, Angel, that she rode down from the north.

"Grandfather", I say, "did you never think about my mother and us all those years? We could have been getting to know each other, spending time together."

The old man clears his throat. "Zarmine chose to leave you know."

"Yes, but you could have tried to see her, or sent a letter. You did find Thea and you were watching her."

"Not all the time. Just after I got back from the cave. It took me a while to find her."

"Was that when my mother was still alive?"

"Umm, I think so,"

I shake my head. "Never mind. It's all over and done. Nothing we can do to change what happened."

A huge sigh escapes the old man. "I'm sorry, Samel. You're right it's too late to change the past." He coughs. "But maybe I can do things differently now." He touches my knee. "I'm an old man, stubborn, selfish. When I started thinking about going in search of the cave, I wanted Thea back here because I thought someone from the family should take over. I didn't know if I'd make it back alive. I wasn't sure I wanted to. But you were unexpected. I mean, I knew you and your sister existed, but I didn't think of you as someone I might want to know or care about. Now I do." He pauses, releases my knee and rubs his face. "I still want to find that cave, there's something about it that draws me." He stares off into the distance. "And I think the cave is important. As you've found out, a lot of odd things have been happening around Schönspitze. I've heard rumours of similar occurrences in other parts of this land. I have a feeling the cave is an important part of that."

"In what way?"

"I don't know. I suppose I hope it will hold answers or even help. Or maybe it's where things started to go badly. I could be wrong. This could be a useless ride." He sighs again and is quiet.

The sun is gone behind the mountains and twilight has arrived. A few stars twinkle. Our fire burns brightly and Tag stirs a pot. Nacht is working in the tent. My fingers twitch and my legs grow restless.

I stand. "I'm going for a short walk. Not far."

I cross to a large rock on the edge of the road. From here I can still see our camp, and I can also see ahead to where we will travel tomorrow. In the distance two mountains lean towards each other as if closing off the road. Nacht has said there's a high pass that will probably have snow in it. Once we get through that the way descends and the going will be easier. If we don't find the cave tomorrow, we'll have to think about returning or the guards will need to do serious hunting so we'll have enough food. I turn to look the way we came today. The mountains close in there, too. We're surrounded by mountains. Is the cave really as important as Grandfather suspects? If so, it could also be very dangerous. Power and magic are complicated, can be good, bad or even in between.

I slide down to sit against the rock so that it hides me from the camp. I put my hand on my belt pouch. There's a slight quivering as if something wants to get out. I reach in and pull out the bracelet, hold it in my hands. It's shining faintly.

"Rowan," I whisper, "I need to talk to you."

But once again I can't reach her, no matter how hard I think of her and picture her in my mind. Am I doing something wrong? Is she angry with me? Or has something happened to her? Maybe she's lost her bracelet. I think of Ali, try seeing her in her room with the black stone I gave her. I can't find her either.

Chapter XXVII
Fire

A loud screech jolts me from sleep. I listen, but it's quiet now except for Grandfather snoring on one side of me. Nacht, on the other, breathes almost silently. I must have been dreaming of Aquila and thought I heard an eagle but can't remember details of the dream.

The smell of the campfire irritates my nose and starts a tickle in my throat. I untangle from blankets and poke my head out of the tent to see what's wrong with the fire, whether someone has put too much green or wet wood on. Arid smoke hangs in the air, making me cough. Usually whoever is on night guard duty sits near the fire or walks close by, but I can't see anyone. I move closer, notice a non-moving hump on the other side of the fire, which is just glowing coals.

Another scream like the one in my dream; is this what the Schönspitze pendants would sound like if we had them here and there was danger? I scramble out of the tent searching for an eagle. Clouds hide most of the stars and the moon, but the sky is oddly orange. I cough again as I reach Tag lying beside the fire. She is not awake; I shake her hard.

Tag mumbles, "What?" Tries to sit up.

A horse neighs loudly, then another. Are we being attacked? I help Tag sit up.

"Talons and beaks something's badly wrong!" I say.

The horses are going crazy. Their neighs are nearly screams, and their hoofs pound. Someone is beside me helping Tag to stand. It's Nacht.

"Fire," Nacht says. "The forest is ablaze." She points. South of us red flickers on a mountainside. A horse, rope trailing, races past me. I'm racked by more coughs.

"Grandfather!" I run for the tent.

The old man is awake and dressed; he usually hasn't undressed much at night on this trip. Which is a good thing.

"Fire?" he asks.

I nod and help him to stand.

"The spring," he says. "We should go there, get as wet as possible. Take blankets."

Both Tag and Nacht lean into the doorway of the tent. "Another horse has run away," Nacht says. "I don't know what to do about them."

"Never mind the horses now. To the spring," Grandfather says.

I grab my belt pouch and strap it on. More smoke in the air makes us all hack and wheeze. As the two guards help Grandfather, I rush to see what is happening to Izmeer. There are no horses tied to the trees where we left them. Most of the ropes are broken except for one that looks as if it has been untied. Izmeer. He always knew how to use his lips and teeth to untie ropes as a camel. I guess he can still do it, even as a horse, or maybe he's transformed again. I hope he'll be all right. The saddles are piled under a tree. On impulse, I grab Izmeer's, and struggling to breathe, lumber toward the spring. Izmeer is there! And he's a horse. I set down the saddle and run to put my arms around his neck.

"Could we put Grandfather on Izmeer and lead him out?" I ask. "How big is the fire do you think?"

"Too hard to tell in the dark," Tag rasps.

"I think it's all round us," Nacht says. "Look at the flames. How could that happen? There was no thunder in the night, not a lightning strike. Perhaps someone was careless. It won't be long before the fire gets here."

"I got Izmeer's saddle, but not the reins. We'll need them to lead or ride Izmeer."

Nacht dashes off. The sky shines red-orange with patches of black smoke hiding stars and moon. Here and there a flicker of flames; they're close. Crackles and crashes and then a roar like a huge gust of wind.

Nacht comes dashing back with the rest of Izmeer's tack.

"We're trapped," Tag yells.

"Keep wetting the blankets," Grandfather says, "and yourselves. The horse, too."

Sparks float through the air now. A few land on our tent. Ash rains down. None of us try to do anything except keep wet, there's no point, and the tent is soon ablaze. Wind whips it up. Wind! I grab for my belt pouch, pull out the bracelet, notice that the leather book is jammed in there along with the flute, and put the bracelet on my left wrist. Then I get the flute and put it to my lips.

"Now's no time for music!" Tag yells over the roar of the wind and the conflagration.

"Leave the boy alone!" Grandfather shouts. He's busy splashing water on Izmeer, who snorts and shows the whites of his eyes.

I play as loudly as I can, watch a puff of ash lift and whirl. The bracelet gleams and that light is growing, but it's very small compared to the inferno of the forest fire. I imagine a huge gust of wind whirling around us, blowing smoke and flames away from us in all directions. Water sprays out from the spring, but the droplets don't get far.

An eagle shrieks, and then another. I look up without stopping my playing. Several great birds soar above us, wings beating. It looks as if they, too are making wind to try and drive the flames back. We huddle in the mid- dle of destruction, but so far we're safe. There's pain in my chest and it's harder to breathe. I have to keep playing, but I don't know how much longer I can do it. One of the eagles dives, lands in front of me. I'm sure it's the young eagle that I freed. He puts out a talon. Is he offering to take a message?

I stop playing for a moment. "It's no use," I say to the eagle. "Even if I send a message with you to Schönspitze, help can't get to us in time."

The eagle screams again, as if in sorrow, and rises into the sky. In the short time that I've stopped playing the flute the fire has drawn closer to our camp. The tent is ash, but there are still trees near us that haven't burned. Can the water of the spring save us? Can I keep playing so that wind holds the flames at bay? Maybe the fire will eventually burn itself out. My body and clothes are soaking – sweat from the heat and water from the spring. I start to play the flute again, making sure to use my body to protect it from water and ash as best I can.

If only my sister were here to help we could try to use the two bracelets together to keep the flames from us. When we were in Hrashak's castle and the old sorcerer attacked, Rowan created a silver bubble that prevented him from getting to us. Could I do something like that on my own? We had the help of others; somehow we connected with distant friends so that drumming and harp music and the thoughts of friends gave us strength. I haven't had any luck connecting with Rowan or Ali lately. Can't do it now.

"Samel!" Grandfather grips my shoulder. "Keep playing, keep summoning wind. Can you make the wind blow the water around us?"

I shrug and close my eyes, imagine white water swirling up, joining the light of the silver bracelet. Wind and water and silver begin to weave together in my mind, forming a rough sphere with us in the middle.

"Yes!" comes Grandfather's voice.

And then I feel him in my mind, a green frog presence that loves and knows water. The cool spray of a spring, the flow of a stream rushing over stones, the roar of a waterfall tumbling from the side of a mountain, and the deep dark pools that hold enough water to protect us for a long time.

Continuing to play, I open my eyes to see a silvery mist surrounding us. Through that mist I can still see flames, but the smoke doesn't penetrate and I can't feel the heat. Breathing is easier.

"Did you make this fog, Samel?" Nacht asks. I nod as I keep playing the flute.

"Is there any way we can move with this around us?" Tag asks. "I think I see a way through the fire along the road back to Schönspitze."

"You think we can get away from the flames?" Nacht says.

"Maybe. If Samel can keep doing whatever he's doing. It's the only way that seems safe. I don't want to stay here and be roasted."

I stop to take a deep breath. The misty silver bubble still holds. I glance at Grandfather. He has his eyes closed and looks tired. Soon he'll need to rest, can't keep doing whatever he's doing to help me much longer.

"All right," I say. "Get Grandfather on Izmeer and let's soak ourselves and the blankets. Then I'll try moving us in the bubble."

"Life is a gift that we're given for a short time," Grandfather says opening his eyes and looking at me. "I wasn't sure that I would return from this journey and I still may not. But remember, Samel, the meaning life has is what we give it and we each have to find our own way. Death comes to us all, taking us away to another place, another life perhaps, or to be absorbed into the world in some way. As food for flowers and grass and trees. We grow and change, the seasons circle, spring to winter, seeds sprout, flowers bloom, berries are eaten, leaves fall. An egg hatches into a tadpole, a tadpole becomes a frog. The cycle of life continues. You have tasks to do yet in this life, Samel; you have to survive." He smiles. "Let's get going."

I put the flute back to my lips and continue to play as we slowly and carefully move into the road. I glance up. There are more eagles now circling and soaring, beating their wings to help hold the flames away. Maybe I can't reach Rowan and Ali, but I have the help of eagles. A couple of the huge birds dive and come close to circle us. These two are adults, not the young one that I helped. They make chittering noises, maybe it's to encourage us. Why do I suddenly think they might be the mother and father of the youngling?

I nod at them and start to play a tune that Papa used to play and sometimes sing to me when I was small and didn't want to go to sleep. It's about a pair of eagles guarding their nest, keeping the eggs and then the hatchlings safe. Feeding them, fanning them with their wings to keep them cool in the day, snuggling with them to keep them warm at night. All the things that good parents try to do for their children. Taking care of them the way Papa has taken care of me all these years. And then one day the hatchlings are big enough and they want to try their wings. It's a long way to the ground if they don't manage to fly. The parents watch and hope and worry. And the hatchlings flutter and tumble and flap and fall and finally glide and stumble to the ground. Safe for the moment, but then they have to find a way to fly back up to the nest, though they won't stay there for long.

I remember a story that Papa told me often. One day when I was quite small we were by the river and Papa noticed a young eaglet huddled crying on the ground under a tree. He threw food to it but didn't touch it because the parents wouldn't like the people smell on them. The poor little bird couldn't fly back up to the nest. But then one of the parents came and picked the eaglet gently up in its talons and flew to the nest.

We are moving along the road. I'm at the head, eyes open, playing the flute as hard as I can, the bracelet shining at my wrist. Grandfather huddles on Izmeer, his eyes closed. Tag and Nacht on either side hold him steady. I still feel Grandfather's presence in my mind, see images of a frog sitting on a lily pad in a pond, diving in with a splash, then surfacing. Cool water, cool mist, cold wind. I hold these pictures in my mind.

"I'll never get to see the cave," Grandfather mumbles sadly.

I am about to stop playing and answer him, tell him that there's not yet an end to hope, when I become aware of someone else in my head. A figure dressed all in scarlet, face shadowed by a hood. Invisible hands push against me, grab my throat. I can't play the flute, can barely breathe. Darkness streaked with flames pushes against our silver bubble. Grandfather coughs, Izmeer stumbles. Tag and Nacht open their mouths to speak or shout but no sound comes out.

"No!" I shout in my mind because I can't say the word aloud.

We have all stopped moving. A thin silvery mist still surrounds us; the dark force has not been able to break through or shrink our protection. A scream, then another. The eagles must still be above us, although I can't see them. Something flutters in front of my face, falls to the ground. I bend. It's an eagle feather, brown-grey with mottled gold, and a tuft of white at the base. I pick it up, run it through my fingers. I had an eagle feather once that I thought an eagle had dropped by accident. I left it behind in Aquila. But what if the dropping of that feather wasn't accidental? Maybe I've had a connection with eagles for longer than I knew. Anyway, I know this feather is a gift. The eagles are letting me know they are there to help. I tuck the feather into my tunic.

The red vision in my mind is growing, but now I push back. Think of eagles' wings beating, eagle talons reaching. My throat feels clear. I put the flute to my lips and blow a triumphant eagle scream. Izmeer neighs loudly in response. My bracelet blazes brightly on my wrist. I hear the splash of a frog jumping into a pond. Slowly we begin to move down the road again.

But the presence is still there, now behind us, now ahead. Is it real or just in my mind? It doesn't matter. I can feel the power – darkness, smoke and fire. And the hunger for our destruction, like a great wolf or bear howling through the mountains. Just keeping on walking is not enough to hold that power and hunger at bay. My arms are heavy as a pile of stones and my legs can barely support me. My feet slow. How can we drive that thing, whatever it is – sorcerer or witch – away?

Many talons and beaks can rend and tear, great strong wings will beat back the darkness. I hear chitters and screams, know what they are saying and thinking.

I stop playing for a few moments, take deep breaths of air that is no longer so smoky, find a bit of strength inside myself. Then I put the flute back at my lips and weave the sounds and sights of eagles into the music, join all that with the brightness of the bracelet. Rowan and I once made cold light. I will do that now; push out frosty radiance against hot fire and smoke. Great gusts of icy wind surge around the silvery mist, rustling and fluttering the red robes, thrusting hard against that presence, beating it back. A gust of snow tosses on the wind. The red-robed figure resists; there is prodigious power. I can't destroy that power, at least not now. But I have to find the strength to keep pushing it away so we can keep moving. Maybe we can get far enough away to be safe. There is less fire ahead of us.

When the world was much younger than it is now, when dragons still roamed and animals could speak like people, when some folk could take the shape of animals there existed in distant mountains a Kingdom of Eagles … The eagles were much mightier than those seen nowadays, even larger than the guardian eagles of the great trading city of Aquila.

I blink my eyes. Tail feathers! Am I really seeing one of those huge eagles from the Leather Book story winging over the mountains toward us amidst a gust of snow? Is this bird real or just my imagination? The answer comes when one swoop of mighty wings flattens burning trees, leaving nothing but smoke. The figure in red surges into the sky between us and the eagle, whirls arms up as if to stop the bird. The eagle lets out a great cry that makes us all clap our hands to our ears. Wind roars through the valley from the north, blasting snow at the fire, flinging the figure south and whirling it away. The last I see of the apparition, it is tumbling through the air in the wake of the fire.

The air still reeks of smoke and burned trees, but we are safe. And exhausted. In the dim light before dawn, we stand for a while just looking at each other – dishevelled, dirty and wet, dusted lightly with snow, shivering. I stare at the barren landscape around us, trying to understand what has just happened.

What was that all about, the fire and the figure? Fire could be a natural thing, a lightning strike or a spark from a careless blaze. But the figure? Was it my imagination or real? Someone wanting to kill us. Or to prevent us from reaching the cave? The only person I can think of who might have wanted to stop us is Hrashak, and he's dead. There are two other people at Hrashak's castle though, his daughter and her mother. The woman, Julina, helped my sister I thought, although Rowan later had her doubts about that help.

"Oh, Rowan!" I shout in my mind. "Where are you? Why can't I hear or see you? What is happening?" But she doesn't respond even though I'm wearing the bracelet and it has shown that its power is still alive.

We start walking slowly back towards Schönspitze, trying to get warm by moving. Sunrise shows us the devastation clearly. Blackened mountain slopes, smoking tree stumps and fallen trees. None of us speaks. I put my flute away and pat Izmeer. His head hangs; he must be weary, too, but he carries Grandfather without complaint. As I gaze at him, it seems to me that he's both a horse and a camel, but I don't know how that can be. A warm breeze dries our wet clothes and blows some of the smoke away. It's easier to breathe now, and Grandfather has stopped coughing. I look at him to make sure he is all right. He's dozing on Izmeer who is a horse. The mist that helped keep the fire from us has dissipated. I look up and see that the eagles have gone. No, there's still one keeping watch over us.

"There should be a stream," Nacht's voice is weary and cracked. "If the fire hasn't dried it completely. I need to drink."

Not too much farther on we find a small trickle of water beside the road. Izmeer slurps and the rest of us crouch to gulp. We take turns bringing water to Grandfather in cupped hands rather than making him get off and on the horse.

"We've got nothing," Tag says. "No food, no tent, not cups or bowls."

"We're alive," Grandfather rasps. "We have the clothes on our backs and I've got a horse to ride."

"And I have my belt knife," Nacht adds.

"It's at least two days to Schönspitze, though," Tag says. "What will we do for food?"

"Once out of this burned area we can find plants to eat," I say. "Rowan taught me a little of that."

I lead the way and we trudge on. Tag keeps muttering under her breath. Her voice is quiet enough that I can't make out the words, but it's irritating anyway. I want to shout at her to shut up, though I know she must be worried and exhausted like the rest of us. The best we can do is to keep going and hope that we'll soon pass out of the devastated area. I look behind now and then to make sure the fire isn't following. I can still see smoke in the south, but no flames. And no red figure.

We stop twice more, once just to rest for a while, stomachs grumbling. There's not a thing around us to eat or drink. Near midday we reach the waterfall I remember from before. Was it only a day ago? It feels like years. But the water is wonderful even if cold, and it fills our bellies.

"It won't hurt us to go a day or two without food," Nacht says from the rock where she's sitting. "We have water at least. People have survived days without food."

No one answers her. Grandfather is dozing again and I wish I could, too. Just stretch out here on the edge of the road. We didn't get to sleep through the whole night after all, and we've been walking through part of the night and half a day.

An eagle chitters, there's a flutter of wings, and a dead rabbit drops to the ground. I look up. My young eagle friend is soaring above us. Tag grabs for the rabbit, but Nacht gets it first. She proceeds to skin it.

"Give me a piece!" Tag puts out a hand.

"You're going to eat it raw?" I shudder.

"I don't see any fire," Tag says, "and I really don't want to. A bit of raw meat is fine."

Nacht hands out thin strips of the rabbit meat. After watching the others chew on theirs I take a nibble of mine. It isn't totally disgusting. I've tasted blood before when I sucked a graze, so I keep chewing. We finish all of the rabbit except for the innards and the fur.

Nacht scrapes the fur as clean as she can and tucks it into her belt. "You never know, might be useful." She tosses the guts to the eagle.

I wish I had food to give Izmeer, but there's not even a single unburned leaf or blade of grass to be found anywhere I look. Still, we step a little livelier now, even Izmeer; the water has done him good, too. And I remember that camels can go a long time without food. It occurs to me that maybe he can choose what he wants to be and for now he chooses horse. It's an intriguing idea.

We pass the place where I think I saw the rock-folk. There isn't any movement up there now. What if the fire woke up a whole bunch of them and they blame us for the destruction of forests? They could be hiding anywhere, just looking like a heap of rocks until they leap on us.

I speed up until I'm nearly running. I glance behind. The others are moving more quickly as well. Another look along the mountainsides. No movement there. Wait, is that a green patch? I squint. I'm sure there is green up on one of the mountains, but it could be just a different colour of rock. I don't say anything to the others because even if it is grass or something similar, it's too far away to do us any good. We won't go clambering up any mountains.

By late afternoon, though, we are definitely getting out of the burnt area. There are more patches of green in the distance, a few undamaged trees, and then a ragged oval of grass by the side of the road. Izmeer spies it before anyone else and is off before we can stop him. Of course, when we realize what he's found we don't want to stop him. Nacht lifts Grandfather off Izmeer and all of us sink onto the green. Izmeer crops grass while Tag chews on a single blade.

"Not bad," Tag says, "but I think I'll wait for something better to eat."

"Umm," I say, "what is that tree over there?"

Tag looks where I'm pointing. "White pine, I think."

"My sister told me about making tea from white pine needles."

"Well, we don't have water or a fire."

"Could we chew the needles?" Grandfather asks. "I could stand to have something in my mouth."

I'm up and by the tree before more words can be said. I break off a small branch to bring back. Put one of the needles in my mouth.

"How is it?" Grandfather asks.

I hand him the branch. "A little lemony." We get lots of lemons in Aquila, make lemonade, lemon cake, lemon pancakes and a lot of other things. I realize how much I've missed having them.

Everyone chews a few of the needles, even Izmeer. They don't really do anything to help our grumbling stomachs, but the taste freshens our mouths. Then on we go again.

Down the road, through the mountains, along a narrow path, and more of the same. I notice other patches of grass and undamaged trees. A rivulet, a spring. I'm feeling quite cheerful until Tag speaks.

"It's going to be cold tonight."

No one else says a word, because of course we know this, but why spoil a day that is slowly getting better? Night will come and we will do what we can. We walk as long as possible, keeping watch for any sort of shelter – a cave, a grove of trees, a patch of soft grass. Tree branches can be used to make a lean-to or for bedding.

The first stars appear and we still keep walking. Tag is no longer grumbling. Maybe she has realized that if the rest of us want to keep going she hasn't much choice.

"There!" It's Grandfather who points, having spied the cave.

It's a shallow one, but large enough for all of us including Izmeer. Nacht drags Tag off to search the area for living trees, bushes or grass. Anything that can be used as bedding. They return with a couple of armfuls. Tag spreads out pine branches for us to lie on. Nacht is working on building a fire using a couple of stones to send sparks into a nest of shredded wood. When she gets the first curl of smoke we all cheer. It's not the most comfortable of nights, but we keep the fire going by taking turns staying up. And I think all of us manage to doze a little now and then.

My sleep is mixed with odd dreams. Visions of fire and smoke, which is not surprising, but also over and over I'm standing in a cave with many tunnels, trying to decide which way to go. There's something missing, something I have to find, but I don't know what it is.

We wake early and start off right away because there's no food or water. If we want it we'll have to find it. As soon as Grandfather is seated on Izmeer, the horse neighs and starts off at a gallop. We all run after, afraid that the old man will fall off, but he's actually laughing as he jounces along.

When we catch up, there's his wide frog grin and he says, "I'm alive. That's astounding."

Nacht estimates that we're a day or so from Schönspitze. It all depends on how long and how steadily we can keep walking. As it turns out, we don't have to walk much further at all. Around a bend we meet two other guards from the city out patrolling.

Tag staggers toward them waving her arms, "Help! We need your help!"

It doesn't take long for us to explain what's happened. The guards say that everyone in Schönspitze saw smoke in the distance, which is why patrols have been sent out to make sure the town isn't in danger. They also share what food and water they have with them. One of the guards stays with us, the other gallops off to bring more help.

We're safe and fed. Grandfather is dozing again on Izmeer. My feet hurt, but I don't even mind. My stomach isn't grumbling and there's a water skin within easy reach. Tag and Nacht are taking turns riding the other horse and talking to the guard who stayed behind and is walking. They ask me if I want to take a turn riding, but I say I'd rather stay beside Izmeer. I give his neck a pat to let him know how much I appreciate him. He didn't run away in fear when the other horses did, and despite having little food or water, he's worked hard giving Grandfather a ride. Izmeer's head swivels and he nuzzles my chest. I wish I had a carrot or an apple to give him, but that will have to wait until we reach the town.

Chapter XXVIII
Return

In late afternoon a clatter of hooves and a hal-
loo signal the return of the guard who rode to
Schönspitze for help. He brings two extra horses.
An ox-drawn wagon and a couple more guards follow.
We settle Grandfather among the blankets and cush-
ions of the cart, tucking him in so that he won't be
jolted too much. A jug of water from the cart makes
the rounds and then one of the guards distributes
dried meat and travel bread. I'm glad we can move in
comfort now, but I keep thinking about that presence
in my head earlier. Will it come back or have the eagles chased it away for good? What did she or he see
in my mind? I wish I could be sure that we will really
be safe, even in Schönspitze.

We reach Schönspitze without trouble in late afternoon. I can hardly wait to get back to the house, feed, water and settle Izmeer. Oh for a hot bath I can sink into, clean clothes and another meal. But there's a throng hanging around the town gate. Have they been waiting there for hours?

One of them says, "A guard blew the horn when you were sighted."

Another yells, "We heard you were almost burned alive!"

Everyone talks at once, jostling, mouths gaping, eyes wide. "Are you all right. How did you get away? What happened to the other horses?"

The oxen keep trudging and I keep riding Izmeer. Tag and Nacht as well as all the guards except the one driving the cart stay at the gate. Thankfully the throng stays with them.

I worry that Tag and Nacht will talk about what I've done with the flute, bringing wind to keep the fire away, surrounding us with a bubble of water. But what if they do? If anyone asks, I'll just say that I don't remember much, that it was all like a dream and we must have had visions from the smoke. I know little about how the people of this city would treat me if they knew of my abilities. They must use spell craft or magic at times, given the mist that hides the city and the safe pass medallions. Rowan and I as well as Thea have kept our special abilities hidden as much as possible, not trusting what others may do or say if they know, but maybe we don't have to here. Anyway, who would believe that giant eagles came to our rescue during the fire?

Our guard drives the cart through the city and into the back yard of Grandfather's house, close to the kitchen door. Grandfather insists that he doesn't have to be carried. While the guard helps the old man hobble off, I take Izmeer to the stable. Bubel is not in sight.

"Soon," I say as I rub Izmeer down, "I'll ask Thea to change you back." He snuffles into my shoulder. "Are you telling me that you can change back yourself whenever you want to?" He nickers softly. "Maybe I'll leave it to you, then."

The guard and the ox cart are rolling out the gate as I cross to the kitchen. The door flies open before I reach it. Thea stands there, hands on hips.

"So," she says, "you knew what you were doing. The guards were going to take care of you." She takes a step toward me and shouts, "You nearly died! What would I have told your father then?"

I shake my head. What is there to say, except, "I'm sorry."

"You think your father would have been content with 'I'm sorry.'?"

"Thea, I need to get clean." She lets me squeeze past her into the kitchen.

No one else is in the room. I wonder if Grandfather is using the bathing room on the second floor. But when I get there it's empty, so I take advantage of that. The water steams and there's a new bar of soap.

Water whirls and foams, rushing out of the spigot. Then it clears so I can see my toes. We might have died of thirst. People have died in the desert, but in the mountains there is usually water. That's what someone said. Was it one of the guards or Grandfather? It doesn't matter. Water collects in hollows, flows in streams, finds holes in the ground and sinks. Lost caves, lost rivers, lost ponds. Maybe we're all lost.

Where am I supposed to be? What am I going to do with my life? Just go back to Aquila, study music, and then what? It might be enough for Papa, but it doesn't feel like enough for me. I have to know more about the bracelet, about its magic and my abilities to work with it, how to protect myself from whoever that was who tried to burn us.

And then I think of sky and air, soaring like eagles, winging along with them. That's what I'd rather be doing than thinking of water. The bracelet helped me to shape water by using wind. Could the bracelet help me to fly? What if the cave holds secrets that would help me with that?

"Samel! Are you going to stay in there forever?"

I can tell she's just outside the door. Is she going to burst in? I check. No, I remembered to hook the door. I sigh. Call, "No, Thea I'm coming out soon."

"I've been invited to Anwalt's house to talk about the businesses and I'm taking the twins. I just wanted to let you know. Helfrith is coming with us, so you and the old man will be alone. See if you can find him and ask what mischief he's planning next. I'd like to keep you both safe at home for a while."

"Yes," I call back.

In a little while doors slam and then it's quiet again. I dress in clean clothes and let the water drain, leave my dirty clothes in the basket which will be sent out to the woman who does the laundry. What I'd really like to do is go up to my room and lie on my bed, sleep for a day or two, but I promised Thea I'd look for Grandfather. I'm also hungry again, so stop in the kitchen and find bread and cheese.

I don't actually have to do much searching. The old man is in the first place I look – in the cellar by the pond. He's just sitting there, squashed into an easy chair, a blanket wrapped around his shoulders. An open bottle of wine and half a beaker full stand beside his chair. He stares at the still, black water.

"No water play today?" I ask. "No dripping and splashing?"

"What's the use," he says. He reaches down grabs the beaker and takes a gulp. "It won't get me anywhere."

"I'm not as interested in water as you are, but I never expected you to give up."

"I'm a very old man, Samel. I've lived a long time, too long probably. But what kept me going was the thought that I could find the cave again. It seemed my destiny, to end my life there while learning some of the secrets of that place."

"What sort of secrets? You've never given details. What exactly did you expect to discover in the cave?"

"Does it matter? I doubt that I'll have time to go there again, and even if I do that creature will probably find a way to stop me."

I sit tailor fashion beside Grandfather's chair. "You saw her, too? The one in red? Do you have an idea who it was?"

He turns from studying the pool to look at me. "It had to be a witch, wizard or sorcerer, don't you think? Who do we know of who fits that description?"

"Hrashak's dead, so you're talking about his former wife, Julina?"

"There could be someone else who is trying to thwart us, but I can't think of anyone."

He turns back to the water and reaches down to stir it. Ruffles spring away from his finger and spread quickly outwards. He picks up a tiny pebble lying beside his chair and drops it into the water. A splash and more ripples. Sudden warmth at my waist that I know instantly is the bracelet. I pull it out.

"Ah," Grandfather says, "did everything start when your parents had those bracelets made or does the origin of whatever this is about go back farther than that?"

"What do you mean? How can we know that?"

"When someone wants power there's usually others who want it, too. Hrashak was one such person and his grievances seemed to go back to his mother. You told me he thought he had the right to rule Aquila because his mother was the Lord's daughter. The old man also found a cave and if it was anything like the one I found there was power there, ancient power. Did someone live in that cave? Did that person have or discover useful secrets? And what about the magic of those bracelets? Where did that come from? Did the smith who crafted them put the power in or did it originate with the silver which came from somewhere underground?" He nods at me and I realize that my mouth is half open. I shut it. "There's so much we don't know. Strange things have been happening here and in other places. How much danger are we in? Is there greater danger for this land and its peoples?" He slaps a hand against his chair arm. "I'm old and tired. I've been thwarted and stopped in my search." He shakes his head and stands. "But you're right, this is no time to give up!"

"What are you going to do? Thea won't let us go again."

He takes another gulp of wine, emptying the beaker. "I'm not sure yet. I'm going to look at my books and think. I want you to think, too, and tell me everything you know about the bracelets. What you've done with them, what they seem to do." He stands, then frowns. "Wait. Perhaps that's where we should start." He sits down again. "Can you give me your bracelet for a moment? Will it allow that?"

"I don't know. When our mother died Rowan found her bracelet and I don't think she's ever given it to anyone else. I found Papa's by accident, and at one point he tried to get it back from me, but it rolled away from him. Hrashak couldn't take the bracelets from us. Maybe it's foolish, but I think they choose who they want to be with. So if Julina wants them, if that's why she tried to burn us, she's not going to succeed."

Grandfather holds out a hand. "I don't want to take the bracelet from you. I merely want to hold it for a few moments. Let's see if it will let me do that."

The silver circlet is in my hand and only slightly warm. Slowly I move my hand and hold it out to Grandfather. He touches the twined ivy leaves. The bracelet flares briefly, then subsides. Grandfather takes a better grip, but gingerly.

"It's warm. I expected it to be hot after that brightness."

"It can make cold fire. Also help me bring wind, and help Rowan and me see and speak to each other when we're far apart. How does it feel to you?"

"It's making my hand tingle slightly."

Grandfather bends forward, touches the bracelet to the water and straightens. A wisp of mist rises from where the silver contacts the pool. Grandfather looks at me and raises an eyebrow. I shrug.

The old man bends down once more. This time he holds the bracelet just over the water without touching it. Usually the water in the pool is dark and opaque, but under the bracelet an oval of clear water appears. I expect to see the bottom of the pool, the cellar floor or perhaps a scattering of pebbles, but instead there's the outline of a familiar tower.

"Hrashak's castle!" I say. "Why is it showing us this?"

Grandfather puts a finger from his other hand to his lips. The oval grows and it's as if we are moving toward the castle and the tower. I identify a window that I think is the one in the tower room where we were imprisoned. Is the bracelet going to show us the inside of that room? Who might be there now? But then one ripple and another cross the scene, and the castle disappears. The water is dark again.

Grandfather hands the bracelet back to me. "It wants you. But, Samel, I think you should try working with your bracelet a lot more. Touch it to things, take it out, look through it. Whatever you can think of."

When the silver touches my hand, I almost drop it because it's as cold as ice and a brief low note sounds in my head. Quickly I wrap it in a part of my tunic. My teeth start to chatter.

"What is it?" Grandfather asks. "Have you seen something else?"

"No, just felt something I haven't felt before. I think you're right. There's bad things going on and we need to find out as much as we can. I'm going up to my room to think and test."

"Good," the old man says. "I'll be down here. I'll can work on a few ideas, too."

"Don't forget to sleep," I say. "I think it's quite late already."

The first thing I do when I'm alone in my room is to light a candle and sit down. I concentrate, trying to see and talk to Rowan. That doesn't work. I think of Ali but can't see her either. There's only darkness when I close my eyes. Is it me or the bracelet or something else that's preventing this? Holding the silver circlet in my cupped hands, I study it: the way the ivy leaves join one to another stem to points, the points themselves, the veins in the leaves. A flare of the candle glances off the bracelet and throws silver lights around the room the way raindrops will reflect sunlight.

In a moment I'm inside a silver bubble and can see only dimly outside it. I feel a nudge against the bubble though I can't see anyone or anything pushing. I hear the faint sound of a soprano flute, but I'm not playing it. Is the music just in my head? The silver light around me brightens and I notice shadows outside, shapes of furniture perhaps and one form that looks like a person.

"Who are you?" I say, then clap my hand over my mouth for the figure turns toward me.

The shadow grows until it hides all the other shapes. I can feel it pressing against my silver bubble, but I'm still safe. My bracelet is strong. I blink and the figure is gone.

My room is gone, too. I'm floating in blue with wisps of white – sky and clouds. Somehow the bracelet is making me fly. I can't tell if this is real, a vision or a dream, but I don't really care. It's amazing! Schönspitze lies below, then as I move along, the scene changes to mountains and valleys; next comes a river. I should be able to see Aquila, but there's a mist where I think the city must be. I can't get closer and I can't see through.

I turn towards the south. Here are more mountains and forests, some burned patches. I can tell where the fire surrounded us. Beyond that should be Hrashak's castle, but again there's a mist I can't penetrate. Someone is preventing me from seeing. I close my eyes and shake my head in hopes of clearing my mind.

When I open my eyes again, I'm lying on my bed in my room in Schönspitze. The bracelet is on the blanket beside me and the candle has nearly burned out. There is no silver bubble around me.

The window is dark and the house quiet. I think it must be the middle of the night. My bracelet is powerful enough to keep whoever that figure was away from me. I'm certain now that Grandfather is right and that it's Julina. Who else? She wants something, maybe the bracelets as Hrashak did, though I have no idea what she wants to do with them. It doesn't feel right or good; I agree with Grandfather on that. Maybe she did try to kill or injure us with the fire, hoping that she'd be able to get my bracelet after I was dead or unable to move.

Well, Julina isn't going to get either of the bracelets, I'm determined on that. Although I think she's preventing Rowan and me from connecting with each other.

Maybe that's because the two of us together could overcome Julina so she has to keep us apart. If she has enough power to do that, I don't have any choice.

I have to go home and get Rowan to help me. Maybe together we can find out what Julina is up to. Grandfather will be disappointed, but I hope he'll understand. I'll tell him first thing in the morning. Maybe he'll want to come with me.

Right now I can barely move or keep my eyes open.

Chapter XXIX
Third Eagle

The full moon hangs like a lantern in a night sky. I'm sitting on a grassy knoll among rolling hills, my silver bracelet gleaming on my wrist brightly enough that I can see the Leather Book on my lap. A breeze ruffles the pages of the book, stops at a story called 'Rings and Other Things.' I begin to read.

Long ago when lightning destroyed a tree, waves capsized a boat, wind blew a roof off a house, or a split in the earth swallowed a horse, of course people reacted with fear, sadness, anger, despair. They also wondered if the gods were punishing them.

"What have we done wrong?" they asked.

A few offered sacrifices in propitiation. Some searched for means of protection. They fashioned amulets, fetishes, protective belts or cloaks; others practised chants or charms, studied magic and spell craft. Still others craved powers of destruction and fear for themselves. Why could they not become like gods? Enchanted swords, spears and rings of power were created.

Hardly any of the people attempted to find sources of power within themselves for this is the longest and most difficult of disciplines. But those who did discovered that certain objects can focus and concentrate this inner power – metals, unusual stones, wood from sacred trees, ancient artifacts. They began to find, make and study such objects. A few succeeded in becoming adepts, but they did not share their knowledge freely because they understood how dangerous it could be. At the same time, they became aware that others sought great power for themselves to subdue and subject the world to their own ends. In order to counter this selfishness, a rare number of the adepts of inner wisdom slowly and carefully sought out those they thought might have a spark of power and could be taught to use it wisely. They needed allies who didn't want power for their own ends, but rather to help others. But these sorts of supporters proved difficult to find.

I turn from the book to my bracelet. It is an object of power, created from a precious metal by a silversmith who disappeared. I haven't thought enough about how it came to be made, haven't wondered much where its magic came from. But if I consider all of the things that have happened around my bracelet and Rowan's it seems to me that we are part of some larger plan. Maybe more than one plan. We've already faced dangers together and apart. What might be coming next? How can I find out more?

"Rowan!" I shout to the moon and the sky. "I need you!"

The scene shivers and breaks apart. I'm resting on my bed in the tower room of the house in Schönspitze. Shadows and light spread across the floor, letting me know it's morning. All is quiet in the house except for rap, rap, rap. I turn my head to the window where a large shadow flutters.

A yellow beak taps and piercing eyes regard me out of a white-feathered head. I leap up to let in the eagle, realizing as I do so, that this sort of event is nearly ordinary for me now. The bird barely manages to squeeze through the round window, bounds in and skids to a stop, talons scraping the wood floor. I kneel down in front of it. As tall as I am kneeling, the fully grown Aquilan eagle holds out a leg. I untie the wad of leather and the eagle chitters.

"I'm sorry, I have no food here, but thank you for delivering the message."

The eagle pecks at the package in my hands. "All right, I'll open it."

They've taken Ali.

Everything goes dark. What has happened to the sun? My body shakes and my teeth chatter. Then I realize that my eyes are closed. I open them and I glance at the end of the letter. There is my sister's scrawled name. Quickly I look back at the beginning.

Samel,

They've taken Ali.

At first no one knew what had happened. Her family

thought she'd gone to the market or to visit her sister or for a wander through the city. They asked if we'd seen her; I had early in the morning as she left their house, but not after that. When evening came and she didn't return home they called on the Lord's Militia to search. And even they couldn't find her. The Militia discovered that she'd been seen talking to two women. A tall woman with black hair that had a reddish streak in it and a younger woman dressed in black leather. As soon as I heard that I told them it had to be Julina and Varonne.

I stare at the eagle. Its golden eyes look back. "Them! What are they up to now? Why Ali?"

So the Militia asked more questions. They didn't learn much except that others had noticed the two women with Ali. No one had seen Julina and Varonne arrive in the city so they might not have come through the gates. They also weren't seen to leave. We know though, that Julina has powers of illusion.

The Commander of the Militia with the approval of the Lord began to organize for searches beyond the city. They didn't tell us details. Perhaps they had news from spies who could tell them more. Or maybe they planned that a troop of cavalry would ride to Hraschak's castle where we all thought the women might have taken Ali.

Then a raven arrived at our house. It was my old raven Mord! I was so glad to see him, and I also thought that he might have come from the castle for I'd heard that ravens were watching there. I'm not like our father; I can't speak with birds, neither eagles nor ravens, but I've always been able to sense what Mord wanted. I wasted some moments trying to figure out what message he might have for me. He kept hopping toward me and bending his head. Well, it was obvious once I paid attention. There was a bit of parchment tied around his neck, hidden in his feathers.

The message from Julina was very short. 'Come to the castle, Rowan, you and Samel with your silver bracelets. Bring your friend Atsu, and Samel can bring the old man who calls himself Grandfather Frog. No one else. If I see any sign of soldiers Ali dies.'

So, Samel, you see that we have no choice. I've sent off this eagle, and my friend Atsu and I have started getting ready to travel to the castle. You don't know about him, but I think he can help. Please meet us at the castle as soon as possible.

Father isn't happy at all, as you can imagine. Neither is the Lord nor his Militia Commander. But we have to do this for Ali and her family.

I think Julina wants to take the bracelets. We'll have to find a way to stop her and save Ali. Hurry.

Rowan

I raise my eyes from the parchment and meet those of the eagle again. Those yellow eyes can be fierce and dangerous, but to me at that moment they look kind and caring. The eagle whistles softly.

"Wait here," I say. "I'll get you food."

Quickly and quietly I run down to the kitchen. My head is full of Ali – her smile, her dark brown hair blowing in the wind, her hands holding paint brushes, the sadness in her eyes when I told her I was leaving. And there is a great ache in my chest, fear coursing through my body, making me shake.

Doors are closed to bedrooms as I move downstairs, and it's still quiet. Thea and the boys as well as the housekeeper must still be asleep. No time now to find Grandfather. Food for the eagle first. I find a few scraps of meat in a wooden bowl in the pantry and take that up to my room. The eagle gobbles the food and raises its head. I expect it to leave now, but it still hunches on my floor, looking at me. It ruffles its feathers, stretches a wing, cocks its head as if asking a question. And I know what that question is.

"Yes, I want you to stay. Can you fly along and watch over us when we go? Stay out of sight so Julina won't know you're there?"

The bird utters a harsh sound, like a door creaking. "I'll take that as a yes. Now go and wait for me outside. We'll leave as soon as we can from the stable."

The eagle squeezes out of the window and I start packing, still thinking of Ali. If Julina has hurt her … No, thinking like that won't help. I hear faint voices – Thea and her twins getting up. She's not going to be happy with me. I have to talk to Grandfather before telling Thea what I'm up to.

I sneak quietly down and check the salon first, but the old man isn't there. Probably hiding out in the cellar. In the kitchen Thea and Helfrith are organizing breakfast.

"Good morning," I say. "Just going down to see Grandfather."

I slip quickly down the back stairs. Behind me I hear Thea ask what's going on. Of course, she suspects something. I ignore her and hurry on. The old man isn't sitting by the pool, but he comes yawning out of his sleeping nook as I pause by the water. I'm trying to think of how to begin to tell him about what I need to do.

"What is it?" he asks. "You look upset."

"Ali, my friend." I take a breath. "I had a letter from my sister by an eagle. My friend, she's been kidnapped. Julina and her daughter did it. Hrashak's former wife."

"Do they know where they took her?"

"The castle. Julina sent a message saying she wants me and Rowan to come, bring our bracelets."

"It's a trap, of course."

"Yes, but what else can we do? I need to leave as soon as I can."

He nods. "You have to go." Takes a step in my direction. "Do you think she'd object if I came, too?"

"No. She, Julina that is, actually said in her note I could 'bring the old man.' So, will you come?"

"Really! More confirmation that she started the fire, as we thought; she's been spying on us and knows who I am. Maybe she hoped to kill us with the fire and take your bracelet. As an alternative plan, she kidnapped your friend. Try and stop me from coming, even if I suspect that Julina has plans for me as well. I won't let you go alone."

"We can't take anyone else, though. She said so, especially no soldiers or Ali dies." My voice breaks and I turn away to hide the tears.

I hear Grandfather's slow shuffle. His hand touches my shoulder briefly. "We'll find a way to save your friend."

The two of us reach the kitchen as Thea and Helfrith are sitting down to eat. We all nod to each other, though Thea is frowning. She doesn't say anything yet, just nudges food closer to us – a plate of pancakes, another of sliced bread, a pot of gruel, butter and honey, fruit. Is Ali getting fed? Are they hurting her? Grandfather and I begin to help ourselves, though I'm not hungry. Still, I need food to keep strong. I'm still not sure how to break the news to Thea.

Grandfather finishes his bowl of gruel and pushes the empty dish away. "Thea and Helfirth," he begins, "I have something to say and I want both of you to listen and not speak until I'm done." They stare at him, but don't utter. Grandfather nods and continues. "Samel has received a message by eagle. His sister needs him and so he has to leave as soon as possible. I'm going with him. We'll leave today. Thea, send a message to Anwalt right away that we need two horses, one for me to ride and a pack horse. Helfrith, get food ready."

Thea shakes her head. "Oh no. You just got back. And you're an old man. Even if it's true that Samel has to go, and he'll have to show me the letter to convince me, there will be no more travelling for you."

Grandfather pushes away from the table and stands. "My dear Thea, I know you worry about me, but there's nothing you can do to stop me. I leave you in the capable hands of Anwalt and Helfrith."

The old man and I leave the kitchen for the front of the house. Thea follows protesting, but we ignore her. We shut ourselves in the salon and Grandfather locks the doors.

"Now," he says, "how long will it take you to pack?"

"I finished before I came down to see you."

"Good. I'll be as quick as I can." He begins rummaging on one of the bookshelves. Turns and sees me standing behind him. He waves his hands. "Shoo, get out of here. Give me an hour or so, then meet me at the stable." He unlocks the door for me, then I hear the key turn again.

I'm aware of Thea chattering in the background, but I don't take in her words. Ali is still in my head and I'm telling her over and over that we'll come for her.

I go upstairs, rummage through my pack to make sure I have everything I might need, but I just don't know. As long as I have the bracelet and the wooden flute, nothing else really matters except that we have to get to Ali as soon as we can. On an impulse I open the secret cupboard and add the box of gemstones to my pack, and then the leather book.

I head out to the stable to explain to Izmeer that I need him for another journey. I don't know if he understands, but he nudges my shoulder. I lean my head into his horsy smell, wishing it were the scent of camel, and wrap my arms around his neck.

"Oh, Izmeer," I say. No more words come.

Then Bubel emerges from a pile of straw, rubbing his eyes. "You need help?" he asks.

"You can saddle Izmeer," I say. "We have to go again."

The extra horses arrive and I leave the boy to get those ready, too. The eagle perches on the wall near the stable. He's tearing at some small animal that he's caught. A rat maybe. If Julina were here I'd set the eagle on her. I feel like yelling and screaming, stamping my feet, tearing at my hair. But none of that will help. It's nearly mid-day by the time we've got the horses saddled and packed. Thea and the boys along with Helfrith stand by the kitchen door and watch us mount and leave the yard. None of them speaks. They must have realized that nothing they could say or do would stop us anyway.

It doesn't take long to ride through the cobblestone streets to the city gate. The guards there are not ones I know. Grandfather hands them our safe conduct pendants, and speaks to them briefly, but I don't hear what he says. Izmeer and I are already through the gate and waiting.

"Ready?" Grandfather asks as he comes alongside towing the pack horse.

"Yes," I say. "But let's not go the way we did with Nacht and Tag. It will be dirty and ugly from the fire. The way I came with the caravan from Aquila leads past Hrashak's castle and Julina may not expect us to come that way. It'll take a little longer, but we're also more likely to meet Rowan and her friend before we reach the castle."

"Sounds good to me," Grandfather says.

Our faces turn south. The horses' hooves thud on the dirt road, the sun glints off snow on distant mountains. Izmeer neighs. Above us an eagle glides.

"Hold on, Ali, we're coming," I whisper.

Regine Haensel's first book in the Leather Book Tales series, *Queen of Fire*, was one of three finalists in the 2015 Young Adult Category of the High Plains Book Awards. The second book in the series, *Child of Dragons*, was published in 2017.

She also has two collections of short stories published: *The Other Place* and *A Rain of Dragonflies*. Her short stories and non-fiction have appeared in magazines and anthologies, and been broadcast on CBC Radio. She has won several Saskatchewan Writers Guild Short Manuscript Awards.

Regine was born in Germany and came to Canada in the 1950's. She has worked as a waitress, teacher, adverting copy-writer, and arts administrator. She lives in Saskatoon, Saskatch-ewan, Canada where she gardens and walks along the river when she isn't writing. She is currently working on Book Four in The Leather Book Tales: *Daughter of Earth*.

Connect with Regine:
Facebook - Regine Haensel writer
Twitter - @RegineHaensel
Blog – serimuse.blogspot.com

www.ingramcontent.com/pod-product-compliance
Lightning Source LLC
Chambersburg PA
CBHW070209260626
47160CB00002B/500